Samuel Johnson, Peter Peterson

Life of Dryden

Samuel Johnson, Peter Peterson

Life of Dryden

ISBN/EAN: 9783337333829

Printed in Europe, USA, Canada, Australia, Japan

Cover: Foto ©Raphael Reischuk / pixelio.de

More available books at **www.hansebooks.com**

JOHNSON'S
LIFE OF DRYDEN

BY

PETER PETERSON, D.Sc.

PROFESSOR OF ORIENTAL LANGUAGES, ELPHINSTONE COLLEGE, BOMBAY

𝔏𝔬𝔫𝔡𝔬𝔫

MACMILLAN AND CO., LIMITED

NEW YORK : THE MACMILLAN COMPANY

1899

NOTE

THE notes marked C.D.P. and enclosed in square brackets have been supplied by Mr. C. D. Punchard, who has also drawn up the summary on pages ix. to xvi.

CONTENTS

SUMMARY OF JOHNSON'S LIFE OF DRYDEN.

1. **Life of Dryden,** pp. 1-41. Dryden was born in Northamptonshire in 1631, brought up as an Anabaptist, and inherited an estate worth two hundred pounds a year.

Educated at Westminster School and Cambridge, and wrote poems at both places.

First public performance, *Heroic Stanzas on Cromwell,* followed by *Astrea Redux,* on the Restoration. (Johnson defends him from the charge of inconstancy.)

Wrote plays from 1663 for thirty-one years.

1. Wild Gallant, unsuccessful.
2. Rival Ladies, first attempt at dramatic rhyme.
3. Indian Emperor, sequel to Howard's *Indian Queen.*

In 1667, *Annus Mirabilis,* in quatrains ; here he begins to commend his own performances.

In 1668 became Laureate and published *Essay on Dramatic Poetry.*

4. Secret Love.
5. Sir Martin Marall, accused of plagiarism.
6. The Tempest, a variation of Shakespeare's play.

In 1673 he attacked Settle's *Empress of Morocco.*

7. An Evening's Love, with a preface on the Drama.
8. Tyrannic Love, severely criticised.
9. Conquest of Granada, majestic and incredible, ridiculed by Clifford.

ix

Elkanah Settle retaliated by attacking the *Conquest of Granada.*

10. Marriage à-la-mode.
11. The Assignation, driven off the stage.
12. Amboyna, to inflame the nation against the Dutch.
13. Troilus and Cressida, imitation of Shakspeare.
14. The Spanish Friar, written against the Papists.
15. The Duke of Guise, offended the Covenanters.
16. Albion and Albanius, a musical drama.
17. The State of Innocence, imitated *Paradise Lost.*
18. Aureng Zebe, his most elaborate drama.
19. All for Love, "the only play he wrote for himself."
20. Limberham, prohibited for indecency.
21. Oedipus, Dryden was helped by Lee.
22. Don Sebastian, one of Dryden's best dramas.
23. Amphitryon, a very diverting play.
24. Cleomenes, mentioned in the *Guardian.*
25. King Arthur, never acted.
26. Love Triumphant, a tragi-comedy, 1694.

Johnson describes the state of the drama, and audiences; the means of profit to the author, viz., dedication, copy, the third night. Dryden often wrote a preface of criticism. His prologues were sought for by the dramatists.

He wrote rapidly; six dramas were published in 1678.

Buckingham and Rochester were his chief enemies.

Buckingham ridiculed him in *The Rehearsal.*

Rochester patronised Settle as a rival of Dryden.

Critics accused him of plagiarism; he offered no defence.

In 1679 Rochester employed men to waylay and beat Dryden.

In 1680 he translated Epistles of Ovid, and wrote a discourse on translation.

In 1681 he turned to politics, and wrote *Absalom and Achitophel* against Shaftesbury and the Duke of Monmouth. This poem was very popular, and universally read. Several replies appeared. *The Medal* also attacked Shaftesbury, and produced *The Medal Reversed* from Elkanah Settle.

On the accession of James II. Dryden embraced popery and wrote *The Hind and Panther*, which was ridiculed by Montague and Prior in *The City Mouse and Country Mouse.*

Britannia Rediviva celebrated the birth of a prince (1688).

The Revolution transferred the Laureateship from Dryden to Shadwell, whom the former attacked in *MacFlecknoe.*

For the rest of his life, Dryden wrote for a living. His last five plays now appeared.

In 1693 he translated Juvenal and Persius, followed by Virgil (1694-7). His last work was his *Fables* (1699). Two *Odes on St. Cecilia's Day* appeared—one in 1687, one in 1697.

Dryden died in 1701.

"A wild story" is told of a practical joke of Lord Jefferies at his funeral (pp. 41-3).

2. Johnson gives a character of Dryden by Congreve, (pp. 44-5). The chief-features described are :

Placability and friendliness; modesty ; magisterial bearing to the young ; slowness in conversation ; fondness of the society of the great.

His writings are licentious, and adulatory—but this may be artificiality only, and not an index of his mind.

He praises others, but laments for himself.

His answers to critics are effusions of genius.

His writings often show a malignity to the priesthood,
which suggests irreverence for religion.

He frequently suffered from want, the cause of which
is doubtful. Tonson paid 250 guineas for his Fables,
and treated Dryden with rudeness; the Ormond family
were liberal to him; his salary as Laureate was very
irregularly paid.

He was the literary monarch at Will's coffee-house.

He frequently shows his belief in astrology.

3. **Dryden as a critic**, pp. 55-64. He first taught the
principles of composition.

Dialogue on the Drama : excellent portraits of English
dramatists, the account of Shakspeare is a model of
criticism. His criticism is that of a poet. Dryden leads
the reader in quest of graceful Truth through fragrance
and flowers : Rymer leads through thorns and brambles
to ungraceful and repulsive truth. Dryden's criticism is
majestic : Rymer's is ferocious.

Dryden wrote with a full mind, and did not elaborate
his work; hence he is not constant. Thus he both
defends and deserts dramatic rhyme.

His remarks on writers are not always trustworthy.
(Johnson gives various examples, pp. 59, 60.)

His literature (literary knowledge) was limited to few
books, and is either obvious, or superficial, or erroneous.

His general knowledge was extensive, resulting from
an active, inquiring mind, a quick apprehension, a
judicious selection, a happy memory, a keen appetite for
knowledge, and a "powerful digestion."

Nearly all his prose consists of criticism.

His style is equable and varied, has no prominent
characteristics, and is not easily imitated.

He continued the work of Waller and Denham, and established the new versification.

4. His **Translations**, pp. 64-5.

Jonson copied the Latin author word by word.

Feltham translated line by line. ·

Sandys struggled to produce an equal number of lines.

Holiday devoted more attention to meaning than to words.

Cowley asserted his liberty, and too boldly left his authors.

Dryden fixed limits of poetical liberty, and gave rules and examples of translation. ·

Languages vary in style and idiom. The translator must express the author's thoughts as the author would have done had he been English. A translator should be like his author, and not try to excel him.

5. **Effect of want on Dryden's works**, pp. 65-7.

Poverty lessened the excellence and increased the number of Dryden's works. Had he written less he might not have written better.

His poems were mostly "occasional"; he could not choose his matter, nor delay the publication; he was circumscribed by the narrowness of his subject. Birth, marriage, funerals, wars, provide no new ideas.

Such compositions merit praise on account of these drawbacks.

6. **Dryden's versification**, pp. 67-77.

He learnt the alternately-rhymed stanza from Davenant.

He is fond of forced conceits. (Johnson gives examples.) ·

His *Aureng Zebe* marks the establishment of his principles of versification.

7. **Absalom and Achitophel**, pp. 77-8. Political and controversial, containing all possible excellences of such a subject. Some lines are improper, many are irreligious : its allegories are strained too far ; it wearies the reader ; historical truth hampered the poet's powers, and prevented a fitting climax.

8. **The Medal**, pp. 78-9. On a narrow plan, though showing the writer's skill. The portrait of Shaftesbury is well delineated and strongly coloured.

9. **Threnodia Augustalis**, pp. 79-80. Defective because the metre is irregular ; is neither tender nor dignified, neither magnificent nor pathetic. Shows too much pleasure at the prospect of the new reign to be a sincere lament over the late King.

10. **Lyric Poems**, pp. 80-2. The poem on Mrs. Killigrew is the noblest ode in our language.

The first *Ode on St. Cecilia's Day* is splendid, vigorous, and striking, but inferior to the second.

Eleonora shows Dryden's skill in elegy, but lacks illustration. The praise is too general because the poet did not know the object of his praises.

11. **Religio Laici**, pp. 82-3. The only voluntary effusion ; rather argumentative than poetical ; a happy example of a "middle kind of writing," neither towering to the skies, nor creeping along the ground.

12. **The Hind and Panther**, pp. 83-6. Dryden's longest poem. Similar in style to *Religio Laici.* The scheme is injudicious and incommodious. It is absurd for one beast to counsel another to believe in the infallibility of the Pope, to discuss the Nicene Fathers, and to declare herself to be the Catholic Church. Montague and Prior detected these incongruities and

properly ridiculed them. Pope, a Catholic, names this
poem as the most correct of Dryden's works. The first
part was intended to be a specimen of majestic poesy.
Some lines are lofty, elegant, and musical : others fail to
carry out the author's intention.

The diction of the second and third parts is familiar
and conversational, but they contain some sonorous
lines. The whole shows smoothness of metre, extensive
knowledge, and abundance of images. Its natural unsuitability and unpopularity have caused it to be neglected,
but it is useful as an example of " poetical ratiocination."

13. **Britannia Rediviva**, p. 86. Remarkable for
extravagant flattery and lack of political foresight.

14. **Translation of Juvenal**, p. 87. Preserves the wit
but lacks the dignity of the original.

15. **Translation of Virgil**, pp. 87-9. "The most
noble and spirited translation that I know in any
language " (Pope). Attacked by Milbourne. Imitated
by many, but not often with success. It will bear the
test of being judged by its general effects and ultimate
result, for in spite of small defects it " keeps the mind
in pleasing captivity."

16. **Fables**, p. 89. These are renovations of some of
Chaucer's Tales.

-17. **Alexander's Feast**, p. 90. Exhibits the highest
flight of fancy and the most exact nicety of art. Stands
without a rival. Was produced in a fortnight.

18. **General survey of Dryden's labours**, pp. 91-100.
i. *His Mind* : comprehensive by nature, enriched with
knowledge ; a strong reason, a vigorous genius, but not
a quick sensibility ; unacquainted with simple, ingenuous
passions.

ii. *Love*: pure, disinterested love did not arouse his faculties; he looked on it as a means or a result of fiercer passions, such as rivalry, ambition, or revenge.

iii. *Pathos*: rare in his works; simplicity he despised; nature had no attractions for him.

iv. *Motives*: to fill the ear; to captivate an audience; to show learning; to engage in disputation and to prolong the argument.

v. *Comedy*: he was not naturally qualified for this; his jests are those of action rather than of sentiment, his humour is acquired by imitation.

vi. *Extravagant imagery*: he approached absurdity, and wrote lines which are almost devoid of meaning. (Johnson gives examples.) These bursts of magnificent extravagance pleased his audience and himself, though he could not approve of them.

vii. *Less noble faults*: frequent use of mythology and fable in connection with religion; pedantic display of knowledge; meanness or confusion of metaphors; vanity in use of French words; negligence in composition, and objection to correct and revise his work.

viii. *Versification*: described in a triplet by Pope. He established the use of Triplets and Alexandrines. His rhymes are rarely open to objection. He enriched his language with a greater variety of models than any other author.

19. **Dryden's observations on Tragedy, pp. 100-8.**

20. **Original letter from Dryden to his so**, pp. 108-10.

JOHNSON'S LIFE OF DRYDEN.

1631–1701.

OF the great poet whose life I am about to delineate, the
curiosity which his reputation must excite will require a
display more ample than can now be given. His contemporaries, however they reverenced his genius, left his life
unwritten ; and nothing therefore can be known beyond
what casual mention and uncertain tradition have supplied.

John Dryden was born August 9, 1631, at Aldwincle,
near Oundle, the son of Erasmus Dryden of Tichmarsh, who
was the third son of Sir Erasmus Dryden, Baronet, of Canons
Ashby. All these places are in Northamptonshire ; but the 10
original stock of the family was in the county of Huntingdon.

He is reported by his last biographer, Derrick, to have
inherited from his father an estate of two hundred a year,
and to have been bred, as was said, an Anabaptist. For
either of these particulars no authority is given. Such a
fortune ought to have secured him from that poverty which
seems always to have oppressed him ; or, if he had wasted
it, to have made him ashamed of publishing his necessities.
But though he had many enemies, who undoubtedly examined his life with a scrutiny sufficiently malicious, I do 20
not remember that he is ever charged with waste of his
patrimony. He was indeed sometimes reproached. for
his first religion: I am therefore inclined to believe that
Derrick's intelligence was partly true, and partly erroneous.

ℭ   A

From Westminster School, where he was instructed as one
of the king's scholars by Dr. Busby, whom he long after
continued to reverence, he was in 1650 elected to one of the
Westminster scholarships at Cambridge.

- Of his school performances has appeared only a poem on
the death of Lord Hastings, composed with great ambition
of such conceits as, notwithstanding the reformation begun
by Waller and Denham, the example of Cowley still kept in
reputation.   Lord Hastings died of the small-pox, and his
10 poet has made of the pustules first rosebuds, and then gems;
at last exalts them into stars ; and says,

> No comet need foretell his change drew on,
> Whose corps might seem a constellation.

At the university he does not appear to have been eager
of poetical distinction, or to have lavished his early wit
either on fictitious subjects or public occasions.   He probably considered that he who purposed to be an author,
ought first to be a student.   He obtained, whatever was the
reason, no fellowship in the college.   Why he was excluded
20 cannot now be known, and it is vain to guess ; had he
thought himself injured, he knew how to complain.   In the
Life of Plutarch he mentions his education in the college
with gratitude ; but in a prologue at Oxford, he has these
lines :

> Oxford to him a dearer name shall be
> Than his own mother-university ;
> Thebes did his rude, unknowing youth engage ;
> He chooses Athens in his riper age.

It was not till the death of Cromwell, in 1658, that he
30 became a public candidate for fame, by publishing Heroic
Stanzas on the late Lord Protector ; which, compared with
the verses of Sprat and Waller on the same occasion, were
sufficient to raise great expectations of the rising poet.

When the king was restored, Dryden, like the other panegyrists of usurpation, changed his opinion, or his profession,
and published Astrea Redux ; a poem on the happy restora-

tion and return of his most sacred Majesty King Charles the Second.

The reproach of inconstancy was, on this occasion, shared with such numbers, that it produced neither hatred nor disgrace ! If he changed, he changed with the nation. It was, however, not totally forgotten when his reputation raised him enemies.

The same year he praised the new king in a second poem on his restoration. In the Astrea was the line,

> An horrid *stillness* first *invades* the *ear*,   10
> And in that silence we a tempest fear—

for which he was persecuted with perpetual ridicule, perhaps with more than was deserved. *Silence* is indeed mere privation ; and, so considered, cannot *invade* ; but privation likewise certainly is *darkness*, and probably *cold* ; yet poetry has never been refused the right of ascribing effects or agency to them as to positive powers. No man scruples to say that *darkness* hinders him from his work ; or that *cold* has killed the plants. Death is also privation ; yet who has made any difficulty of assigning to Death a dart 20 and the power of striking ?

In settling the order of his works there is some difficulty ; for, even when they are important enough to be formally offered to a patron, he does not commonly date his dedication ; the time of writing and publishing is not always the same ; nor can the first editions be easily found, if even from them could be obtained the necessary information.

The time at which his first play was exhibited is not certainly known, because it was not printed till it was, some years afterwards, altered and revived ; but since the 30 plays are said to be printed in the order in which they were written, from the dates of some, those of others may be inferred ; and thus it may be collected, that in 1663, in the thirty-second year of his life, he commenced a writer for the stage ; compelled undoubtedly by necessity, for he appears

*

never to have loved that exercise of his genius, or to have much pleased himself with his own dramas.

Of the stage, when he had once invaded it, he kept possession for many years; not indeed without the competition of rivals who sometimes prevailed, or the censure of critics, which was often poignant and often just; but with such a degree of reputation as made him at least secure of being heard, whatever might be the final determination of the public.

His first piece was a comedy called the Wild Gallant.
10 He began with no happy auguries; for his performance was so much disapproved, that he was compelled to recall it, and change it from its imperfect state to the form in which it now appears, and which is yet sufficiently defective to vindicate the critics.

I wish that there were no necessity of following the progress of his theatrical fame, or tracing the meanders of his mind through the whole series of his dramatic performances; it will be fit, however, to enumerate them, and to take especial notice of those that are distinguished by any
20 peculiarity, intrinsic or concomitant; for the composition and fate of eight-and-twenty dramas include too much of a poetical life to be omitted.

In 1664 he published the Rival Ladies, which he dedicated to the Earl of Orrery a man of high reputation both as a writer and a statesman. In this play he made his essay of dramatic rhyme, which he defends, in his dedication, with sufficient certainty of a favourable hearing; for Orrery was himself a writer of rhyming tragedies.

He then joined with Sir Robert Howard in the Indian
30 Queen, a tragedy in rhyme. The parts which either of them wrote are not distinguished.

The Indian Emperor was published in 1667. It is a tragedy in rhyme, intended for a sequel to Howard's Indian Queen. Of this connection notice was given to the audience by printed bills, distributed at the door; an expedient supposed to be ridiculed in the Rehearsal, when Bayes tells

how many reams he has printed, to instil into the audience
some conception of his plot.

In this play is the description of Night, which Rymer has
made famous by preferring it to those of all other poets.

The practice of making tragedies in rhyme was introduced
soon after the Restoration, as it seems by the Earl of Orrery,
in compliance with the opinion of Charles the Second, who
had formed his taste by the French theatre ; and Dryden,
who wrote, and made no difficulty of declaring that he wrote,
only to please, and who perhaps knew that by his dexterity 10
of versification he was more likely to excel others in rhyme
than without it, very readily adopted his master's preference.
He therefore made rhyming tragedies, till, by the prevalence
of manifest propriety, he seems to have grown ashamed of
making them any longer.

To this play is prefixed a very vehement defence of dramatic rhyme, in confutation of the preface to the Duke of
Lerma, in which Sir Robert Howard had censured it.

In 1667 he published Annus Mirabilis, the Year of
Wonders, which may be esteemed one of his most elaborate 20
works.

It is addressed to Sir Robert Howard by a letter, which is
not properly a dedication ; and, writing to a poet, he has
interspersed many critical observations, of which some are
common, and some perhaps ventured without much consideration. He began, even now, to exercise the domination
of conscious genius, by recommending his own performance :
" I am satisfied that as the Prince and General [Rupert and
Monk] are incomparably the best subjects I ever had,
so what I have written on them is much better than what I 30
have performed on any other. As I have endeavoured to
adorn my poem with noble thoughts, so much more to express
those thoughts with elocution."

It is written in quatrains, or heroic stanzas of four lines ;
a measure which he had learned from the Goudibert of
Davenant, and which he then thought the most majestic

that the English language affords. Of this stanza he mentions the encumbrances, increased as they were by the
exactness which the age required. It was, throughout his
life, very much his custom to recommend his works by
representation of the difficulties that he had encountered,
without appearing to have sufficiently considered, that where
there is no difficulty there is no praise.

There seems to be, in the conduct of Sir Robert Howard
and Dryden towards each other, something that is not now
10 easily to be explained. Dryden, in his dedication to the
Earl of Orrery, had defended dramatic rhyme ; and Howard,
in the preface to a collection of plays, had censured his
opinion. Dryden vindicated himself in his Dialogue on
Dramatic Poetry : Howard, in his preface to the Duke of
Lerma, animadverted on the Vindication ; and Dryden, in
a preface to the Indian Emperor, replied to the Animadversions with great asperity, and almost with contumely.
The dedication to this play is dated the year in which the
Annus Mirabilis was published. Here appears a strange
20 inconsistency ; but Langbaine affords some help, by relating
that the answer to Howard was not published in the first
edition of the play, but was added when it was afterwards
reprinted ; and as the Duke of Lerma did not appear till
1668, the same year in which the dialogue was published,
there was time enough for enmity to grow up between
authors, who, writing both for the theatre, were naturally
rivals.

He was now so much distinguished, that in 1668 he succeeded Sir William Davenant as poet-laureat. The salary of
30 the laureat had been raised in favour of Jonson, by Charles
the First, from an hundred marks to one hundred pounds a
year and a tierce of wine ; a revenue in those days not
inadequate to the conveniences of life.

The same year, he published his Essay on Dramatic Poetry,
an elegant and instructive dialogue, in which we are told, by
Prior, that the principal character is meant to represent the

Duke of Dorset. This work seems to have given Addison a model for his Dialogues upon Medals.

Secret Love, or the Maiden Queen (1668), is a tragicomedy. In the preface he discusses a curious question, whether a poet can judge well of his own productions? and determines very justly, that, of the plan and disposition, and all that can be reduced to principles of science, the author may depend upon his own opinion; but that, in those parts where fancy predominates, self-love may easily deceive. He might have observed that what is good only 10 because it pleases, cannot be pronounced good till it has been found to please.

Sir Martin Marall (1668) is a comedy, published without preface or dedication, and at first without the name of the author. Langbaine charges it, like most of the rest, with plagiarism; and observes, that the song is translated from Voiture, allowing however that both the sense and measure are exactly observed.

The Tempest (1670) is an alteration of Shakspeare's play, made by Dryden in conjunction with Davenant, 20 "whom," says he, "I found of so quick a fancy, that nothing was proposed to him in which he could not suddenly produce a thought extremely pleasant and surprising; and those first thoughts of his, contrary to the Latin proverb, were not always the least happy; and as his fancy was quick, so likewise were the products of it remote and new. He borrowed not of any other; and his imaginations were such as could not easily enter into any other man."

The effect produced by the conjunction of these two powerful minds was, that to Shakspeare's monster, Caliban, 30 is added a sister-monster, Sicorax; and a woman, who, in the original play, had never seen a man, is in this brought acquainted with a man that had never seen a woman.

About this time, in 1673, Dryden seems to have had his quiet much disturbed by the success of the Empress of Morocco, a tragedy written in rhyme by Elkanah Settle;

which was so much applauded, as to make him think his supremacy of reputation in some danger. Settle had not only been prosperous on the stage, but, in the confidence of success, had published his play, with sculptures and a preface of defiance. Here was one offence added to another ; and, for the last blast of inflammation, it was acted at Whitehall by the court-ladies.

Dryden could not now repress these emotions, which he called indignation, and others jealousy ; but wrote upon the
10 play and the dedication such criticism as malignant impatience could pour out in haste.

Of Settle he gives this character : " He's an animal of a most deplored understanding, without conversation. His being is in a twilight of sense, and some glimmering of thought which he can never fashion into, wit or English. His style is boisterous and rough-hewn, his rhyme incorrigibly lewd, and his numbers perpetually harsh and illsounding. The little talent which he has, is fancy. He sometimes labours with a thought ; but, with the pudder he
20 makes to ring it into the world, 'tis commonly still-born ; so that, for want of learning and elocution, he will never be able to express any thing either naturally or justly."

This is not very decent ; yet this is one of the pages in which criticism prevails most over brutal fury. He proceeds : " He has a heavy hand at fools, and a great felicity in writing nonsense for them. Fools they will be in spite of him. His King, his two Empresses, his Villain, and his Sub-villain, nay his Hero, have all a certain natural cast of the father—their folly was born and bred in them, and
30 something of the Elkanah will be visible."

This is Dryden's general declamation ; I will not withhold from the reader a particular remark. Having gone through the first act, he says, " To conclude this act with the most rumbling piece of nonsense spoken yet :

To flattering lightning our feign'd smiles conform,
Which, back'd with thunder, do but gild a storm.

Conform a smile to lightning, make a *smile* imitate *lightning,* and *flattering lightning* ; lightning sure is a threatening thing. And this lightning must *gild a storm.* Now, if I must conform my smiles to lightning, then my smiles must gild a storm too : to *gild* with *smiles* is a new invention of gilding. And gild a storm by being *backed with thunder.* Thunder is part of the storm ; so one part of the storm must help to *gild* another part, and help by *backing ;* as if a man would gild a thing the better for being backed, or having a load upon his back. So that here is *gilding* by *conforming,* 10 *smiling, lightning, backing,* and *thundering.* The whole is as if I should say thus : I will make my counterfeit smiles look like a flattering stone-horse, which, being backed with a trooper, does but gild the battle. I am mistaken if nonsense is not here pretty thick sown. Sure the poet writ these two lines aboard some smack in a storm, and, being sea-sick, spewed up a good lump of clotted nonsense at once."

Here is perhaps a sufficient specimen ; but as the pamphlet, though Dryden's, has never been thought worthy of re-publication, and is not easily to be found, it may gratify 20 curiosity to quote it more largely :

> `           ` " Whene'er she bleeds,
> He no severer a damnation needs,
> That dares pronounce the sentence of her death,
> Than the infection that attends that breath.

That attends that breath.——The poet is at *breath* again ; *breath* can never 'scape him ; and here he brings in a *breath* that must be *infectious* with *pronouncing* a sentence ; and this sentence is not to be pronounced till the condemned party *bleeds ;* that is, she must be executed first, and 30 sentenced after ; and the *pronouncing* of this *sentence* will be infectious ; that is, others will catch the disease of that sentence, and this infecting of others will torment a man's self. The whole is thus : *when she bleeds, thou needest no greater hell or torment to thyself, than infecting of others by pronouncing a sentence upon her.* What hodge-podge does he make here ! Never was Dutch grout such clogging, thick, indigestible stuff. But this is but a taste to stay the stomach ; we shall have a more plentiful mess presently.

"Now to dish up the poet's broth that I promised ;

> For when we're dead, and our freed souls enlarged,
> Of nature's grosser burden we're discharged,
> Then, gentle as a happy lover's sigh,
> Like wand'ring meteors through the air we'll fly,
10 > And, in our airy walk, as subtle guests,
> We'll steal into our cruel fathers' breasts,
> There read their souls, and track each passion's sphere ;
> See how Revenge moves there, Ambition here ;
> And in their orbs view the dark characters
> Of sieges, ruins, murders, blood, and wars.
> We'll blot out all these hideous draughts, and write
> Pure and white forms ; then with a radiant light
> Their breasts encircle, till their passions be
> Gentle as nature in its infancy ;
20 > Till, soften'd by our charms, their furies cease,
> And their revenge resolves into a peace.
> Thus by our death their quarrel ends,
> Whom living we made foes, dead we'll make friends.

If this be not a very liberal mess, I will refer myself to the stomach of any moderate guest. And a rare mess it is, far excelling any Westminster white-broth. It is a kind of giblet porridge, made of the giblets of a couple of young geese, stodged full of *meteors, orbs, spheres, track, hideous draughts, dark characters, white forms,* and *radiant lights,*
30 designed not only to please appetite, and indulge luxury, but it is also physical, being an approved medicine, for it is propounded, by Morena, as a receipt to cure their fathers of their choleric humours ; and, were it written in characters as barbarous as the words, might very well pass for a doctor's bill. To conclude : it is porridge, 'tis a receipt, 'tis I know not what : for, certainly, never anyone that pretended to write sense had the impudence before to put such stuff as

this into the mouths of those that were to speak it before an audience, whom he did not take to be all fools ; and after that to print it too, and expose it to the examination of the world.   But let us see what we can make of this stuff.

For when we're dead, and our freed souls enlarged—

Here he tells us what it is to be *dead* ; it is to have *our freed souls set free*.   Now, if to have a soul set free, is to be dead ; then to have a *freed soul* set free, is to have a dead man die.

Then, gentle as a happy lover's sigh—

They two like one *sigh*, and that one *sigh* like two wandering 10 meteors,
           —Shall fly through the air—

That is, they shall mount above like falling stars, or else they shall skip like two Jacks with lanthorns, or Will with a wisp, and Madge with a candle.

"*And in their airy walk steal into their cruel fathers' breasts, like subtle guests.*   So that their *fathers' breasts* must be in an *airy walk*, an *airy walk* of a *flier*.   *And there they will read their souls, and track the spheres of their passions.*   That is, these walking fliers, Jack with a lanthorn, etc., will put on 20 his spectacles, and fall a *reading souls*, and put on his pumps, and fall a *tracking of spheres:* so that he will read and run, walk and fly, at the same time !   Oh ! Nimble Jack !   *Then he will see, how revenge here, how ambition there*——The birds will hop about.   *And then view the dark characters of sieges, ruins, murders, blood, and wars, in their orbs: Track the characters* to their forms !   Oh ! rare sport for Jack !   Never was place so full of game as these breasts !   You cannot stir, but flush a sphere, start a character, or unkennel an orb !"   30

Settle's is said to have been the first play embellished with sculptures ; those ornaments seem to have given poor Dryden great disturbance.   He tries however to ease his pain, by venting his malice in a parody.

"The poet has not only been so imprudent to expose all
.this stuff, but so arrogant to defend it with an epistle ; like
a saucy booth-keeper, that, when he had put a cheat upon
the people, would wrangle and fight with any that would
not like it, or would offer to discover it ; for which arrogance
our poet receives this correction ; and, to jerk him a little
the sharper, I will not transpose his verse, but by the help
of his own words trans-non-sense sense, that, by my stuff,
people may judge the better what his is :

10   Great Boy, thy tragedy and sculptures done
             From press, and plates in fleets do homeward come :
             And, in ridiculous and humble pride,
             Their course in ballad-singers' baskets guide,
             Whose greasy twigs do all new beauties take,
             From the gay shows thy dainty sculptures make.
             Thy lines a mess of rhyming nonsense yield,
             A senseless tale, with flattering fustian fill'd.
             No grain of sense does in one line appear,
             Thy words big bulks of boisterous bombast bear.
20   With noise they move, and from players' mouths rebound,
             When their tongues dance to thy words' empty sound.
             By thee inspired the rumbling verses roll,
             As if that rhyme and bombast lent a soul :
             And with that soul they seem taught duty too,
             To huffing words does humble nonsense bow,
             As if it would thy worthless worth enhance,
             To th' lowest rank of fops thy praise advance ;
             To whom, by instinct, all thy stuff is dear :
             Their loud claps echo to the theatre.
30   From breaths of fools thy commendation spreads,
             Fame sings thy praise with mouths of logger-heads.
             With noise and laughing each thy fustian greets,
             'Tis clapt by quires of empty-headed cits,
             Who have their tribute sent, and homage given,
             As men in whispers send loud noise to Heaven.

"Thus I have daubed him with his own puddle : and now
we are come from aboard his dancing, masking, rebounding,
breathing fleet ; and, as if we had landed at Gotham, we
meet nothing but fools and nonsense."

Such was the criticism to which the genius of Dryden could be reduced, between rage and terror; rage with little provocation, and terror with little danger. To see the highest mind thus levelled with the meanest may produce some solace to the consciousness of weakness, and some mortification to the pride of wisdom. But let it be remembered, that minds are not levelled in their powers but when they are first levelled in their desires. Dryden and Settle had both placed their happiness in the claps of multitudes.

An Evening's Love, or the Mock Astrologer, a comedy 10 (1671), is dedicated to the illustrious Duke of Newcastle, whom he courts by adding to his praises those of his lady, not only as a lover but a partner of his studies. It is unpleasing to think how many names, once celebrated, are since forgotten. Of Newcastle's works nothing is now known but his Treatise on Horsemanship.

The Preface seems very elaborately written, and contains many just remarks on the Fathers of the English drama. Shakspeare's plots, he says, are in the hundred novels of Cinthio; those of Beaumont and Fletcher in Spanish Stories; 20 Jonson only made them for himself. His criticisms upon tragedy, comedy, and farce, are judicious and profound. He endeavours to defend the immorality of some of his comedies by the example of former writers; which is only to say that he was not the first nor perhaps the greatest offender. Against those that accused him of plagiarism he alleges a favourable expression of the king: "He only desired that they who accuse me of thefts, would steal him plays like mine"; and then relates how much labour he spends' in fitting for the English stage what he borrows from others. 30

Tyrannic Love, or the Virgin Martyr (1672), was another tragedy in rhyme, conspicuous for many passages of strength and elegance, and many of empty noise and ridiculous turbulence. The rants of Maximin have been always the sport of criticism; and were at length (1681), if his own confession may be trusted, the shame of the writer.

Of this play he takes care to let the reader know, that
it was contrived and written in seven weeks. Want of time
was often his excuse, or perhaps shortness of time was his
private boast in the form of an apology.

It was written before the Conquest of Granada, but
published after it. The design is to recommend piety. "I
considered that pleasure was not the only end of Poesy; and
that even the instructions of morality were not so wholly
the business of a poet, as that precepts and examples of
piety were to be omitted; for to leave that employment
altogether to the clergy, were to forget that religion was
first taught in verse, which the laziness or dulness of succeeding priesthood turned afterwards into prose." Thus
foolishly could Dryden write, rather than not show his
malice to the parsons.

The two parts of the Conquest of Granada (1672), are
written with a seeming determination to glut the public
with dramatic wonders, to exhibit in its highest elevation a
theatrical meteor of incredible love and impossible valour,
20 and to leave no room for a wilder flight to the extravagance
of posterity. All the rays of romantic heat, whether
amorous or warlike, glow in Almanzor by a kind of con-
centration. He is above all laws; he is exempt from all
restraints; he ranges the world at will, and governs where-
ever he appears. He fights without inquiring the cause,
and loves in spite of the obligations of justice, of rejection
by his mistress, and of prohibition from the dead. Yet the
scenes are, for the most part, delightful; they exhibit a
kind of illustrious depravity, and majestic madness, such as,
30 if it is sometimes despised, is often reverenced, and in which
the ridiculous is mingled with the astonishing.

In the epilogue to the second part of the Conquest of
Granada, Dryden indulges his favourite pleasure of discrediting his predecessors; and this epilogue he has defended
by a long postscript. He had promised a second dialogue,
in which he should more fully treat of the virtues and faults

of the English poets, who have written in the dramatic,
epic, or lyric way. This promise was never formally performed ; but, with respect to the dramatic writers, he has
given us in his prefaces and in this postscript, something
equivalent ; but his purpose being to exalt himself by the
comparison, he shows faults distinctly, and only praises
excellence in general terms.

A play thus written, in professed defiance of probability,
naturally drew down upon itself the vultures of the theatre.
One of the critics that attacked it was Martin Clifford, to 10
whom Sprat addressed the Life of Cowley, with such veneration of his critical powers as might naturally excite great
expectations of instruction from his remarks. But let honest
credulity beware of receiving characters from contemporary
writers. Clifford's remarks, by the favour of Dr. Percy,
were at last obtained ; and, that no man may ever want
them more, I will extract enough to satisfy all reasonable
desire.

In the first letter his observation is only general : "You
do live," says he, "in as much ignorance and darkness as 20
you did in the womb ; your writings are like a Jack-of-
all-trades' shop ; they have a variety, but nothing of value ;
and if thou art not the dullest plant-animal that ever
the earth produced, all that I have conversed with are
strangely mistaken in thee."

In the second he tells him that Almanzor is not more
copied from Achilles than from Ancient Pistol. "But I
am," says he, "strangely mistaken if I have not seen this
very Almanzor of yours in some disguise about this town,
and passing under another name. Pr'ythee tell me true, 30
was not this Huffcap once the Indian Emperor ? and
at another time did he not call himself Maximin ? Was
not Lyndaraxa once called Almeira ? I mean under Montezuma the Indian Emperor. I protest and vow they are
either the same, or so alike that I cannot, for my heart, distinguish one from the other. You are therefore a strange

unconscionable thief ; thou art not content to steal from
others, but dost rob thy poor wretched self too."

Now was Settle's time to take his revenge. He wrote
a vindication of his own lines ; and, if he is forced to yield
anything, makes reprisals upon his enemy. To say that
his answer is equal to the censure, is no high commendation.
To expose Dryden's method of analyzing his expressions,
he tries the same experiment upon the description of the
ships in the Indian Emperor, of which however he does
10 not deny the excellence ; but intends to show, that by
studied misconstruction everything may be equally represented as ridiculous. After so much of Dryden's elegant
animadversions, justice requires that something of Settle's
should be exhibited. The following observations are therefore extracted from a quarto pamphlet of ninety-five pages :

> " Fate after him below with pain did move,
> And victory could scarce keep pace above.

These two lines, if he can show me any sense or thought in,
or anything but bombast and noise, he shall make me believe
20 every word in his observations on Morocco sense.

"In the Empress of Morocco were these lines :

> I'll travel then to some remoter sphere,
> Till I find out new worlds, and crown you there—

on which Dryden made this remark : 'I believe our learned
author takes a sphere for a country ; the sphere of Morocco !
as if Morocco were the globe of earth and water ; but a
globe is no sphere neither, by his leave,' etc. So *sphere* must
not be sense, unless it relate to a circular motion about a
globe, in which sense the astronomers use it. I would desire
30 him to expound those lines in Granada :

> I'll to the turrets of the palace go,
> And add new fire to those that fight below.
> Thence, hero-like, with torches by my side,
> (Far be the omen tho') my Love I'll guide.

No, like his better fortune I'll appear,
With open arms, loose vail, and flowing hair,
Just flying forward from my rowling sphere.

I wonder, if he be so strict, how he dares make so bold with
sphere himself, and be so critical in other men's writings.
Fortune is fancied standing on a globe, not on a *sphere*,
as he told us in the first act.

"Because *Elkanah's similes are the most unlike things to
what they are compared in the world*, I'll venture to start
a simile in his Annus Mirabilis : he gives this poetical 10
description of the ship called the London :

The goodly London in her gallant trim,
The Phenix-daughter of the vanquisht old,
Like a rich bride does to the ocean swim,
And on her shadow rides in floating gold.
Her flag aloft spread ruffling in the wind,
And sanguine streamers seem'd the flood to fire :
The weaver, charm'd with what his loom design'd,
Goes on to sea, and knows not to retire.
With roomy decks her guns of mighty strength,   20
Whose low-laid mouths each mounting billow laves,
Deep in her draught, and warlike in her length,
She seems a sea-wasp flying on the waves.

What a wonderful pother is here, to make all these poetical
beautifications of a ship ; that is, a *phenix* in the first stanza,
band but a *wasp* in the last : nay, to make his humble comparison of a *wasp* more ridiculous, he does not say it flies
upon the waves as nimbly as a wasp, or the like, but it
seemed a *wasp*. But our author at the writing of this was
not in his altitudes, to compare ships to floating palaces ; 30
a comparison to the purpose was a perfection he did not
arrive to till his Indian Emperor's days. But perhaps his
similitude has more in it than we imagine ; this ship had
a great many guns in her, and they, put all together, made
the sting in the wasp's tail : for this is all the reason I
can guess, why it seemed a *wasp*. But, because we will

B

allow him all we can to help out, let it be a *phenix sea-wasp*, and the rarity of such an animal may do much towards heightening the fancy.

"It had been much more to his purpose, if he had designed to render the senseless play little, to have searched for some such pedantry as this :

> Two ifs scarce makes one possibility.
> If justice will take all, and nothing give,
> Justice, methinks, is not distributive.
> To die or kill you is the alternative.
> Rather than take your life, I will not live.

10

"Observe how prettily our author chops logic in heroic verse. Three such fustian canting words as *distributive*, *alternative*, and *two ifs*, no man but himself would have come within the noise of. But he's a man of general learning, and all comes into his play.

"'Twould have done well too if he could have met with the rant or two, worth the observation : such as,

> Move swiftly, Sun, and fly a lover's pace,
> Leave months and weeks behind thee in thy race.

20

"But surely the Sun, whether he flies a lover's or not a lover's pace, leaves weeks and months, nay years too behind him in his race.

"Poor Robin, or any other of the philo-mathema would have given him satisfaction in the point.

> If I could kill thee now, thy fate's so low,
> That I must stoop ere I can give the blow :
> But mine is fixt so far above thy crown,
> That all thy men,
> Piled on thy back, can never pull it down.

30

"Now where that is, Almanzor's fate is fixed, I cannot guess ; but, wherever it is, I believe Almanzor, and think that all Abdalla's subjects, piled upon one another, might not pull down his fate so well as without piling ; besides, I

think Abdalla so wise a man, that, if Almanzor had told
him piling his men upon his back might do the feat, he
would scarcely bear such a weight, for the pleasure of the
exploit ; but it is a huff, and let Abdalla do it if he dare.

> The people like a headlong torrent go,
> And every dam they break or overflow.
> But, unopposed, they either lose their force,
> Or wind in volumes to their former course ;

a very pretty allusion, contrary to all sense or reason. Tor-
rents, I take it, let them wind never so much, can never 10
return to their former course, unless he can suppose that
fountains can go upwards, which is impossible ; nay, more,
in the foregoing page he tells us so too ; a trick of a very
unfaithful memory,

> But can no more than fountains upward flow ;

which of a *torrent*, which signifies a rapid stream, is much
more impossible. Besides, if he goes to quibble, and say
that it is possible by art water may be made return, and
the same water run twice in one and the same channel, then
he quite confutes what he says : for it is by being opposed, 20
that it runs into its former course ; for all engines that
make water so return, do it by compulsion and opposition.
Or, if he means a headlong torrent for a tide, which would
be ridiculous, yet they do not wind in volumes, but come
foreright back (if their upright lies straight to their former
course), and that by opposition of the sea-water, that drives
them back again.

"And for fancy, when he lights of anything like it, 'tis a
wonder if it be not borrowed. As here, for example of, I
find this fanciful thought in his Annus Mirabilis :   30

> Old father Thames raised up his reverend head :
> But fear'd the fate of Simoeis would return ;
> Deep in his ooze he sought his sedgy bed,
> And shrunk his waters back into his urn.

" This is stolen from Cowley's Davideis, p. 9.

Swift Jordan started, and straight backward fled,
Hiding amongst thick reeds his aged head.
And when the Spaniards their assault begin,
At once beat those without and those within.

" This Almanzor speaks of himself; and sure for one man
to conquer an army within the city, and another without the
city, at once, is something difficult : but this flight is pardon-
able to some we meet with in Granada : Osmin, speaking of
10 Almanzor,

Who, like a tempest that outrides the wind,
Made a just battle, ere the bodies join'd.

Pray, what does this honourable person mean by a *tempest
that outrides the wind!* a tempest that outrides itself. To
suppose a tempest without wind, is as bad as supposing a
man to walk without feet ; for if he supposes the tempest to
be something distinct from the wind, yet, as being the effect
of wind only, to come before the cause is a little prepos-
terous ; so that, if he takes it one way, or if he takes it the
20 other, those two *ifs* will scarce make one *possibility.*" Enough
of Settle.

Marriage Alamode (1673) is a comedy dedicated to the
Earl of Rochester, whom he acknowledges not only as the
defender of his poetry, but the promoter of his fortune.
Langbaine places this play in 1673.   The Earl of Rochester,
therefore, was the famous Wilmot, whom yet tradition always
represents as an enemy to Dryden, and who is mentioned by
him with some disrespect in the preface to Juvenal.

The Assignation, or Love in a Nunnery, a comedy
30 (1673), was driven off the stage, *against the opinion,* as the
author says, *of the best judges.*   It is dedicated, in a very
elegant address, to Sir Charles Sedley ; in which he finds an
opportunity for his usual complaint of hard treatment and
unreasonable censure.

Amboyna (1673) is a tissue of mingled dialogue in verse

and prose, and was perhaps written in less time than The
Virgin Martyr; though the author thought not fit either
ostentatiously or mournfully to tell how little labour it cost
him, or at how short a warning he produced it. It was a
temporary performance, written in the time of the Dutch
war, to inflame the nation against their enemies; to whom
he hopes, as he declares in his epilogue, to make his poetry
not .less destructive than that by which Tyrtæus of old
animated the Spartans. This play was written in the second
Dutch war in 1673.　　　　　　　　　　　　　　　　　　　10

Troilus and Cressida (1679) is a play altered from Shakspeare ; but so altered, that, even in Langbaine's opinion,
"the last scene in the third act is a master-piece." It is
introduced by a discourse "on the Grounds of Criticism in
Tragedy," to which I suspect that Rymer's book had given
occasion.

The Spanish Friar (1681) is a tragi-comedy, eminent
for the happy coincidence and coalition of the two plots. As
it was written against the papists, it would naturally at that
time have friends and enemies ; and partly by the popularity 20
which it obtained at first, and partly by the real power both
of the serious and risible part, it continued long a favourite
of the public.

It was Dryden's opinion, at least, for some time, and he
maintains it in the dedication of this play, that the drama
required an alternation of comic and tragic scenes ; and that
it is necessary to mitigate by alleviations of merriment the
pressure of ponderous events, and the fatigue of toilsome
passions. "Whoever," says he, "cannot perform both parts,
is but half a writer for the stage."　　　　　　　　　　　30

The Duke of Guise, a tragedy (1683), written in conjunction with Lee, as Œdipus had been before, seems to
deserve notice only for the offence which it gave to the
remnant of the Covenanters, and in general to the enemies
of the court, who attacked him with great violence, and were
answered by him ; though at last he seems to withdraw from

the conflict, by transferring the greater part of the blame or
merit to his partner. It happened that a contract had been
made between them, by which they were to join in writing
a play ; and "he happened," says Dryden, "to claim the
promise just upon the finishing of a poem, when I would
have been glad of a little respite. —*Two*-thirds of it belonged
to him ; and to me only the first scene of the play, the whole
fourth act, and the first half, or somewhat more, of the fifth."

This was a play written professedly for the party of the
10 Duke of York, whose succession was then opposed. A
parallel is intended between the Leaguers of France and the
Covenanters of England; and this intention produced the
controversy.

Albion and Albanius (1685) is a musical drama or opera,
written, like the Duke of Guise, against the Republicans.
With what success it was performed, I have not found.

The State of Innocence and Fall of Man (1675) is
termed by him an opera : it is rather a tragedy in heroic
rhyme, but of which the personages are such as cannot
20 decently be exhibited on the stage. Some such production
was foreseen by Marvel, who writes thus to Milton :

> Or if a work so infinite be spann'd,
> Jealous I was least some less skilful hand
> (Such as disquiet always what is well,
> And by ill-imitating would excel),
> Might hence presume the whole creation's day
> To change in scenes, and show it in a play.

It is another of his hasty productions ; for the heat of his
imagination raised it in a month.

30   This composition is addressed to the Princess of Modena,
then Duchess of York, in a strain of flattery which disgraces
genius, and which it was wonderful that any man that knew
the meaning of his own words could use without self-
detestation. It is an attempt to mingle earth and heaven,
by praising human excellence in the language of religion.

The preface contains an apology for heroic verse and

poetic licence; by which is meant not any liberty taken in contracting or extending words, but the use of bold fictions and ambitious figures.

The reason which he gives for printing what was never acted cannot be overpassed : " I was induced to it in my own defence, many hundred copies of it being dispersed abroad without my knowledge or consent ; and every one gathering new faults, it became at length a libel against me." These copies, as they gathered faults, were apparently manuscript ; and he lived in an age very unlike ours, if 10 many hundred copies of fourteen hundred lines were likely to be transcribed.   An author has a right to print his own works, and needs not seek an apology in falsehood ; but he that could bear to write the dedication felt no pain in writing the preface.

Aureng Zebe (1676) is a tragedy founded on the actions of a great prince then reigning, but over nations not likely to employ their critics upon the transactions of the English stage.   If he had known and disliked his own character, our trade was not in those times secure from his resentment. 20 His country is at such a distance, that the manners might be safely falsified, and the incidents feigned ; for remoteness of place is remarked, by Racine, to afford the same conveniences to a poet as length of time.

This play is written in rhyme ; and has the appearance of being the most elaborate of all the dramas.   The personages are imperial ; but the dialogue is often domestic, and therefore susceptible of sentiments accommodated to familiar incidents.   The complaint of life is celebrated ; and there are many other passages that may be read with pleasure.   30

The play is addressed to the Earl of Mulgrave, afterwards Duke of Buckingham, himself, if not a poet, yet a writer of verses, and a critic.   In this address Dryden gave the first hints of his intention to write an epic poem.   He mentions his design in terms so obscure, that he seems afraid lest his plan should be purloined, as he says, happened to him when he told it more plainly in his preface to Juvenal. "The design," says he, "you know is great, the story English, and neither too near the present times, nor too distant from them."

All for Love, or the World well Lost (1678), a tragedy founded upon the story of Antony and Cleopatra, he tells us, "is the only play which he wrote for himself": the rest were given to the people. It is by universal consent accounted the work in which he has admitted the fewest
10 improprieties of style or character; but it has one fault equal to many, though rather moral than critical, that, by admitting the romantic omnipotence of love, he has recom- mended, as laudable and worthy of imitation, that conduct which, through all ages, the good have censured as vicious, and the bad despised as foolish.

Of this play the prologue and the epilogue, though written upon the common topics of malicious and ignorant criticism, and without any particular relation to the characters or incidents of the drama, are deservedly celebrated for their
20 elegance and sprightliness.

Limberham, or the Kind Keeper (1680), is a comedy, which, after the third night, was prohibited as too indecent for the stage. What gave offence, was in the printing, as the author says, altered or omitted. Dryden confesses that its indecency was objected to; but Langbaine, who yet seldom favours him, imputes its expulsion to resentment, because it "so much exposed the keeping part of the town."

Œdipus (1679) is a tragedy formed by Dryden and Lee, in conjunction, from the works of Sophocles, Seneca, and
30 Corneille. Dryden planned the scenes, and composed the first and third acts.

Don Sebastian (1690) is commonly esteemed either the first or second of his dramatic performances. It is too long to be all acted, and has many characters and many incidents; and though it is not without sallies of frantic dignity, and more noise than meaning, yet, as it makes approaches to the

possibilities of real life, and has some sentiments which leave
a strong impression, it continued long to attract attention.
Amidst the distresses of princes, and the vicissitudes of
empire, are inserted several scenes which the writer intended
for comic ; but which, I suppose, that age did not much
commend, and this would not endure. There are, however,
passages of excellence universally acknowledged ; the dispute
and the reconciliation of Dorax and Sebastian has always
been admired.

This play was first acted in 1690, after Dryden had for 10
some years discontinued dramatic poetry.

Amphitryon is a comedy derived from Plautus and
Molière. The dedication is dated Oct. 1690. This play
seems to have succeeded at its first appearance ; and was, I
think, long considered as a very diverting entertainment.

Cleomenes (1692) is a tragedy, only remarkable as it
occasioned an incident related in the Guardian, and allusively
mentioned by Dryden in his preface. As he came out from
the representation, he was accosted thus by some airy strip-
ling : "Had I been left alone with a young beauty, I would 20
not have spent my time like your Spartan." "That, sir,"
said Dryden, "perhaps is true ; but give me leave to tell
you, that you are no hero."

King Arthur (1691) is another opera. It was the last
work that Dryden performed for King Charles, who did not
live to see it exhibited, and it does not seem to have been
ever brought upon the stage. In the dedication to the
Marquis of Halifax, there is a very elegant character of
Charles, and a pleasing account of his latter life. When this
was first brought upon the stage, news that the Duke of 30
Monmouth had landed was told in the theatre ; upon which
the company departed, and Arthur was exhibited no more.

His last drama was Love Triumphant, a tragi-comedy.
In his dedication to the Earl of Salisbury he mentions "the
lowness of fortune to which he has voluntarily reduced himself, and of which he has no reason to be ashamed."

This play appeared in 1694. It is said to have been unsuccessful. The catastrophe, proceeding merely from a change
of mind, is confessed by the author to be defective. Thus
he began and ended his dramatic labours with ill success.

From such a number of theatrical pieces, it will be
supposed, by most readers, that he must have improved
his fortune; at least, that such diligence with such abilities
must have set penury at defiance. But in Dryden's time
the drama was very ·far from that universal approbation
10 which it has now obtained. The playhouse was abhorred
by the Puritans, and avoided by those who desired the
character of seriousness or decency. A grave lawyer would
have debased his dignity, and a young trader would have
impaired his credit, by appearing in those mansions of
dissolute licentiousness. The profits of the theatre, when
so many classes of the people were deducted from the
audience, were not great; and the poet had, for a long
time, but a single night. The first that had two nights
was Southern ; and the first that had three was Rowe.
20 There were, however, in those days, arts of improving a
poet's profit, which Dryden forbore to practise ; and a play
therefore seldom produced him more than a hundred pounds,
by the accumulated gain of the third night, the dedication,
and the copy.

Almost every piece had a dedication, written with such
elegance and luxuriance of praise, as neither haughtiness
nor avarice could be imagined able to resist. But he seems
to have made flattery too cheap. That praise is worth
nothing of which the price is known.

30 To increase the value of his copies, he often accompanied
his work with a preface of criticism ; a kind of learning
then almost new in the English language, and which he,
who had considered with great accuracy the principles of
writing, was able to distribute copiously as occasions arose.
By these dissertations the public judgment must have been
much improved ; and Swift, who conversed with Dryden,

relates that he regretted the success of his own instructions, and found his readers made suddenly too skilful to be easily satisfied.

His prologues had such reputation, that for some time a play was considered as less likely to be well received, if some of his verses did not introduce it. The price of a prologue was two guineas, till, being asked to write one for Mr. Southern, he demanded three ; "Not," said he, "young man, out of disrespect to you, but the players have had my goods too cheap." 10

Though he declares, that in his own opinion his genius was not dramatic, he had great confidence in his own fertility ; for he is said to have engaged, by contract, to furnish four plays a year.

It is certain that in one year, 1678, he published All for Love, Assignation, two parts of the Conquest of Granada, Sir Martin Marall, and the State of Innocence, six complete plays, with a celerity of performance, which, though all Langbaine's charges of plagiarism should be allowed, shows such facility of composition, such readiness of language, 20 and such copiousness of sentiment, as, since the time of Lopez de Vega, perhaps no other author has possessed.

He did not enjoy his reputation, however great, nor his profits, however small, without molestation. He had critics to endure, and rivals to oppose. The two most distinguished wits of the nobility, the Duke of Buckingham and Earl of Rochester, declared themselves his enemies.

Buckingham characterized him, in 1671, by the name of Bayes in the Rehearsal : a farce which he is said to have written with the assistance of Butler, the author of Hudi- 30 bras ; Martin Clifford, of the Charter-house ; and Dr. Sprat, the friend of Cowley, then his chaplain. Dryden and his friends laughed at the length of time, and the number of hands employed upon this performance ; in which, though by some artifice of action it yet keeps possession of the stage, it is not possible now to find anything that might not

have been written without so long delay, or a confederacy
so numerous.

To adjust the minute events of literary history is tedious
and troublesome ; it requires indeed no great force of understanding, but often depends upon inquiries which there is
no opportunity of making, or is to be fetched from books
and pamphlets not always at hand.

The Rehearsal was played in 1671, and yet is represented
as ridiculing passages in the Conquest of Granada and Assig-
10 nation, which were not published till 1678, in Marriage Alamode, published in 1673, and in Tyrannic Love, of 1677.
These contradictions show how rashly satire is applied.

It is said that this farce was originally intended against
Davenant, who, in the first draught, was characterized by
the name of Bilboa. Davenant had been a soldier and an
adventurer.

There is one passage in the Rehearsal still remaining,
which seems to have related originally to Davenant. Bayes
hurts his nose, and comes in with brown paper applied to
20 the bruise ; how this affected Dryden, does not appear.
Davenant's nose had suffered such diminution, that a patch
upon that part evidently denoted him.   ————

It is said likewise that Sir Robert Howard was once
meant. The design was probably to ridicule the reigning
poet, whoever he might be.

Much of the personal satire, to which it might owe its
first reception, is now lost or obscured. Bayes probably
imitated the dress, and mimicked the manner, of Dryden ;
the cant words which are so often in his mouth may be
30 supposed to have been Dryden's habitual phrases, or customary exclamations. Bayes, when he is to write, is blooded
and purged ; this, as Lamotte relates himself to have heard,
was the real practice of the poet.

There were other strokes in the Rehearsal by which
malice was gratified ; the debate between Love and Honour,
which keeps Prince Volscius in a single boot, is said to

have alluded to the misconduct of the Duke of Ormond, who lost Dublin to the rebels while he was toying with a mistress.

The Earl of Rochester, to suppress the reputation of Dryden, took Settle into his protection, and endeavoured to persuade the public that its approbation had been to that time misplaced. Settle was a while in high reputation ; his Empress of Morocco, having first delighted the town (1673), was carried in triumph to Whitehall, and played by the ladies of the court. Now was the poetical meteor at the 10 highest : the next moment began its fall. Rochester with-drew his patronage ; seeming resolved, says one of his biographers, "to have a judgement contrary to that of the town" ; perhaps being unable to endure any reputation beyond a certain height, even when he had himself con-tributed to raise it.

Neither critics nor rivals did Dryden much mischief, unless they gained from his own temper the power of vexing him, which his frequent bursts of resentment give reason to suspect. He is always angry at some past, or afraid 20 some future censure ; but he lessens the smart of his wounds by the balm of his own approbation, and endeavours to repel the shafts of criticism by opposing a shield of adamantine confidence.

The perpetual accusation produced against him was that of plagiarism, against which he never attempted any vigorous defence ; for though he was perhaps sometimes injuriously censured, he would, by denying part of the charge, have con-fessed the rest ; and, as his adversaries had the proof in their own hands, he, who knew that wit had little power 30 against facts, wisely left, in that perplexity which generality produces, a question which it was his interest to suppress, and which, unless provoked by vindication, few were likely to examine.

Though the life of a writer, from about thirty-five to sixty-three, may be supposed to have been sufficiently busied

by the composition of eight-and-twenty pieces for the stage.
Dryden found room in the same space for many other under-
takings.

But how much soever he wrote, he was at least once
suspected of writing more ; for in 1679, a paper of verses,
called An Essay on Satire, was shown about in manuscript,
by which the Earl of Rochester, the Duchess of Portsmouth,
and others, were so much provoked, that, as was supposed
(for the actors were never discovered), they procured Dryden,
10 whom they suspected as the author, to be waylaid and
beaten.   This incident is mentioned by the Duke of Buckinghamshire, the true writer, in his Art of Poetry ; where he
says of Dryden,

> Though praised and beaten for another's rhymes,
> His own deserves as great applause sometimes.

His reputation in time was such, that his name was
thought necessary to the success of every poetical or literary
performance, and therefore he was engaged to contribute
something, whatever it might be, to many publications.   He
20 prefixed the Life of Polybius to the translation of Sir Henry
Sheers ; and those of Lucian and Plutarch, to versions of
their works by different hands.   Of the English Tacitus he
translated the first book ; and, if Gordon be credited, translated it from the French.   Such a charge can hardly be
mentioned without some degree of indignation ; but it is
not, I suppose, so much to be inferred, that Dryden wanted
the literature necessary to the perusal of Tacitus, as that,
considering himself as hidden in a crowd, he had no awe of
the public ; and, writing merely for money, was contented
30 to get it by the nearest way.

In 1680, the Epistles of Ovid being translated by the poets
of the time, among which one was the work of Dryden, and
another of Dryden and Lord Mulgrave, it was necessary to
introduce them by a preface ; and Dryden, who on such
occasions was regularly summoned, prefixed a discourse upon

translation, which was then struggling for the liberty that
it now enjoys. Why it should find any difficulty in breaking
the shackles of verbal interpretation, which must for ever
debar it from elegance, it would be difficult to conjecture,
were not the power of prejudice every day observed. The
authority of Jonson, Sandys, and Holiday, had fixed the
judgment of the nation ; and it was not easily believed that
a better way could be found than they had taken, though
Fanshaw, Denham, Waller, and Cowley had tried to give
examples of a different practice.   10

In 1681, Dryden became yet more conspicuous by uniting
politics with poetry, in the memorable satire called Absalom
and Achitophel, written against the faction which, by Lord
Shaftesbury's incitement, set the Duke of Monmouth at its
head.

Of this poem, in which personal satire was applied to the
support of public principles, and in which therefore every
mind was interested, the reception was eager, and the sale so
large, that my father, an old bookseller, told me, he had not
known it equalled but by Sacheverell's trial.   20

The reason of this general perusal Addison has attempted
to derive from the delight which the mind feels in the in-
vestigation of secrets; and thinks that curiosity to decipher
the names procured readers to the poem. There is no need
to inquire why those verses were read, which, to all the
attractions of wit, elegance, and harmony, added the co-
operation of all the factious passions, and filled every mind
with triumph or resentment.

It could not be supposed that all the provocation given by
Dryden would be endured without resistance or reply. Both   30
his person and his party were exposed in their turns to the
shafts of satire, which, though neither so well pointed, nor
perhaps so well aimed, undoubtedly drew blood.

One of these poems is called Dryden's Satire on his Muse;
ascribed, though, as Pope says, falsely, to Somers, who was
afterwards chancellor. The poem, whose soever it was, has

much virulence, and some sprightliness. The writer tells all
the ill that he can collect both of Dryden and his friends.

The poem of Absalom and Achitophel had two answers,
now both forgotten ; one called Azaria and Hushai ; the
other Absalom Senior. Of these hostile compositions, Dryden
apparently imputes Absalom Senior to Settle, by quoting in
his verses against him the second line. Azaria and Hushai
was, as Wood says, imputed to him, though it is somewhat
unlikely that he should write twice on the same occasion.
10 This is a difficulty which I cannot remove, for want of a
minuter knowledge of poetical transactions.

The same year he published The Medal, of which the
subject is a medal struck on Lord Shaftesbury's escape from
a prosecution, by the ignoramus of a grand jury of Londoners.
In both poems he maintains the same principles, and saw
them both attacked by the same antagonist. Elkanah Settle,
who had answered Absalom, appeared with equal courage in
opposition to The Medal, and published an answer called
The Medal Reversed, with so much success in both en-
20 counters, that he left the palm doubtful, and divided the
suffrages of the nation. Such are the revolutions of fame, or
such is the prevalence of fashion, that the man whose works
have not yet been thought to deserve the care of collecting
them, who died forgotten in an hospital, and whose latter
years were spent in contriving shows for fairs, and carrying
an elegy or epithalamium, of which the beginning and end
were occasionally varied, but the intermediate parts were
always the same, to every house where there was a funeral
or a wedding, might with truth have had inscribed upon his
30 stone,

Here lies the Rival and Antagonist of Dryden.

Settle was, for this rebellion, severely chastised by Dryden
under the name of Doeg, in the second part of Absalom and
Achitophel ; and was perhaps for his factious audacity made
the city poet, whose annual office was to describe the glories
of the Mayor's day. Of these bards he was the last, and

seems not much to have deserved even this degree of regard,
if it was paid to his political opinions; for he afterwards
wrote a panegyric on the virtues of Judge Jefferies; and
what more could have been done by the meanest zealot for
prerogative?

Of translated fragments, or occasional poems, to enumerate
the titles, or settle the dates, would be tedious, with little
use. It may be observed that, as Dryden's genius was commonly excited by some personal regard, he rarely writes
upon a general topic. 10

Soon after the accession of King James, when the design
of reconciling the nation to the Church of Rome became
apparent, and the religion of the court gave the only effica-
cious title to its favours, Dryden declared himself a convert
to popery. This at any other time might have passed with
little censure. Sir Kenelm Digby embraced popery; the two
Rainolds reciprocally converted one another; and Chillingworth himself was a while so entangled in the wilds of controversy, as to retire for quiet to an infallible church. If men
of argument and study can find such difficulties, or such 20
motives, as may either unite them to the Church of Rome, or
detain them in uncertainty, there can be no wonder that a
man, who perhaps never inquired why he was a protestant,
should by an artful and experienced disputant be made a
papist, overborne by the sudden violence of new and un-
expected arguments, or deceived by a representation which
shows only the doubts on one part, and only the evidence on
the other.

That conversion will always be suspected that apparently
concurs with interest. He that never finds his error till 30
it hinders his progress towards wealth or honour, will not
be thought to love truth only for herself. Yet it may
easily happen that information may come at a commodious
time; and, as truth and interest are not by any fatal
necessity at variance, that one may by accident introduce
the other. When opinions are struggling into popularity,

C

the arguments by which they are opposed or defended
become more known; and he that changes his profession
would perhaps have changed it before, with the like opportunities of instruction. This was then the state of popery;
every artifice was used to show it in its fairest form; and
it must be owned to be a religion of external appearance
sufficiently attractive.

It is natural to hope that a comprehensive is likewise an
elevated soul, and that whoever is wise is also honest. I
10 am willing to believe that Dryden, having employed his
mind, active as it was, upon different studies, and filled it,
capacious as it was, with other materials, came unprovided
to the controversy, and wanted rather skill to discover
the right than virtue to maintain it. But enquiries into
the heart are not for man; we must now leave him to his
Judge.

The priests, having strengthened their cause by so powerful an adherent, were not long before they brought him into
action. They engaged him to defend the controversial
20 papers found in the strong box of Charles the Second;
and, what yet was harder, to defend them against Stillingfleet.

With hopes of promoting popery, he was employed to
translate Maimbourg's History of the League; which he
published with a large introduction. His name is likewise
prefixed to the English Life of Francis Xavier; but I know
not that he ever owned himself the translator. Perhaps the
use of his name was a pious fraud, which however seems not
to have had much effect; for neither of the books, I believe,
30 was ever popular.

The version of Xavier's Life is commended by Brown, in a
pamphlet not written to flatter; and the occasion of it is
said to have been, that the queen, when she solicited a son,
made vows to him as her tutelary saint.

He was supposed to have undertaken to translate Varillas's
History of Heresies; and, when Burnet published remarks

upon it, to have written an Answer; upon which Burnet makes the following observation :

" I have been informed from England, that a gentleman, who is famous both for poetry and several other things, had spent three months in translating M. Varillas's History; but that, as soon as my Reflections appeared, he discontinued his labour, finding the credit of his author was gone. Now, if he thinks it is recovered by his Answer, he will perhaps go on with his translation; and this may be, for aught I know, as good an entertainment for him as the conversation that he had set on between the Hinds and Panthers and all the rest of animals, for whom M. Varillas may serve well enough as an author : and this history and that poem are such extraordinary things of their kind, that it will be but suitable to see the author of the worst poem become likewise the translator of the worst history that the age has produced. If his grace and his wit improve both proportionably, he will hardly find that he has gained much by the change he has made, from having no religion, to chuse one of the worst. It is true, he had somewhat to sink from in matter of wit; but, as for his morals, it is scarce possible for him to grow a worse man than he was. He has lately wreaked his malice on me for spoiling his three months' labour ; but in it he has done me all the honour that any man can receive from him, which is to be railed at by him. If I had ill-nature enough to prompt me to wish a very bad wish for him, it should be, that he would go on and finish his translation. By that it will appear, whether the English nation, which is the most competent judge in this matter, has, upon the seeing our debate, pronounced in M. Varillas's favour, or in mine. It is true, Mr. D. will suffer a little by it ; but at least it will serve to keep him in from other extravagances ; and if he gains little honour by this work, yet he cannot lose so much by it as he has done by his last employment."

Having probably felt his own inferiority in theological controversy, he was desirous of trying whether, by bringing

poetry to aid his arguments, he might become a more effica-
cious defender of his new profession. To reason in verse
was, indeed, one of his powers; but subtilty and harmony,
united, are still feeble, when opposed to truth.

Actuated therefore by zeal for Rome, or hope of fame, he
published the Hind and Panther (1687), a poem in which the
Church of Rome, figured by the *milk-white Hind*, defends her
tenets against the Church of England, represented by the
Panther, a beast beautiful, but spotted.

10   A fable, which exhibits two beasts talking theology,
appears at once full of absurdity; and it was accordingly
ridiculed in the City Mouse and Country Mouse, a parody,
written by Montague, afterwards Earl of Halifax, and Prior,
who then gave the first specimen of his abilities.

The conversion of such a man, at such a time, was not
likely to pass uncensured. Three dialogues were published
by the facetious Thomas Brown, of which the two first were
called Reasons of Mr. Bayes's changing his religion : and the
third, the Reasons of Mr. Hains the Player's Conversion
20 and Re-conversion. The first was printed in 1688, the
second not till 1690, the third in 1691. The clamour seems
to have been long continued, and the subject to have
strongly fixed the public attention.

In the two first dialogues Bayes is brought into the
company of Crites and Eugenius, with whom he had formerly debated on dramatic poetry. The two talkers in the
third are Mr. Bayes and Mr. Hains.

Brown was a man not deficient in literature, nor destitute
of fancy; but he seems to have thought it the pinnacle of
30 excellence to be a *merry fellow*; and therefore laid out his
powers upon small jests or gross buffoonery; so that his
performances have little intrinsic value, and were read only
while they were recommended by the novelty of the event
that occasioned them.

These dialogues are like his other works : what sense or
knowledge they contain is disgraced by the garb in which it

is exhibited. One great source of pleasure is to call Dryden _little Bayes._ Ajax, who happens to be mentioned, is "he that wore as many cow-hides upon his shield as would have furnished half the king's army with shoe-leather."

Being asked whether he has seen the Hind and Panther, Crites answers: "Seen it! Mr. Bayes; why I can stir nowhere but it pursues me : it haunts me worse than a pewter-buttoned serjeant does a decayed cit. Sometimes I meet it in a bandbox, when my laundress brings home my linen ; sometimes, whether I will or no, it lights my pipe at 10 a coffee-house ; sometimes it surprises me in a trunk-maker's shop, and sometimes it refreshes my memory for me on the backside of a Chancery-lane parcel. For your comfort too, Mr. Bayes, I have not only seen it, as you may perceive, but have read it too, and can quote it as freely upon occasion as a frugal tradesman can quote that noble treatise the Worth of a Penny to his extravagant 'prentice, that revels in stewed apples and penny custards."

The whole animation of these compositions arises from a profusion of ludicrous and affected comparisons.   20

Brown does not wholly forget past transactions : "You began," says Crites to Bayes, "with a very indifferent religion, and have not mended the matter in your last choice. It was but reason that your Muse, which appeared first in a Tyrant's quarrel, should employ her last efforts to justify the usurpation of the Hind."

Next year the nation was summoned to celebrate the birth of the Prince. Now was the time for Dryden to rouse his imagination, and strain his voice. Happy days were at hand, and he was willing to enjoy and diffuse the anticipated 30 blessings. He published a poem, filled with predictions of greatness and prosperity; predictions, of which it is not necessary to tell how they have been verified.

A few months passed after these joyful notes, and every blossom of popish hope was blasted for ever by the Revolution. A papist now could be no longer Laureat. The revenue

which he had enjoyed with so much pride and praise, was
transferred to Shadwell, an old enemy, whom he had formerly stigmatised by the name of Og. Dryden could not
decently complain that he was deposed ; but seemed very
angry that Shadwell succeeded him, and has therefore celebrated the intruder's inauguration in a poem exquisitely
satirical, called Mac Flecknoe ; of which the Dunciad, as
Pope himself declares, is an imitation, though more extended
in its plan, and more diversified in its incidents.

10   It is related by Prior, that Lord Dorset, when as chamberlain he was constrained to eject Dryden from his office, gave
him from his own purse an allowance equal to the salary.
This is no romantic or incredible act of generosity; an
hundred a year is often enough given to claims less cogent
by men less famed for liberality.   Yet Dryden always represented himself as suffering under a public infliction; and
once particularly demands respect for the patience with
which he endured the loss of his little fortune.   His patron
might, indeed, enjoin him to suppress his bounty; but if he
20 suffered nothing, he should not have complained.

During the short reign of King James, he had written
nothing for the stage, being, in his opinion, more profitably
employed in controversy and flattery.   Of praise he might
perhaps have been less lavish without inconvenience, for
James was never said to have much regard for poetry : he
was to be flattered only by adopting his religion.

Times were now changed : Dryden was no longer the
court-poet, and was to look back for support to his former
trade ; and having waited about two years, either considering
30 himself as discountenanced by the public, or perhaps expect-
ing a second Revolution, he produced Don Sebastian in
1690 ; and in the next four years four dramas more.

In 1693 appeared a new version of Juvenal and Persius.
Of Juvenal he translated the first, third, sixth, tenth, and
sixteenth satires ; and of Persius the whole work.   On
this occasion he introduced his two sons to the public, as

nurslings of the Muses. The fourteenth of Juvenal was the work of John and the seventh of Charles Dryden. He prefixed a very ample preface, in the form of a dedication to Lord Dorset; and there gives an account of the design which he had once formed to write an epic poem on the actions either of Arthur or the Black Prince. He considered the epic as necessarily including some kind of supernatural *clever* agency, and had imagined a new kind of contest between the guardian angels of kingdoms, of whom he conceived that each might be represented zealous for his charge, 10 without any intended opposition to the purposes of the Supreme Being, of which all created minds must in part be ignorant.

This is the most reasonable scheme of celestial interposition that ever was formed. The surprises and terrors of enchantments which have succeeded to the intrigues and oppositions of Pagan deities, afford very striking scenes, and open a vast extent to the imagination; but, as Boileau observes (and Boileau will be seldom found mistaken), with this incurable defect, that, in a contest between Heaven and 20 Hell, we know at the beginning which is to prevail; for this reason we follow Rinaldo to the enchanted wood with more curiosity than terror.

In the scheme of Dryden there is one great difficulty, which yet he would perhaps have had address enough to surmount. In a war justice can be but on one side; and, to entitle the hero to the protection of angels, he must fight in the defence of indubitable right. Yet some of the celestial beings, thus opposed to each other, must have been represented as defending guilt. 30

That this poem was never written, is reasonably to be lamented. It would doubtless have improved our numbers, and enlarged our language; and might perhaps have contributed by pleasing instruction to rectify our opinions, and purify our manners.

What he required as the indispensable condition of such

an undertaking, a public stipend, was not likely in those
times to be obtained. Riches were not become familiar to
us; nor had the nation yet learned to be liberal.

This plan he charged Blackmore with stealing; "only,"
says he, "the guardian angels of kingdoms were machines
too ponderous for him to manage."

In 1694, he began the most laborious and difficult of all
his works, the translation of Virgil; from which he borrowed
two months, that he might turn Fresnoy's Art of Painting
10 into English prose. The preface, which he boasts to have
written in twelve mornings, exhibits a parallel of poetry
and painting, with a miscellaneous collection of critical
remarks, such as cost a mind stored like his' no labour to
produce them.

In 1697, he published his version of the works of Virgil;
and, that no opportunity of profit might be lost, dedicated
the Pastorals to the Lord Clifford, the Georgics to the Earl
of Chesterfield, and the Eneid to the Earl of Mulgrave.
This economy of flattery, at once lavish and discreet, did not
20 pass without observation.

This translation was censured by Milbourne, a clergyman,
styled, by Pope, "the fairest of critics," because he exhibited his own version to be compared with that which
he condemned.

His last work was his Fables, published in 1699, in consequence, as is supposed, of a contract now in the hands
of ·Mr. Tonson; by which he obliged himself, in consideration
of three hundred pounds, to finish for the press ten thousand
verses.

30   In this volume is comprised the well-known Ode on St.
Cecilia's day, which, as appeared by a letter communicated
to Dr. Birch, he spent a fortnight in composing and correct-
ing. But what is this to the patience and diligence of
Boileau, whose Equivoque, a poem of only three hundred
forty six lines, took from his life eleven months to write it,
and three years to revise it.

Part of this book of Fables is the first Iliad in English,
intended as a specimen of a version of the whole. Considering
into what hands Homer was to fall, the reader cannot but
rejoice that this project went no further.

The time was now at hand which was to put an end to all
his schemes and labours. On the first of May, 1701, having
been some time, as he tells us, a cripple in his limbs, he died,
in Gerard-street, of a mortification in his leg.

There is extant a wild story relating to some vexatious
events that happened at his funeral, which, at the end of 10
Congreve's Life, by a writer of I know not what credit, are
thus related, as I find the account transferred to a biographical
dictionary.

"Mr. Dryden dying on the Wednesday morning, Dr.
Thomas Sprat, then Bishop of Rochester and Dean of Westminster, sent the next day to the Lady Elizabeth Howard,
Mr. Dryden's widow, that he would make a present of the
ground, which was forty pounds, with all the other Abbey
fees. The Lord Halifax likewise sent to the Lady Elizabeth,
and Mr. Charles Dryden her son, that, if they would give 20
him leave to bury Mr. Dryden, he would inter him with a
gentleman's private funeral, and afterwards bestow five
hundred pounds on a monument in the Abbey ; which, as
they had no reason to refuse, they accepted. On the Saturday
following the company came; the corpse was put into a
velvet hearse ; and eighteen mourning coaches, filled with
company, attended. When they were just ready to move,
the Lord Jefferies, son of the Lord Chancellor Jefferies,
with some of his rakish companions, coming by, asked whose
funeral it was : and being told Mr. Dryden's, he said, 'What, 30
shall Dryden, the greatest honour and ornament of the
nation, be buried after this private manner ! No, gentlemen,
let all that loved Mr. Dryden, and honour his memory,
alight and join with me in gaining my lady's consent to let
me have the honour of his interment, which shall be after
another manner than this ; and I will bestow a thousand

pounds on a monument in the Abbey for him.' The gentlemen in the coaches, not knowing of the Bishop of Rochester's
favour, nor of the Lord Halifax's generous design (they both
having, out of respect to the family, enjoined the Lady
Elizabeth, and her son, to keep their favour concealed to the
world, and let it pass for their own expense), readily came
out of their coaches, and attended Lord Jefferies up to the
lady's bedside, who was then sick. He repeated the purport
of what he had before said ; but she absolutely refusing, he
10 fell on his knees, vowing never to rise till his request was
granted. The rest of the company by his desire kneeled also ;
and the lady, being under a sudden surprise, fainted away.
As soon as she recovered her speech, she cried, *No, no.*
Enough, gentlemen, replied he; my lady is very good, she
says, *Go, go.* She repeated her former words with all her
strength, but in vain, for her feeble voice was lost in their
acclamations of joy ; and the Lord Jefferies ordered the
hearsemen to carry the corpse to Mr. Russel's, an undertaker's
in Cheapside, and leave it there till he should send orders for
20 the embalmment, which, he added, should be after the royal
manner. His directions were obeyed, the company dispersed,
and Lady Elizabeth and her son remained inconsolable. The
next day Mr. Charles Dryden waited on the Lord Halifax,
and the Bishop, to excuse his mother and himself, by relating
the real truth. But neither his Lordship nor the Bishop
would admit of any plea: especially the latter, who had the
Abbey lighted, the ground opened, the choir attending, an
anthem ready set, and himself waiting for sometime without
any corpse to bury. The undertaker, after three days' ex-
30 pectance of orders for embalmment without receiving any,
waited on the Lord Jefferies ; who pretending ignorance of
the matter, turned it off with an ill-natured jest, saying, that
those who observed the orders of a drunken frolic deserved
no better; that he remembered nothing at all of it ; and that
he might do what he pleased with the corpse. Upon this,
the undertaker waited upon the Lady Elizabeth and her son,

and threatened to bring the corpse home, and set it before the door. They desired a day's respite, which was granted. Mr. Charles Dryden wrote a handsome letter to the Lord Jefferies, who returned it with this cool answer: 'That he knew nothing of the matter, and would be troubled no more about it.' He then addressed the Lord Halifax and the Bishop of Rochester, who absolutely refused to do anything in it. In this distress Dr. Garth sent for the corpse to the College of Physicians, and proposed a funeral by subscription, to which himself set a most noble example. At last a day, 10 about three weeks after Mr. Dryden's decease, was appointed for the interment. Dr. Garth pronounced a fine Latin oration, at the College, over the corpse; which was attended to the Abbey by a numerous train of coaches. When the funeral was over, Mr. Charles Dryden sent a challenge to the Lord Jefferies, who refusing to answer it, he sent several others, and went often himself; but could neither get a letter delivered, nor admittance to speak to him; which so incensed him, that he resolved, since his lordship refused to answer him like a gentleman, that he would watch an opportunity 20 to meet and fight off-hand, though with all the rules of honour; which his lordship hearing, left the town: and Mr. Charles Dryden could never have the satisfaction of meeting him, though he sought it till his death with the utmost application."

This story I once intended to omit, as it appears with no great evidence; nor have I met with any confirmation, but in a letter of Farquhar; and he only relates that the funeral of Dryden was tumultuary and confused.

Supposing the story true, we may remark, that the gradual 30 change of manners, though imperceptible in the process, appears great when different times, and those not very distant, are compared. If at this time a young drunken lord should interrupt the pompous regularity of a magnificent funeral, what would be the event, but that he would be justled out of the way, and compelled to be quiet? If he

should thrust himself into a house, he would be sent roughly
away; and, what is yet more to the honour of the present
time, I believe that those, who had subscribed to the funeral
of a man like Dryden, would not, for such an accident, have
withdrawn their contributions.

He was buried among the poets in Westminster Abbey,
where, though the Duke of Newcastle had, in a general
dedication prefixed by Congreve to his dramatic works,
accepted thanks for his intention of erecting him a monument,
10 he lay long without distinction, till the Duke of Buckinghamshire gave him a tablet, inscribed only with the name of
DRYDEN.

He married (1663) the Lady Elizabeth Howard, daughter
of the Earl of Berkshire, with circumstances, according to
the satire imputed to Lord Somers, not very honourable to
either party ; by her he had three sons, Charles, John, and
Henry.   Charles was usher of the palace to Pope Clement
the XIth; and visiting England in 1704, was drowned in an
attempt to swim across the Thames at Windsor.
20   John was author of a comedy.   He is said to have died at
Rome.   Henry entered into some religious order.   It is some
proof of Dryden's sincerity in his second religion, that he
taught it to his sons.   A man, conscious of hypocritical
profession in himself, is not likely to convert others ; and,
as his sons were qualified in 1693 to appear among the
translators of Juvenal, they must have been taught some
religion before their father's change.

Of the person of Dryden I know not any account : of his
mind, the portrait which has been left by Congreve, who
30 knew him with great familiarity, is such as adds our love of
his manners to our admiration of his genius.   "He was,"
we are told, "of a nature exceedingly humane and com-
passionate, ready to forgive injuries, and capable of a sincere
reconciliation with those that had offended him.   His friendship, where he professed it, went beyond his professions.
He was of a very easy, of very pleasing access ; but somewhat

slow, and, as it were, diffident, in his advances to others; he had
that in his nature which abhorred intrusion into any society
whatever. He was therefore less known, and consequently
his character became more liable to misapprehensions and
misrepresentations : he was very modest, and very easily
to be discountenanced in his approaches to his equals or
superiors. As his reading had been very extensive, so was he
very happy in a memory tenacious of everything that he had
read. He was not more possessed of knowledge than he was
communicative of it; but then his communication was by no 10
means pedantic, or imposed upon the conversation, but just
such, and went so far as, by the natural turn of the conversation in which he was engaged, it was necessarily
promoted or required. He was extreme ready and gentle
in his correction of the errors of any writer who thought fit
to consult him, and full as ready and patient to admit of the
reprehensions of others, in respect of his own oversights or
mistakes."

To this account of Congreve nothing can be objected but
the fondness of friendship; and to have excited that fondness 20
in such a mind is no small degree of praise. The disposition
of Dryden, however, is shown in this character rather as it
exhibited itself in cursory conversation, than as it operated
on the more important parts of life. His placability and
his friendship indeed were solid virtues ; but courtesy and
good humour are often found with little real worth. Since
Congreve, who knew him well, has told us no more, the rest
must be collected as it can from other testimonies, and
particularly from those notices which Dryden has very
liberally given us of himself.   30

The modesty which made him so slow to advance, and so
easy to be repulsed, was certainly no suspicion of deficient
merit, or unconsciousness of his own value : he appears
to have known, in its whole extent, the dignity of his
character, and to have set a very high value on his own
powers and performances. He probably did not offer his

conversation, because he expected it to be solicited ; and he
retired from a cold reception, not submissive but indignant,
with such reverence of his own greatness as made him
unwilling to expose it to neglect or violation.

His modesty was by no means inconsistent with osten-
tatiousness ; he is diligent enough to remind the world of his
merit, and expresses with very little scruple his high opinion
of his own powers ; but his self-commendations are read
without scorn or indignation ; we allow his claims, and love
10 his frankness.

Tradition, however, has not allowed that his confidence
in himself exempted him from jealousy of others. He
is accused of envy and insidiousness ; and is particularly
charged with inciting Creech to translate Horace, that he
might lose the reputation which Lucretius had given him.

Of this charge we immediately discover that it is merely
conjectural ; the purpose was such as no man would confess ; and a crime that admits no proof, why should we
believe ?

20 He has been described as magisterially presiding over the
younger writers ; and assuming the distribution of poetical
fame ; but he who excels has a right to teach, and he whose
judgment is incontestable may without usurpation examine
and decide.

Congreve represents him as ready to advise and instruct ;
but there is reason to believe that his communication was
rather useful than entertaining. He declares of himself that
he was saturnine and not one of those whose sprightly
sayings diverted company ; and one of his censurers makes
30 him say,

> Nor wine nor love could ever see me gay ;
> To writing bred, I knew not what to say.

There are men whose powers operate only at leisure and
in retirement, and whose intellectual vigour deserts them
in conversation ; whom merriment confuses, and objection
disconcerts ; whose bashfulness restrains their exertion, and

suffers them not to speak till the time of speaking is past;
or whose attention to their own character makes them
unwilling to utter at hazard what has not been considered,
and cannot be recalled.

Of Dryden's sluggishness in conversation it is vain to
search or to guess the cause. He certainly wanted neither
sentiments nor language : his intellectual treasures were
great, though they were locked up from his own use. "His
thoughts," when he wrote, " flowed in upon him so fast, that
his only care was which to chuse and which to reject." 10
Such rapidity of composition naturally promises a flow of
talk ; yet we must be content to believe what an enemy says
of him, when he likewise says it of himself. But, whatever
was his character as a companion, it appears that he lived in
familiarity with the highest persons of his time. It is related
by Carte of the Duke of Ormond, that he used often to pass
a night with Dryden, and those with whom Dryden con-
sorted : who they were, Carte has not told, but certainly the
convivial table at which Ormond sat was not surrounded
with a plebeian society. He was indeed reproached with 20
boasting of his familiarity with the great ; and Horace will
support him in the opinion, that to please superiors is not
the lowest kind of merit.

The merit of pleasing must, however, be estimated by the
means. Favour is not always gained by good actions or
laudable qualities. Caresses and preferments are often
bestowed on the auxiliaries of vice, the procurers of pleasure,
or the flatterers of vanity. Dryden has never been charged
with any personal agency unworthy of a good character : he
abetted vice and vanity only with his pen. One of his enemies 30
has accused him of lewdness in his conversation ; but, if
accusation without proof be credited, who shall be innocent ?

His works afford too many examples of dissolute licentiousness, and abject adulation : but they were probably, like his
merriment, artificial and constrained : the effects of study
and meditation, and his trade rather than his pleasure.

Of the mind that can trade in corruption, and can
deliberately pollute itself with ideal wickedness for the sake
of spreading the contagion in society, I wish not to conceal
or excuse the depravity.—Such degradation of the dignity
of genius, such abuse of superlative abilities, cannot be
contemplated but with grief and indignation. What consolation can be had, Dryden has afforded, by living to repent,
and to testify his repentance.

Of dramatic immorality he did not want examples among
10 his predecessors, or companions among his contemporaries:
but, in the meanness and servility of hyperbolical adulation,
I know not whether, since the days in which the Roman
emperors were deified, he has been ever equalled except by
Afra Behn in an address to Eleanor Gwyn. When once he
has undertaken the task of praise, he no longer retains shame
in himself, nor supposes it in his patron. As many odor-
iferous bodies are observed to diffuse perfumes from year to
year, without sensible diminution of bulk or weight, he
appears never to have impoverished his mint of flattery by
20 his expenses, however lavish. He had all the forms of
excellence, intellectual and moral, combined in his mind,
with endless variation; and, when he had scattered on the
hero of the day the golden shower of wit and virtue, he had
ready for him, whom he wished to court on the morrow, new
wit and virtue with another stamp. Of this kind of meanness he never seems to decline the practice, or lament the
necessity: he considers the great as entitled to encomiastic
homage, and brings praise rather as a tribute than a gift,
more delighted with the fertility of his invention than
30 mortified by the prostitution of his judgment. It is indeed
not certain, that on these occasions his judgment much
rebelled against his interest. There are minds which easily
sink into submission, that look on grandeur with undistin-
guishing reverence, and discover no defect where there is
elevation of rank and affluence of riches.

With his praises of others and of himself is always intermingled a strain of discontent and lamentation, a sullen growl of resentment, or a querulous murmur of distress. His works are under-valued, his merit is unrewarded, and "he has few thanks to pay his stars that he was born among Englishmen." To his critics he is sometimes contemptuous, sometimes resentful, and sometimes submissive. The writer who thinks his works formed for duration, mistakes his interest when he mentions his enemies. He degrades his own dignity by showing that he was affected by their censures, and gives lasting importance to names, which, left 10 to themselves, would vanish from remembrance. From this principle Dryden did not oft depart; his complaints are for the greater part general; he seldom pollutes his page with an adverse name. He condescended indeed to a controversy with Settle, in which he perhaps may be considered rather as assaulting than repelling; and since Settle is sunk into oblivion, his libel remains injurious only to himself.

Among answers to critics, no poetical attacks, or altercations, are to be included; they are like other poems, effusions of genius, produced as much to obtain praise as to obviate 20 censure. These Dryden practised, and in these he excelled.

Of Collier, Blackmore, and Milbourne, he has made mention in the preface of his Fables. To the censure of Collier, whose remarks may be rather termed admonitions than criticisms, he makes little reply; being, at the age of sixty-eight, attentive to better things than the claps of a playhouse. He complains of Collier's rudeness, and the "horse-play of his raillery"; and asserts, that, "in many places he has perverted by his glosses the meaning" of what he censures; but in other things he confesses that he is 30 justly taxed; and says, with great calmness and candour, "I have pleaded guilty to all thoughts or expressions of mine that can be truly accused of obscenity, immorality, or profaneness, and retract them. If he be my enemy, let him triumph; if he be my friend, he will be glad of my repentance." Yet as our best dispositions are imperfect,

D

he left standing in the same book a reflection on Collier of
great asperity, and indeed of more asperity than wit.

Blackmore he represents as made his enemy by the poem
of Absalom and Achitophel, which "he thinks a little hard
upon his fanatic patrons"; and charges him with borrowing
the plan of his Arthur from the preface to Juvenal, "though
he had," says he, "the baseness not to acknowledge his
benefactor, but instead of it to traduce me in a libel."

The libel in which Blackmore traduced him was a Satire
10 upon Wit; in which, having lamented the exuberance of
false wit and the deficiency of true, he proposes that all wit
should be re-coined, before it is current, and appoints
masters of assay who shall reject all that is light or debased.

> 'Tis true, that when the coarse and worthless dross
> Is purged away, there will be mighty loss;
> Ev'n Congreve, Southern, manly Wycherley,
> When thus refined, will grievous sufferers be;
> Into the melting pot when Dryden comes,
> What horrid stench will rise, what noisome fumes!
20 > How will he shrink, when all his lewd allay,
> And wicked mixture, shall be purged away!

Thus stands the passage in the last edition; but in the
original there was an abatement of the censure, beginning
thus:

> But what remains will be so pure, 'twill bear
> Th' examination of the most severe.

Blackmore, finding the censure resented, and the civility
disregarded, ungenerously omitted the softer part. Such
variations discover a writer who consults his passions more
30 than his virtue; and it may be reasonably supposed that
Dryden imputes his enmity to its true cause.

Of Milbourne he wrote only in general terms, such as are
always ready at the call of anger, whether just or not: a
short extract will be sufficient. "He pretends a quarrel to
me, that I have fallen foul upon priesthood; if I have, I am

only to ask pardon of good priests, and am afraid his share of the reparation will come to little. Let him be satisfied that he shall never be able to force himself upon me for an adversary; I contemn him too much to enter into competition with him.

"As for the rest of those who have written against me, they are such scoundrels that they deserve not the least notice to be taken of them. Blackmore and Milbourne are only distinguished from the crowd by being remembered to their infamy."   10

Dryden indeed discovered, in many of his writings, an affected and absurd malignity to priests and priesthood, which naturally raised him many enemies, and which was sometimes as unseasonably resented as it was exerted. Trapp is angry that he calls the sacrificer in the Georgics "The Holy Butcher"; the translation is indeed ridiculous; but Trapp's anger arises from his zeal, not for the author, but the priest; as if any reproach of the follies of paganism could be extended to the preachers of truth.

Dryden's dislike of the priesthood is imputed by Langbaine, 20 and I think by Brown, to a repulse which he suffered when he solicited ordination; but he denies, in the preface to his Fables, that he ever designed to enter into the church; and such a denial he would not have hazarded, if he could have been convicted of falsehood.

Malevolence to the clergy is seldom at a great distance from irreverence of religion, and Dryden affords no exception to this observation. His writings exhibit many passages, which, with all the allowance that can be made for characters and occasions, are such as piety would not have 30 admitted, and such as may vitiate light and unprincipled minds. But there is no reason for supposing that he disbelieved the religion which he disobeyed. He forgot his duty rather than disowned it. His tendency to profaneness is the effect of levity, negligence, and loose conversation, with a desire of accommodating himself to the corruption of

the times, by venturing to be wicked as far as he durst.
When he professed himself a convert to popery, he did not
pretend to have received any new conviction of the funda-
mental doctrines of Christianity.

The persecution of critics was not the worst of his vexa-
tions; he was much more disturbed by the importunities of
want. His complaints of poverty are so frequently repeated,
either with the dejection of weakness sinking in helpless
misery, or the indignation of merit claiming its tribute from
10 mankind, that it is impossible not to detest the age which
could impose on such a man the necessity of such solicitations, or not to despise the man who could submit to such
solicitations without necessity.

Whether by the world's neglect, or his own imprudence, I
am afraid that the greatest part of his life was passed in
exigencies. Such outcries were surely never uttered but in
severe pain. Of his supplies or his expenses no probable
estimate can now be made. Except the salary of the Laureat,
to which King James added the office of Historiographer,
20 perhaps with some additional emoluments, his whole revenue
seems to have been casual; and it is well known that he
seldom lives frugally who lives by chance. Hope is always
liberal; and they that trust her promises make little scruple
of revelling to-day on the profits of the morrow.

Of his plays the profit was not great; and of the produce
of his other works very little intelligence can be had. By
discoursing with the late amiable Mr. Tonson, I could not
find that any memorials of the transactions between his
predecessor and Dryden had been preserved, except the
30 following papers :

"I do hereby promise to pay John Dryden, Esq., or order,
on the 25th of March, 1699, the sum of two hundred and
fifty guineas, in consideration of ten thousand verses, which
the said John Dryden, Esq., is to deliver to me, Jacob
Tonson, when finished, whereof seven thousand five hundred
verses, more or less, are already in the said Jacob Tonson's

possession. And I do hereby farther promise, and engage myself, to make up the said sum of two hundred and fifty guineas three hundred pounds sterling to the said John Dryden, Esq., his executors, administrators, or assigns, at the beginning of the second impression of the said ten thousand verses.

"In witness whereof I have hereunto set my hand and seal, this 20th day of March, 169⅞.

"JACOB TONSON.

"Sealed and delivered, being   10
first duly stampt, pursuant to
the acts of parliament for
that purpose, in the presence
of
      "Ben. Portlock,
      "Will. Congreve."

"March 24, 1698.

"Received then of Mr. Jacob Tonson the sum of two hundred sixty-eight pounds fifteen shillings, in pursuance of an agreement for ten thousand verses, to be delivered 20 by me to the said Jacob Tonson, whereof I have already delivered to him about seven thousand five hundred, more or less; he the said Jacob Tonson being obliged to make up the foresaid sum of two hundred sixty-eight pounds fifteen shillings three hundred pounds, at the beginning of the second impression of the foresaid ten thousand verses ;

      "I say, received by me
          "JOHN DRYDEN.
"Witness, Charles Dryden."

Two hundred and fifty guineas, at $1l.$ $1s.$ $6d.$ is $268l.$ $15s.$ 30
It is manifest, from the dates of this contract, that it relates to the volume of Fables, which contains about twelve thousand verses, and for which therefore the payment must have been afterwards enlarged.

I have been told of another letter yet remaining, in which
he desires Tonson to bring him money, to pay for a watch
which he had ordered for his son, and which the maker
would not leave without the price.

The inevitable consequence of poverty is dependence.
Dryden had probably no recourse in his exigencies but to
his bookseller.   The particular character of Tonson I do not
know; but the general conduct of traders was much less
liberal in those times than in our own; their views were
10 narrower, and their manners grosser.   To the mercantile
ruggedness of that race, the delicacy of the poet was sometimes exposed.   Lord Bolingbroke, who in his youth had
cultivated poetry, related to Dr. King of Oxford, that one
day, when he visited Dryden, they heard, as they were
conversing, another person entering the house.   "This," said
Dryden, "is Tonson.   You will take care not to depart before
he goes away : for I have not completed the sheet which
I promised him ; and, if you leave me unprotected, I must
suffer all the rudeness to which his resentment can prompt
20 his tongue."

What rewards he obtained for his poems, besides the
payment of the bookseller, cannot be known.   Mr. Derrick,
who consulted some of his relations, was informed that his
Fables obtained five hundred pounds from the Duchess of
Ormond; a present not unsuitable to the magnificence of
that splendid family; and he quotes Moyle, as relating that
forty pounds were paid by a musical society for the use of
Alexander's Feast.

In those days the economy of government was yet
30 unsettled, and the payments of the exchequer were dilatory
and uncertain ; of this disorder there is reason to believe
that the Laureat sometimes felt the effects ; for in one of his
prefaces he complains of those, who, being intrusted with
the distribution of the prince's bounty, suffer those that
depend upon it to languish in penury.

Of his petty habits or slight amusements, tradition has

retained little. Of the only two men whom I have found
to whom he was personally known, one told me, that at the
house which he frequented, called Will's coffee-house, the
appeal upon any literary dispute was made to him; and the
other related, that his armed chair, which in the winter
had a settled and prescriptive place by the fire, was in
the summer placed in the balcony, and that he called the
two places his winter and his summer seat.   This is all the
intelligence which his two survivors afforded me.

One of his opinions will do him no honour in the present 10
age, though in his own time, at least in the beginning of it,
he was far from having it confined to himself. He put great
confidence in the prognostications of judicial astrology.   In
the appendix to the Life of Congreve, is a narrative of some
of his predictions wonderfully fulfilled ; but I know not the
writer's means of information, or character of veracity.   That
he had the configurations of the horoscope in his mind, and
considered them as influencing the affairs of men, he does not
forbear to hint.

> The utmost malice of the stars is past.—   20
> Now frequent *trines* the happier lights among,
> And *high-rais'd Jove*, from his dark prison freed,
> Those weights took off that on his planet hung,
> Will gloriously the new-laid works succeed.

He has elsewhere shown his attention to the planetary
powers ; and in the preface to his Fables has endeavoured
obliquely to justify his superstition, by attributing the same
to some of the ancients.   The letter added to this narrative
leaves no doubt of his notions or practice [p. 108].

So slight and so scanty is the knowledge which I have 30
been able to collect concerning the private life and domestic
manners of a man, whom every English generation must
mention with reverence as a critic and a poet.

Dryden may be properly considered as the father of
English criticism, as the writer who first taught us to

determine upon principles the merit of composition. Of
our former poets, the greatest dramatist wrote without
rules, conducted through life and nature by a genius, that
rarely misled, and rarely deserted him. Of the rest, those
who knew the laws of propriety had neglected to teach them.

Two Arts of English Poetry were written in the days of
Elizabeth by Webb and Puttenham, from which something
might be learned, and a few hints had been given by Jonson
and Cowley ; but Dryden's Essay on Dramatic Poetry
10 was the first regular and valuable treatise on the art of
writing.

He who, having formed his opinions in the present age of
English literature, turns back to peruse this dialogue, will
not perhaps find much increase of knowledge, or much
novelty of instruction ; but he is to remember that critical
principles were then in the hands of a few, who had gathered
them partly from the ancients, and partly from the Italians
and French. The structure of dramatic poems was not then
generally understood. Audiences applauded by instinct ;
20 and poets perhaps often pleased by chance.

A writer who obtains his full purpose loses himself in his
own lustre. Of an opinion which is no longer doubted, the
evidence ceases to be examined. Of an art universally
practised, the first teacher is forgotten. Learning once
made popular is no longer learning ; it has the appearance
of something which we have bestowed upon ourselves, as the
dew appears to rise from the field which it refreshes.

To judge rightly of an author, we must transport ourselves
to his time, and examine what were the wants of his contem-
30 poraries, and what were his means of supplying them. That
which is easy at one time was difficult at another. Dryden
at least imported his science, and gave his country what it
wanted before ; or, rather, he imported only the materials,
and manufactured them by his own skill.

The Dialogue on the Drama was one of his first essays
of criticism, written when he was yet a timorous candidate

for reputation, and therefore laboured with that diligence
which he might allow himself somewhat to remit, when his
name gave sanction to his positions, and his awe of the public
was abated, partly by custom, and partly by success. It will
not be easy to find, in all the opulence of our language, a
treatise so artfully variegated with successive representations
of opposite probabilities, so enlivened with imagery, so
brightened with illustrations. His portraits of the English
dramatists are wrought with great spirit and diligence. The
account of Shakspeare may stand as a perpetual model of 10
encomiastic criticism; exact without minuteness, and lofty
without exaggeration. The praise lavished by Longinus, on
the attestation of the heroes of Marathon, by Demosthenes,
fades away before it. In a few lines is exhibited a character,
so extensive in its comprehension, and so curious in its
limitations, that nothing can be added, diminished, or reformed; nor can the editors and admirers of Shakspeare, in
all their emulation of reverence, boast of much more than of
having diffused and paraphrased this epitome of excellence,
of having changed Dryden's gold for baser metal, of lower 20
value, though of greater bulk.
    In this, and in all his other essays on the same subject, the
criticism of Dryden is the criticism of a poet; not a dull
collection of theorems, nor a rude detection of faults, which
perhaps the censor was not able to have committed; but a
gay and vigorous dissertation, where delight is mingled with
instruction, and where the author proves his right of judgment by his power of performance.
    The different manner and effect with which critical know-
ledge may be conveyed was perhaps never more clearly 30
exemplified than in the performances of Rymer and Dryden.
It was said of a dispute between two mathematicians,
" malim cum Scaligero errare, quam cum Clavio recte
sapere "; that " it was more eligible to go wrong with one,
than right with the other." A tendency of the same kind
every mind must feel at the perusal of Dryden's prefaces and

Rymer's discourses. With Dryden we are wandering in quest of Truth; whom we find, if we find her at all, dressed in the graces of elegance; and, if we miss her, the labour of the pursuit rewards itself; we are led only through fragrance and flowers. Rymer, without taking a nearer, takes a rougher way; every step is to be made through thorns and brambles; and Truth, if we meet her, appears repulsive by her mien, and ungraceful by her habit. Dryden's criticism has the majesty of a queen; Rymer's has the ferocity of a 10 tyrant.

As he had studied with great diligence the art of Poetry, and enlarged or rectified his notions, by experience perpetually increasing, he had his mind stored with principles and observations; he poured out his knowledge with little labour; for of labour, notwithstanding the multiplicity of his productions, there is sufficient reason to suspect that he was not a lover. To write *con amore*, with fondness for the employment, with perpetual touches and retouchés, with unwillingness to take leave of his own idea, and an unwearied 20 pursuit of unattainable perfection, was, I think, no part of his character.

His criticism may be considered as general or occasional. In his general precepts, which depend upon the nature of things, and the structure of the human mind, he may doubtless be safely recommended to the confidence of the reader; but his occasional and particular positions were sometimes interested, sometimes negligent, and sometimes capricious. It is not without reason that Trapp, speaking of the praises which he bestows on Palamon and Arcite, says, "Novimus 30 judicium Drydeni de poemate quodam Chauceri, pulchro sane illo, et admodum laudando, nimirum quod non modo vere epicum sit, sed Iliada etiam atque Æneada æquet, imo superet. Sed novimus eodem tempore viri illius maximi non semper accuratissimas esse censuras, nec ad severissimam critices normam exactas : illo judice id plerumque optimum est, quod nunc præ manibus habet, et in quo nunc occupatur."

He is therefore by no means constant to himself. His
defence and desertion of dramatic rhyme is generally known.
Spence, in his remarks on Pope's Odyssey, produces what he
thinks an unconquerable quotation from Dryden's preface to
the Eneid, in favour of translating an epic poem into blank
verse ; but he forgets that when his author attempted the
Iliad, some years afterwards, he departed from his own
decision, and translated into rhyme.

When he has any objection to obviate, or any licence to
defend, he is not very scrupulous about what he asserts, nor 10
very cautious, if the present purpose be served, not to
entangle himself in his own sophistries. But when all arts
are exhausted, like other hunted animals, he sometimes
stands at bay ; when he cannot disown the grossness of one
of his plays, he declares that he knows not any law that
prescribes morality to a comic poet.

His remarks on ancient or modern writers are not always
to be trusted. His parallel of the versification of Ovid with
that of Claudian has been very justly censured by Sewel.[1]
His comparison of the first line of Virgil with the first of 20
Statius is not happier. Virgil, he says, is soft and gentle,
and would have thought Statius mad, if he had heard him
thundering out

> Quæ superimposito moles geminata colosso.

Statius perhaps heats himself, as he proceeds, to exaggera-
tions somewhat hyperbolical ; but undoubtedly Virgil would
have been too hasty, if he had condemned him to straw for
one sounding line. Dryden wanted an instance, and the first
that occurred was imprest into the service.

What he wishes to say, he says at hazard: he cited 30
Gorbuduc, which he had never seen; gives a false account
of Chapman's versification ; and discovers, in the preface to
his Fables, that he translated the first book of the Iliad
without knowing what was in the second.

It will be difficult to prove that Dryden ever made any

[1] Preface to Ovid's Metamorphoses.

great advances in literature. As having distinguished himself at Westminster under the tuition of Busby, who advanced
his scholars to a height of knowledge very rarely attained in
grammar-schools, he resided afterwards at Cambridge ; it is
not to be supposed, that his skill in the ancient languages
was deficient, compared with that of common students, but
his scholastic acquisitions seem not proportionate to his
opportunities and abilities.   He could not, like Milton or
Cowley, have made his name illustrious merely by his
10 learning.   He mentions but few books, and those such as
lie in the beaten track of regular study ; from which if
ever he departs, he is in danger of losing himself in unknown regions.

In his Dialogue on the Drama, he pronounces with great
confidence that the Latin tragedy of Medea is not Ovid's,
because it is not sufficiently interesting and pathetic. (He
might have determined the question upon surer evidence)
for it is quoted by Quintilian as .the work of Seneca ; and
the only line which remains of Ovid's play, for one line is
20 left us, is not there to be found.   There was therefore no
need of the gravity of conjecture, or the discussion of plot
or sentiment, to find what was already known upon higher
authority than such discussions can ever reach.

His literature, though not always free from ostentation,
will be commonly·found either obvious, and made his own
by the art of dressing it ; or superficial, which, by what he
gives, shows what he wanted ; or erroneous, hastily collected,
and negligently scattered.

Yet it cannot be said that his genius is ever unprovided
30 of matter, or that his fancy languishes in penury of ideas.
His works, abound with knowledge,·and sparkle with illustrations.   There is scarcely any science or faculty that does
not supply him with occasional images and lucky similitudes ;
every page discovers a mind very widely acquainted both
with art and nature, and in full possession of great stores
of intellectual wealth.   Of him that knows much it is natural

to suppose that he has read with diligence : yet I rather
believe that the knowledge of Dryden was gleaned from
accidental intelligence and various conversation, by a quick
apprehension, a judicious selection, and a happy memory, a
keen appetite of knowledge, and a powerful digestion ; by
vigilance that permitted nothing to pass without notice, and
a habit of reflection that suffered nothing useful to be lost.
A mind like Dryden's, always curious, always active, to
which every understanding was proud to be associated, and
of which every one solicited the regard, by an ambitious **10**
display of himself, had a more pleasant, perhaps a nearer
way to knowledge than by the silent progress of solitary
reading. I do not suppose that he despised books, or in-
tentionally neglected them ; but that he was carried out,
·by the impetuosity of his genius, to more vivid and speedy
instructors ; and that his studies were rather desultory and
fortuitous than constant and systematical.

It must be confessed that he scarcely ever appears to
want book learning but when he mentions books ; and to
him may be transferred the praise which he gives his **20**
master Charles :

> His conversation, wit, and parts,
> His knowledge in the noblest useful arts,
> Were such, dead authors could not give,
> But habitudes of those that live;'
> Who, lighting him, did greater lights receive:
> He drain'd from all, and all they knew,
> His apprehension quick, his judgment true:
> That the most learn'd with shame confess
> His knowledge more, his reading only less.

30

Of all this, however, if the proof be demanded, I will not
undertake to give it ; the atoms of probability, of which my
opinion has been formed, lie scattered over all his works ;
and by him who thinks the question worth his notice, his
works must be perused with very close attention.

Criticism, either didactic or defensive, occupies almost all

his prose, except those pages which he has devoted to his
patrons; but none of his prefaces were ever thought tedious.
They have not the formality of a settled style, in which the
first half of the sentence betrays the other.   The clauses are
never balanced, nor the periods modelled : every word seems
to drop by chance, though it falls into its proper place.
Nothing is cold or languid ; the whole is airy, animated,
and vigorous; what is little, is gay; what is great, is
splendid.   He may be thought to mention himself too fre-
10 quently ; but, while he forces himself upon our esteem, we
cannot refuse him to stand high in his own.   Everything
is excused by the play of images, and the sprightliness of
expression.   Though all is easy, nothing is feeble ; though
all seems careless, there is nothing harsh ; and though, since
his earlier works more than a century has passed, they have
nothing yet uncouth or obsolete.

He who writes much will not easily escape a manner, such
a recurrence of particular modes as may be easily noted.
Dryden is always *another and the same* ; he does not exhibit
20 a second time the same elegancies in the same form, nor
appears to have any art other than that of expressing with
clearness what he thinks with vigour.   His style could not
easily be imitated, either seriously or ludicrously ; for, being
always equable and always varied, it has no prominent or
discriminative characters.   The beauty who is totally free
from disproportion of parts and features cannot be ridiculed
by an overcharged resemblance.

From his prose, however, Dryden derives only his accidental and secondary praise ; the veneration with which his
30 name is pronounced by every cultivator of English literature,
is paid to him as he refined the language, improved the
sentiments, and tuned the numbers of English poetry.

After about half a century of forced thoughts, and rugged
metre, some advances towards nature and harmony had been
already made by Waller and Denham ; they had shown that
long discourses in rhyme grew more pleasing when they were

broken into couplets, and that verse consisted (not only in the number but the arrangement of syllables.)

But though they did much, who can deny that they left much to do? Their works were not many, nor were their minds of very ample comprehension. More examples of more modes of composition were necessary for the establishment of regularity, and the introduction of propriety in word and thought.

Every language of a learned nation necessarily divides itself into diction scholastic and popular, grave and familiar, 10 elegant and gross; and from a nice distinction of these different parts arises a great part of the beauty of style. But, if we except a few minds, (the favourites of nature,) to whom (their own original rectitude) was in the place of rules, this delicacy of selection was little known to our authors; our speech lay before them in a heap of confusion; and every man took for every purpose what chance might offer him.

There was, therefore, before the time of Dryden no poetical diction, no system of words at once refined from the gross- 20 ness of domestic use, and free from the harshness of terms appropriated to particular arts. Words too familiar, or too remote, defeat the purpose of a poet. From those sounds which we hear on small or on coarse occasions, we do not easily receive strong impressions, or delightful images; and words to which we are nearly strangers, whenever they occur, draw that attention on themselves which they should transmit to things.

Those happy combinations of words which distinguish poetry from prose had been rarely attempted: we had few 30 elegancies or flowers of speech; the roses had not yet been plucked from the bramble, or different colours had not been joined to enliven one another.

It may be doubted whether Waller and Denham could have overborne the prejudices which had long prevailed, and which even then were sheltered by the protection of

Cowley. The new versification, as it was called, may be considered as owing its establishment to Dryden; from whose time it is apparent that English poetry has had no tendency to relapse to its former savageness.

. The affluence and comprehension of our language is very illustriously displayed in our poetical translations of ancient writers; a work which the French seem to relinquish in despair, and which we were long unable to perform with dexterity. Ben Jonson thought it necessary to copy Horace

10 almost word by word; Feltham, his contemporary and adversary, considers it as indispensably requisite in a translation to give line for line. It is said that Sandys, whom Dryden calls the best versifier of the last age, has struggled hard to comprise every book of his English Metamorphoses in the same number of verses with the original. Holyday had nothing in view but to show that he understood his author, with so little regard to the grandeur of his diction, or the volubility of his numbers, that his metres can hardly be called verses; they cannot be read without reluctance, nor

20 will the labour always be rewarded by understanding them. Cowley saw that such copiers were a servile race; he asserted his liberty, and spread his wings so boldly that he left his authors. It was reserved for Dryden to fix the limits of poetical liberty, and give us just rules and examples of translation.

When languages are formed upon different principles, it is impossible that the same modes of expression should always be elegant in both. While they run on together, the closest translation may be considered as the best; but when

30 they divaricate, each must take its natural course. Where correspondence cannot be obtained, it is necessary to be content with something equivalent. "Translation, therefore," says Dryden, "is not so loose as paraphrase, nor so close as metaphrase."

All polished languages have different styles; the concise, the diffuse, the lofty, and the humble. In the proper choice

of style consists the resemblance which Dryden principally
exacts from the translator. He is to exhibit his author's
thoughts in such a dress of diction as the author would have
given them, had his language been English : rugged magnificence is not to be softened ; hyperbolical ostentation is not
to be repressed; nor sententious affectation to have its points
blunted.   A translator is to be like his author ; it is not his
business to excel him.

The reasonableness of these rules seems sufficient for their
vindication ; and the effects produced by observing them 10
were so happy, that I know not whether they were ever
opposed by Sir Edward Sherburne, a man whose learning
was greater than his powers of poetry, and who, being better
qualified to give the meaning than the spirit of Seneca, has
introduced his version of three tragedies by a defence of
close translation.   The authority of Horace, which the new
translators cited in defence of their practice, he, has, by a
judicious explanation, taken fairly from them ; but reason
wants not Horace to support it.

It seldom happens that all the necessary causes concur to 20
any great effect : will is wanting to power, or power to will,
or both are impeded by external obstructions.   The exigencies in which Dryden was condemned to pass his life
are reasonably supposed to have blasted his genius, to have
driven out his works in a state of immaturity, and to have
intercepted the full-blown elegance which longer growth
would have supplied.   -

Poverty, like other rigid powers, is sometimes too hastily
accused.   If the excellence of Dryden's works was lessened
by his indigence, their number was increased ; and I know 30
not how it will be proved, that if he had written less he
would have written better ; or that indeed he would have
undergone the toil of an author, if he had not been solicited
by something more pressing than the love of praise.

But, as is said by his Sebastian,

What had been is unknown ; what is appears.

E

We know that Dryden's several productions were so many
successive expedients for his support ; his plays were therefore often borrowed ; and his poems were almost all
occasional.

In an occasional performance no height of excellence can
be expected from any mind, however fertile in itself, and
however stored with acquisitions. He whose work is general
and arbitrary has the choice of his matter, and takes that
which his inclination and his studies have best qualified him
to display and decorate. He is at liberty to delay his publication till he has satisfied his friends and himself, till he
has reformed his first thoughts by subsequent examination, and polished away those faults which the precipitance
of ardent composition is likely to leave behind it. Virgil is
related to have poured out a great number of lines in the
morning, and to have passed the day in reducing them
to fewer.

The occasional poet is circumscribed by the narrowness of
his subject. Whatever can happen to man has happened so
often that little remains for fancy or invention. We have
been all born ; we have most of us been married ; and so
many have died before us, that our deaths can supply but
few materials for a poet. In the fate of princes the public
has an interest; and what happens to them of good or evil,
the poets have always considered as business for the Muse.
But after so many inauguratory gratulations, nuptial hymns,
and funeral dirges, he must be highly favoured by nature,
or by fortune, who says anything not said before. Even
war and conquest, however splendid, suggest no new images ;
the triumphal chariot of a victorious monarch can be decked
only with those ornaments that have graced his predecessors.

Not only matter but time is wanting. The poem must
not be delayed till the occasion is forgotten. The lucky
moments of animated imagination cannot be attended ;
elegances and illustrations cannot be multiplied by gradual
accumulation ; the composition must be despatched while

conversation is yet busy, and admiration fresh ; and haste
is to be made, lest some other event should lay hold upon
mankind.

Occasional compositions may however secure to a writer
the praise both of learning and facility ; for they cannot be
the effect of long study and must be furnished immediately
from the treasures of the mind.

The death of Cromwell was the first public event which
called forth Dryden's poetical powers. His heroic stanzas
have beauties and defects ; the thoughts are vigorous, and, 10
though not always proper, show a mind replete with ideas;
the numbers are smooth ; and the diction, if not altogether
correct, is elegant and easy.

Davenant was perhaps at this time his favourite author,
though Gondibert never appears to have been popular ; and
from Davenant he learned to please his ear with the stanza
of four lines alternately rhymed.

Dryden very early formed his versification ; there are in
this early production no traces of Donne's or Jonson's
ruggedness ; but he did not so soon free his mind from the 20
ambition of forced conceits. In his verses on the Restoration,
he says of the King's exile,

> He, toss'd by Fate—
> Could taste no sweets of youth's desired age,
> But found his life too true a pilgrimage.

And afterwards, to show how virtue and wisdom are increased by adversity, he makes this remark :

> Well might the ancient poets then confer
> On Night the honour'd name of *counsellor*,
> Since, struck with rays of prosperous fortune blind,   30
> We light alone in dark afflictions find.

His praise of Monk's dexterity comprises such a cluster of
thoughts unallied to one another, as will not elsewhere be
easily found :

> 'Twas Monk, whom Providence designed to loose
> Those real bonds false freedom did impose.

The blessed saints that watch'd this turning scene,
Did from their stars with joyful wonder lean,
To see small clues draw vastest weights along,
Not in their bulk, but in their order strong.
Thus pencils can by one slight touch restore
Smiles to that changed face that wept before.
With ease such fond chimæras we pursue,
As fancy frames for fancy to subdue :
But, when ourselves to action we betake,
10   It shuns the mint like gold that chymists make :
How hard was then his task, at once to be
What in the body natural we see !
Man's Architect distinctly did ordain
The charge of muscles, nerves, and of the brain,
Through viewless conduits spirits to dispense
The springs of motion from the seat of sense.
'Twas not the hasty product of a day,
But the well-ripen'd fruit of wise delay.
He, like a patient angler, ere he strook,
20   Would let them play a-while upon the hook.
Our healthful food the stomach labours thus,
At first embracing what it straight doth crush.
Wise leeches will not vain receipts obtrude,
While growing pains pronounce the humours crude ;
Deaf to complaints, they wait upon the ill,
Till some safe crisis authorize their skill.

He had not yet learned, indeed he never learned well, to forbear the improper use of mythology.) After having rewarded the heathen deities for their care,

30   With Alga who the sacred altar strows?
To all the sea-gods Charles an offering owes ;
A bull to thee, Portunus, shall be slain ;
A ram to you, ye Tempests of the Main.

He tells us, in the language of religion,

Prayer storm'd the skies, and ravish'd Charles from thence,
As heaven itself is took by violence.

And afterwards mentions one of the most awful passages of

Sacred History.   Other (conceits) there are, too curious to be quite omitted ; as,

> For by example most we sinn'd before,
> And, glass-like, clearness mix'd with frailty bore.

How far he was yet from thinking it necessary to found his sentiments on nature, appears from the extravagance of his fictions and hyperboles :

> The winds, that never moderation knew,
> Afraid to blow too much, too faintly blew ;
> Or, out of breath with joy, could not enlarge   10
> Their straiten'd lungs.—
>
> It is no longer motion cheats your view ;
> As you meet it, the land approacheth you ;
> The land returns, and in the white it wears
> The marks of penitence and sorrow bears.

I know not whether this fancy, however little be its value, was not borrowed.   A French poet read to Malherbe some verses, in which he represents France as moving out of its place to receive the King. "Though this," said Malherbe, "was in my time, I do not remember it."   20

His poem on the Coronation has a more even tenour of thought. Some lines deserve to be quoted :

> You have already quench'd sedition's brand,
> And zeal, that burnt it, only warms the land ;
> The jealous sects that durst not trust their cause
> So far from their own will as to the laws,
> Him for their umpire and their synod take,
> And their appeal alone to Cæsar make.

Here may be found one particle of that old versification, of which, I believe, in all his works, there is not another :   30

> Nor is it duty, or our hope alone,
> Creates that joy, but full *fruition*.

In the verses to the Lord Chancellor Clarendon, two years afterwards, is a conceit so hopeless at the first view, that few

would have attempted it ; and so successfully laboured, that
though at last it gives the reader more perplexity than
pleasure, and seems hardly worth the study that it costs, yet
it must be valued as a proof of a mind at once subtle and
comprehensive :

> In open prospect nothing bounds our eye,
> Until the earth seems join'd unto the sky :
> So in this hemisphere our utmost view
> Is only bounded by our king and you :
> 10   Our sight is limited where you are join'd,
> And beyond that no farther Heaven can find.
> So well your virtues do with his agree,
> That though your orbs of different greatness be,
> Yet both are for each other's use disposed.
> His to enclose, and yours to be enclosed.
> Nor could another in your room have been,
> Except an emptiness had come between.

The comparison of the Chancellor to the Indies leaves all
resemblance too far behind it :

> 20   And as the Indies were not found before
> Those rich perfumes which from the happy shore
> The winds upon their balmy wings conveyed,
> Whose guilty sweetness first their world betray'd ;
> So by your counsels we are brought to view
> A new and undiscover'd world in you.

There is another comparison, for there is little else in the
poem, of which, though perhaps it cannot be explained into
plain prosaic meaning, the mind perceives enough to be
delighted, and readily forgives its obscurity for its mag-
30 nificence :

> How strangely active are the arts of peace,
> Whose restless motions less than wars do cease :
> Peace is not freed from labour, but from noise ;
> And war more force, but not more pains employs.
> Such is the mighty swiftness of your mind,
> That, like the earth's, it leaves our sense behind,
> While you so smoothly turn and rowl our sphere,
> That rapid motion does but rest appear.

> For as in nature's swiftness, with the throng
> Of flying orbs while ours is borne along,
> All seems at rest to the deluded eye,
> Mov'd by the soul of the same harmony :
> So carry'd on by our unwearied care,
> We rest in peace, and yet in motion share.

To this succeed four lines, which perhaps afford Dryden's first attempt at those penetrating remarks on human nature, for which he seems to have been peculiarly formed :

> Let envy then those crimes within you see,   10
> From which the happy never must be free ;
> Envy that does with misery reside,
> The joy and the revenge of ruin'd pride.

Into this poem he seems to have collected all his powers ; and after this he did not often bring upon his anvil such stubborn and unmalleable thoughts ; but, as a specimen of his abilities to unite the most unsociable matter, he has concluded with lines of which I think not myself obliged to tell the meaning :

> Yet unimpair'd with labours, or with time,   20
> Your age but seems to a new youth to climb.
> Thus heavenly bodies do our time beget,
> And measure change, but share no part of it :
> And still it shall without a weight increase,
> Like this new year, whose motions never cea...
> For since the glorious course you have begun
> Is led by Charles, as that is by the sun,
> It must both weightless and immortal prove,
> Because the centre of it is above.

In the Annus Mirabilis he returned to the quatrain, which 30 from that time he totally quitted, perhaps from this experience of its inconvenience, for he complains of its difficulty. This is one of his greatest attempts. He had subjects equal to his abilities, a great naval war, and the Fire of London. Battles have always been described in heroic poetry ; but a sea-fight and artillery had yet something of novelty. New arts are long in the world before poets describe them ; for they borrow everything from their predecessors, and commonly derive very little from nature or from life. Boileau was the first French writer that had ever hazarded in verse the mention of modern war, or the effects of gunpowder. We, who are less afraid of novelty, had already possession of those dreadful images : Waller had described a sea-fight. Milton had not yet transferred the invention of fire-arms to the rebellious angels.

This poem is written with great diligence, yet does not
10 fully answer the expectation raised by such subjects and such a writer. With the stanza of Davenant he has sometimes his vein of parenthesis, and incidental disquisition, and stops his narrative for a wise remark.

The general fault is, that he affords more sentiment than description, and does not so much impress scenes upon the fancy, as deduce consequences and make comparisons.

The initial stanzas have rather too much resemblance to the first lines of Waller's poem on the war with Spain ; perhaps such a beginning is natural, and could not be avoided
20 without affectation. Both Waller and Dryden might take their hint from the poem on the civil war of Rome, "Orbem jam totum," etc.

Of the king collecting his navy, he says,

> It seems as every ship their sovereign knows,
> His awful summons they so soon obey ;
> So hear the scaly herds when Proteus blows,
> And so to pasture follow through the sea.

It would not be hard to believe that Dryden had written the two first lines seriously, and that some wag had added
30 the two latter in burlesque. Who would expect the lines that immediately follow, which are indeed perhaps indecently hyperbolical, but certainly in a mode totally different ?

> To see this fleet upon the ocean move,
> Angels drew wide the curtains of the skies ;
> And Heaven, as if there wanted lights above,
> For tapers made two glaring comets rise.

The description of the attempt at Bergen will afford a very complete specimen of the descriptions in this poem :

And now approach'd their fleet from India, fraught
    With all the riches of the rising sun :
And precious sand from southern climates brought,
    The fatal regions where the war begun.

Like hunted castors, conscious of their store,
    Their way-laid wealth to Norway's coast they bring ;
Then first the North's cold bosom spices bore,
    And winter brooded on the eastern spring.   10

By the rich scent we found our perfum'd prey,
    Which, flank'd with rocks, did close in covert lie :
And round about their murdering cannon lay,
    At once to threaten and invite the eye.

Fiercer than cannon, and than rocks more hard,
    The English undertake th' unequal war :
Seven ships alone, by which the port is barr'd,
    Besiege the Indies, and all Denmark dare.

These fight like husbands, but like lovers those :
    These fain would keep, and those more fain enjoy ;   20
And to such height their frantic passion grows,
    That what both love, both hazard to destroy :

Amidst whole heaps of spices lights a ball,
    And now their odours arm'd against them fly :
Some preciously by shatter'd porcelain fall,
    And some by aromatic splinters die.

And though by tempests of the prize bereft,
    In Heaven's inclemency some ease we find :
Our foes we vanquish'd by our valour left,
    And only yielded to the seas and wind.   30

In this manner is the sublime too often mingled with the ridiculous. The Dutch seek a shelter for a wealthy fleet : this surely needed no illustration ; yet they must fly, not like all the rest of mankind on the same occasion, but " like hunted castors " ; and they might with strict propriety be hunted ; for we winded them by our noses—their *perfumes*

betrayed them. The *husband* and the *lover*, though of more
dignity than the castor, are images too domestic to mingle
properly with the horrors of war. The two quatrains that
follow are worthy of the author.

The account of the different sensations with which the
two fleets retired, when the night parted them, is one of the
fairest flowers of English poetry:

> The night comes on, we eager to pursue
> The combat still, and they asham'd to leave:
> 'Till the last streaks of dying day withdrew,
> And doubtful moonlight did our rage deceive.
>
> In th' English fleet each ship resounds with joy,
> And loud applause of their great leader's fame:
> In fiery dreams the Dutch they still destroy,
> And, slumbering, smile at the imagined flame.
>
> Not so the Holland fleet, who, tired and done,
> Stretch'd on their decks, like weary oxen lie:
> Faint sweats all down their mighty members run,
> (Vast bulks, which little souls but ill supply).
>
> In dreams they fearful precipices tread,
> Or, shipwreck'd, labour to some distant shore:
> Or, in dark churches, walk among the dead;
> They wake with horror, and dare sleep no more.

It is a general rule in poetry, that all appropriated terms
of art should be sunk in general expressions, because poetry
is to speak an universal language. This rule is still stronger
with regard to arts not liberal, or confined to few, and therefore far removed from common knowledge; and of this kind,
certainly is technical navigation. Yet Dryden was of opinion,
that a sea-fight ought to be described in the nautical language; "and certainly," says he, "as those, who in a logical
disputation keep to general terms, would hide a fallacy, so
those who do it in any poetical description would veil their
ignorance."

Let us then appeal to experience; for by experience at
last we learn as well what will please as what will profit. In

the battle, his terms seem to have been blown away ; but he
deals them liberally in the dock :

> So here some pick out bullets from the side,
> Some drive old *oakum* thro' each *seam* and rift :
> Their left-hand does the *calking-iron* guide,
> The rattling *mallet* with the right they lift.

> With boiling pitch another near at hand
> (From friendly Sweden brought) the *seams instops* ;
> Which, well laid o'er, the salt-sea waves withstand,
> And shake them from the rising beak in drops.   10

> Some the *gall'd* ropes with dauby *marling* blind,
> Or sear-cloth masts with strong *tarpawling* coats :
> To try new *shrouds* one mounts into the wind,
> And one below their ease or stiffness notes.

I suppose here is not one term which every reader does
not wish away.

His digression to the original and progress of navigation,
with his prospect of the advancement which it shall receive
from the Royal Society, then newly instituted, may be considered as an example seldom equalled of seasonable excursion 20
and artful return.

One line, however, leaves me discontented ; he says, that,
by the help of the philosophers,

> Instructed ships shall sail to quick commerce,
> By which remotest regions are allied—

Which he is constrained to explain in a note, "by a more exact
measure of longitude." It had better become Dryden's
learning and genius to have laboured science into poetry,
and have shown, by explaining longitude, that verse did not
refuse the ideas of philosophy.   30

His description of the Fire is painted by resolute meditation, out of a mind better formed to reason than to feel.
The conflagration of a city, with all its tumults of concomitant
distress, is one of the most dreadful spectacles which this
world can offer to human eyes ; yet it seems to raise little

emotion in the breast of the poet, he watches the flame
coolly from street to street, with now a reflection, and now a
simile, till at last he meets the king, for whom he makes a
speech, rather tedious in a time so busy; and then follows
again the progress of the fire.

There are, however, in this part some passages that deserve attention ; as in the beginning :

        The diligence of trades and noiseful gain,
        And luxury, more late asleep were laid ;
10   All was the Night's, and in her silent reign
        No sound the rest of Nature did invade
        In this deep quiet——

The expression "All was the Night's" is taken from
Seneca, who remarks on Virgil's line,

        Omnia noctis erant placida composta quiete,

that he might have concluded better,

        Omnia noctis erant.

The following quatrain is vigorous and animated ;

        The ghosts of traitors from the bridge descend
20   With bold fanatic spectres to rejoice ;
        About the fire into a dance they bend,
        And sing their sabbath notes with feeble voice.

His prediction of the improvements which shall be made
in the new city is elegant and poetical, and with an event
which poets cannot always boast has been happily verified.
The poem concludes with a simile that might have better
been omitted.

Dryden, when he wrote this poem, seems not yet fully
to have formed his versification, or settled his system of
30 propriety.

From this time he addicted himself almost wholly to the
stage, "to which," says he, "my genius never much inclined
me," merely as the most profitable market for poetry. By

writing tragedies in rhyme, he continued to improve his diction and his numbers. According to the opinion of Harte, who had studied his works with great attention, he settled his principles of versification in 1676, when he produced the play of Aureng Zebe ; and according to his own account of the short time in which he wrote Tyrannic Love, and the State of Innocence, he soon obtained the full effect of diligence, and added facility to exactness.

Rhyme has been so long banished from the theatre, that we know not its effect upon the passions of an audience ; but it has this convenience, that sentences stand more independent on each other, and striking passages are therefore easily selected and retained. Thus the description of Night in the Indian Emperor, and the rise and fall of empire in the Conquest of Granada, are more frequently repeated than any lines in All for Love or Don Sebastian.

To search his plays for vigorous sallies and sententious elegances, or to fix the dates of any little pieces which he wrote by chance, or by solicitation, were labour too tedious and minute.

His dramatic labours did not so wholly absorb his thoughts, but that he promulgated the laws of translation in a preface to the English Epistles of Ovid ; one of which he translated himself, and another in conjunction with the Earl of Mulgrave.

Absalom and Achitophel is a work so well known, that particular criticism is superfluous. If it be considered as a poem political and controversial, it will be found to comprise all the excellences of which the subject is susceptible ; acrimony of censure, elegance of praise, artful delineation of characters, variety and vigour of sentiment, happy turns of language, and pleasing harmony of numbers ; and all these raised to such a height as can scarcely be found in any other English composition.

It is not, however, without faults ; some lines are inelegant or improper, and too many are irreligiously licentious. The original structure of the poem was defective; allegories drawn to great length will always break; Charles could not run continually parallel with David.

The subject had likewise another inconvenience : it admitted little imagery or description; and a long poem of mere sentiments easily becomes tedious; though all the parts are forcible, and every line kindles new rapture, the reader, if not relieved by the interposition of something that soothes the fancy, grows weary of admiration, and defers the
10 rest.

As an approach to historical truth was necessary, the action and catastrophe were not in the poet's power ; there is therefore an unpleasing disproportion between the beginning and the end. We are alarmed by a faction formed out of many sects, various in their principles, but agreeing in their purpose of mischief, formidable for their numbers, and strong by their supports ; while the king's friends are few and weak. The chiefs on either part are set forth to view; but when expectation is at the height, the king makes
20 a speech, and

Henceforth a series of new times began.

Who can forbear to think of an enchanted castle, with a wide moat and lofty battlements, walls of marble and gates of brass which vanishes at once into air, when the destined knight blows his horn before it ?

In the second part, written by Tate, there is a long insertion, which, for poignancy of satire, exceeds any part of the former. Personal resentment, though no laudable motive to satire, can add great force to general principles. Self-love
30 is a busy prompter.

The Medal, written upon the same principles with Absalom and Achitophel, but upon a narrower plan, gives less pleasure, though it discovers equal abilities in the writer. The superstructure cannot extend beyond the foundation ; a single character or incident cannot furnish as many ideas,

as a series of events, or multiplicity of agents. This poem
therefore, since time has left it to itself, is not much read,
nor perhaps generally understood ;) yet it abounds with
touches both of humorous and serious satire) The picture of
a man whose propensions to mischief are such, that his best
actions are but inability of wickedness, is very skilfully
delineated and strongly coloured :)

> Power was his aim: but, thrown from that pretence,
> The wretch turn'd loyal in his own defence,
> And malice reconcil'd him to his prince.   10
> Him, in the anguish of his soul, he served ;
> Rewarded faster still than he deserv'd :
> Behold him now exalted into trust ;
> His counsels oft convenient, seldom just.
> Ev'n in the most sincere advice he gave,
> He had a grudging still to be a knave.
> The frauds he learnt in his fanatic years,
> Made him uneasy in his lawful gears ;
> At least as little honest as he cou'd :
> And, like white witches, mischievously good.   20
> To this first bias, longingly, he leans ;
> And rather would be great by wicked means.

The Threnodia, which by a term I am afraid neither
authorised nor analogical, he calls Augustalis, is not among
his happiest productions. Its first and obvious defect is the
irregularity of its metre) to which the ears of that age,
however, were accustomed. What is worse, it has neither
tenderness nor dignity ; it is neither magnificent nor pathetic.
He seems to look round him for images which he cannot find,
and what he has he distorts by endeavouring to enlarge 30
them. "He is," he says, "petrified with grief," but the
marble sometimes relents, and trickles in a joke.

> The sons of art all med'cines try'd,
> And every noble remedy apply'd ;
> With emulation each essay'd
> His utmost skill ; *nay, more, they pray'd* :
> Was never losing game with better conduct play'd.

He had been a little inclined to merriment before, upon
the prayers of a nation for their dying sovereign ; (nor was
he serious enough to keep heathen fables out of his religion :)

> With him th' innumerable crowd of armed prayers
> Knock'd at the gates of heaven, and knock'd aloud ;
> *The first well-meaning rude petitioners*
> All for his life assail'd the throne,
> All would have brib'd the skies by offering up their own.
> So great a throng not heaven itself could bar ;
> 'Twas almost borne by force *as in the giants war.*
> The pray'rs, at least, for his reprieve were heard ;
> His death, like Hezekiah's, was deferr'd.

10 (margin)

There is throughout the composition a desire of splendour
without wealth.   In the conclusion he seems too much
pleased with the prospect of the new reign to have lamented
his old master with much sincerity.

He did not miscarry in this attempt for want of skill either
in lyric or elegiac poetry.   His poem on the death of Mrs.
Killigrew is undoubtedly the noblest ode that our language
ever has produced. (The first part flows with a torrent of
enthusiasm.) *Fervet immensusque ruit.*   All the stanzas
indeed are not equal. (An imperial crown cannot be one
continued diamond.   The gems must be held together by
some less valuable matter.)

20 (margin)

In his first ode for Cecilia's day, which is lost in the
splendour of the second, there are passages which would
have dignified any other poet.   The first stanza is vigorous
and elegant; though the word *diapason* is too technical, and
the rhymes are too remote from one another.

> From harmony, from heavenly harmony,
> This universal frame began :
> When nature underneath a heap of jarring atoms lay,
> And could not heave her head,
> The tuneful voice was heard from high,
> Arise ye more than dead.
> Then cold and hot, and moist and dry,

30 (margin)

In order to their stations leap,
And music's power obey.
From harmony, from heavenly harmony,
This universal frame began :
From harmony to harmony
Through all the compass of the notes it ran,
The diapason closing full in man.

The conclusion is likewise striking ; but it includes an image so awful in itself, that it can owe little to poetry ; and I could wish the antithesis of *music untuning* had found 10 some other place.

As from the power of sacred lays
The spheres began to move,
And sung the great Creator's praise
To all the bless'd above.
So when the last and dreadful hour
This crumbling pageant shall devour,
The trumpet shall be heard on high,
The dead shall live, the living die,
And music shall untune the sky.   20

Of his skill in elegy he has given a specimen in his Eleonora, of which the following lines discover their author :

Though all these rare endowments of the mind
Were in a narrow space of life confin'd,
The figure was with full perfection crown'd ;
Though not so large an orb, as truly round :
As when in glory, through the public place,
The spoils of conquer'd nations were to pass,
And but one day for triumph was allow'd,
The consul was constrain'd his pomp to crowd ;   30
And so the swift procession hurry'd on,
That all, though not distinctly, might be shown ;
So in the straiten'd bounds of life confin'd,
She gave but glimpses of her glorious mind :
And multitudes of virtues pass'd along ;
Each pressing foremost in the mighty throng,
Ambitious to be seen, and then make room
For greater multitudes that were to come.

F

Yet unemploy'd no minute slipp'd away;
Moments were precious in so short a stay.
The haste of Heaven to have her was so great,
That some were single acts, though each complete;
And every act stood ready to repeat.

This piece, however, is not without its faults; there is so much likeness in the initial comparison, that there is no illustration. As a king would be lamented, Eleonora was lamented:

10   As when some great and gracious monarch dies,
     Soft whispers, first, and mournful murmurs rise
     Among the sad attendants; then the sound
     Soon gathers voice, and spreads the news around,
     Through town and country, till the dreadful blast
     Is blown to distant colonies at last;
     Who, then, perhaps, were offering vows in vain,
     For his long life, and for his happy reign:
     So slowly, by degrees, unwilling Fame,
     Did matchless Eleonora's fate proclaim
20   Till public as the loss the news became.

This is little better than to say in praise of a shrub, that it is as green as a tree; or of a brook, that it waters a garden, as a river waters a country.

Dryden confesses that he did not know the lady whom he celebrates: the praise being therefore inevitably general fixes no impression upon the reader, nor excites any tendency to love, nor much desire of imitation. Knowledge of the subject is to the poet what durable materials are to the architect.

The Religio Laici, which borrows its title from the Religio
30 Medici of Browne, is almost the only work of Dryden which can be considered as a voluntary effusion; in this, therefore, it might be hoped, that the full effulgence of his genius would be found. But unhappily the subject is rather argumentative than poetical; he intended only a specimen of metrical disputation:

     And this unpolish'd rugged verse I chose,
     As fittest for discourse, and nearest prose.

This, however, is a composition of great excellence in its kind, in which the familiar is very properly diversified with the solemn, and the grave with the humorous; in which metre has neither weakened the force, nor clouded the perspicuity of argument; nor will it be easy to find another example equally happy of this middle kind of writing, which, though prosaic in some parts, rises to high poetry in others, and neither towers to the skies, nor creeps along the ground.

Of the same kind, or not far distant from it, is the Hind 10 and Panther, the longest of all Dryden's original poems; an allegory intended to comprise and to decide the controversy between the Romanists and the Protestants. The scheme of the work is injudicious and incommodious; for what can be more absurd than that one beast should counsel another to rest her faith upon a pope and council? He seems well enough skilled in the usual topics of argument, endeavours to show the necessity of an infallible judge, and reproaches the reformers with want of unity; but is weak enough to ask why, since we see without knowing how, we may not have 20 an infallible judge without knowing where.

The Hind at one time is afraid to drink at the common brook, because she may be worried; but, walking home with the Panther, talks by the way of the Nicene Fathers, and at last declares herself to be the Catholic Church.

This absurdity was very properly ridiculed in the City Mouse and Country Mouse of Montague and Prior; and in the detection and censure of the incongruity of the fiction chiefly consists the value of their performance, which, whatever reputation it might obtain by the help of temporary 30 passions, seems, to readers almost a century distant, not very forcible or animated.

Pope, whose judgment was perhaps a little bribed by the subject, used to mention this poem as the most correct specimen of Dryden's versification. It was indeed written when he had completely formed his manner, and may be supposed to exhibit, negligence excepted, his deliberate and ultimate scheme of metre.

We may therefore reasonably infer, that he did not approve the perpetual uniformity which confines the sense to couplets, since he has broken his lines in the initial paragraph.

> A milk-white Hind, immortal and unchanged,
> Fed on the lawns, and in the forest ranged :
> Without unspotted, innocent within,
> 10   She fear'd no danger, for she knew no sin.
> Yet had she oft been chased with horns and hounds,
> And Scythian shafts, and many winged wounds
> Aim'd at her heart ; was often forced to fly,
> And doom'd to death, though fated not to die.

These lines are lofty, elegant, and musical, notwithstanding the interruption of the pause, of which the effect is rather increase of pleasure by variety, than offence by ruggedness.

To the first part it was his intention, he says, " to give the majestic turn of heroic poesy " ; and perhaps he might have 20 executed his design not unsuccessfully, had not an opportunity of satire, which he cannot forbear, fallen sometimes in his way. The character of a Presbyterian, whose emblem is the Wolf, is not very heroically majestic :

> More haughty than the rest, the wolfish race
> Appear with belly gaunt and famish'd face ;
> Never was so deform'd a beast of grace.
> His ragged tail betwixt his legs he wears,
> Close clapp'd for shame ; but his rough crest he rears,
> And pricks up his predestinating ears.

30 His general character of the other sorts of beasts that never go to church, though sprightly and keen, has, however, not much of heroic poesy :

> These are the chief ; to number o'er the rest,
> And stand like Adam naming every beast,
> Were weary work ; nor will the Muse describe
> A slimy-born, and sun-begotten tribe,

Who, far from steeples and their sacred sound,
In fields their sullen conventicles found.
These gross, half-animated, lumps I leave
Nor can I think what thoughts they can conceive ;
But, if they think at all, tis sure no higher
Than matter, put in motion, may aspire ;
Souls that can scarce ferment their mass of clay ;
So drossy, so divisible are they,
As would but serve pure bodies for allay ;
Such souls as shards produce, such beetle things   10
As only buz to heaven with evening wings ;
Strike in the dark, offending but by chance ;
Such are the blindfold blows of ignorance.
They know not beings, and but hate a name ;
To them the Hind and Panther are the same.

One more instance, and that taken from the narrative part, where style was more in his choice, will show how steadily he kept his resolution of heroic dignity.

For when the herd, suffic'd, did late repair
To ferny heaths and to their forest lair,   20
She made a mannerly excuse to stay,
Proffering the Hind to wait her half the way :
That, since the sky was clear, an hour of talk
Might help her to beguile the tedious walk.
With much good-will the motion was embraced,
To chat awhile on their adventures past :
Nor had the grateful Hind so soon forgot
Her friend and fellow-sufferer in the plot.
Yet, wondering how of late she grew estranged,
Her forehead cloudy and her count'nance changed,   30
She thought this hour th' occasion would present
To learn her secret cause of discontent,
Which well she hoped might be with ease redress'd.
Considering her a well-bred civil beast,
And more a gentlewoman than the rest.
After some common talk what rumours ran,
The lady of the spotted muff began.

The second and third parts he professes to have reduced to diction more familiar and more suitable to dispute and

conversation ; the difference is not, however, very easily
perceived ; the first has familiar, and the two others have
sonorous, lines.   The original incongruity runs through
the whole ; the King is now *Cæsar*, and now the *Lyon* ; and
the name *Pan* is given to the Supreme Being.

But when this constitutional absurdity is forgiven, the
poem must be confessed to be written with great smoothness
of metre, a wide extent of knowledge, and an abundant
multiplicity of images ; the controversy is embellished with
10 pointed sentences, diversified by illustrations, and enlivened
by sallies of invective.   Some of the facts to which allusions
are made are now become obscure, and perhaps there may
be many satirical passages little understood.

As it was by its nature a work of defiance, a composition
which would naturally be examined with the utmost acrimony of criticism, it was probably laboured with uncommon
attention, and there are, indeed, few negligences in the
subordinate parts.   The original impropriety and the
subsequent unpopularity of the subject, added to the
20 ridiculousness of its first elements, has sunk it into neglect ;
but it may be usefully studied, as an example of poetical
ratiocination, in which the argument suffers little from
the metre.

In the poem on the Birth of the Prince of Wales, nothing
is very remarkable but the exorbitant adulation, and that
insensibility of the precipice on which the king was then
standing, which the laureate apparently shared with the rest
of the courtiers.   A few months cured him of controversy,
dismissed him from court, and made him again a playwright
30 and translator.

Of Juvenal there had been a translation by Stapylton, and
another by Holiday ; neither of them is very poetical.
Stapylton is more smooth ; and Holiday's is more esteemed
for the learning of his notes.   A new version was proposed
to the poets of that time and undertaken by them in conjunction.   The main design was conducted by Dryden, whose

reputation was such that no man was unwilling to serve the Muses under him.

The general character of this translation will be given, when it is said to preserve the wit, but to want the dignity, of the original. The peculiarity of Juvenal is a mixture of gaiety and stateliness, of pointed sentences, and declamatory grandeur. His points have not been neglected ; but his grandeur none of the band seemed to consider as necessary to be imitated, except Creech, who undertook the thirteenth satire. It is therefore perhaps possible to give a better 10 representation of that great satirist, even in those parts which Dryden himself has translated, some passages excepted, which will never be excelled.

With Juvenal was published Persius, translated wholly by Dryden. This work, though like all the other productions of Dryden it may have shining parts, seems to have been written merely for wages, in an uniform mediocrity, without any eager endeavour after excellence, or laborious effort of the mind.

There wanders an opinion among the readers of poetry, that one of these satires is an exercise of the school. Dryden 20 says that he once translated it at school ; but not that he preserved or published the juvenile performance.

Not long afterwards he undertook perhaps the most arduous work of its kind, a translation of Virgil, for which he had shown how well he was qualified by his version of the Pollio, and two episodes, one of Nisus and Euryalus, the other of Mezentius and Lausus.

In the comparison of Homer and Virgil, the discriminative excellence of Homer is elevation and comprehension of thought, and that of Virgil is grace and splendour of diction. 30 The beauties of Homer are therefore difficult to be lost, and those of Virgil difficult to be retained. The massy trunk of sentiment is safe by its solidity, but the blossoms of elocution easily drop away. The author, having the choice of his own images, selects those which he can best adorn ; the translator must, at all hazards, follow his original, and express thoughts which perhaps he would not have chosen. When to this primary difficulty is added the inconvenience of a language so much inferior in harmony to the Latin, it cannot be expected that they who read the Georgic and the Eneid should be much delighted with any version.

All these obstacles Dryden saw, and all these he determined to encounter. The expectation of his work was undoubtedly great; the nation considered its honour as interested in the event. One gave him the different editions 10 of his author, and another helped him in the subordinate parts. The arguments of the several books were given him by Addison.

The hopes of the public were not disappointed. He produced, says Pope, "the most noble and spirited translation that I know in any language." It certainly excelled whatever had appeared in English, and appears to have satisfied his friends, and, for the most part, to have silenced his enemies. Milbourne, indeed, a clergyman, attacked it; but his outrages seem to be the ebullitions of a mind agitated by 20 stronger resentment than bad poetry can excite, and previously resolved not to be pleased.

When admiration had subsided, the translation was more coolly examined, and found, like all others, to be sometimes erroneous, and sometimes licentious. Those who could find faults, thought they could avoid them; and Dr. Brady attempted in blank verse a translation of the Eneid, which, when dragged into the world, did not live long enough to cry. I have never seen it; but that such a version there is, or has been, perhaps some old catalogue informed me.

30　　With not much better success, Trapp, when his Tragedy and his Prelections had given him reputation, attempted another blank version of the Eneid; to which, notwithstanding the slight regard with which it was treated, he had afterwards perseverance enough to add the Eclogues and Georgics. His book may continue its existence as long as it is the clandestine refuge of school-boys.

Since the English ear has been accustomed to the mellifluence of Pope's numbers, and the diction of poetry has become more splendid, new attempts have been made to translate Virgil; and all his works have been attempted by men better qualified to contend with Dryden. I will not engage myself in an invidious comparison, by opposing one passage to another; a work of which there would be no end, and which might be often offensive without use.

It is not by comparing line with line that the merit of great works is to be estimated, but by their general effects and ultimate result. It is easy to note a weak line, and write one more vigorous in its place; to find a happiness of expression in the original, and transplant it by force into the version; but what is given to the parts may be subducted from the whole, and the reader may be weary, though the critic may commend. Works of imagination excel by their allurement and delight; by their power of attracting and detaining the attention. That book is good in vain, which the reader throws away. He only is the master, who keeps the mind in pleasing captivity; whose pages are perused with eagerness, and in hope of new pleasure are perused again; and whose conclusion is perceived with an eye of sorrow, such as the traveller casts upon departing day.

By his proportion of this predomination I will consent that Dryden should be tried; of this, which, in opposition to reason, makes Ariosto the darling and the pride of Italy; of this, which, in defiance of criticism, continues Shakspeare the sovereign of the drama.

His last work was his Fables, in which he gave us the first example of a mode of writing which the Italians call *refaccimento, a renovation of ancient writers, by modernizing their language.* Thus the old poem of Boiardo has been new-dressed by Domenichi and Berni. The works of Chaucer, upon which this kind of rejuvenescence has been bestowed by Dryden, require little criticism. The tale of the Cock seems hardly worth revival; and the story of Palamon and

Arcite, containing an action unsuitable to the times in which
it is placed, can hardly be suffered to pass without censure of
the hyperbolical commendation which Dryden has given it in
the general Preface, and in a poetical Dedication, a piece
where his original fondness of remote conceits seems to have
revived.

Of the three pieces, borrowed from Boccace, Sigismunda
may be defended by the celebrity of the story. Theodore
and Honoria, though it contains not much moral, yet afforded
10 opportunities of striking description. And Cymon was
formerly a tale of such reputation, that at the revival of
letters it was translated into Latin by one of the Beroalds.

Whatever subjects employed his pen, he was still improving our measures and embellishing our language.

In this volume are interspersed some short original poems,
which, with his prologues, epilogues, and songs, may be
comprised in Congreve's remark, that even those, if he had
written nothing else, would have entitled him to the praise
of excellence in his kind.

20   One-composition must however be distinguished. The
Ode for St. Cecilia's Day, perhaps the last effort of his poetry,
has been always considered as exhibiting the highest flight
of fancy, and the exactest nicety of art. This is allowed to
stand without a rival. If indeed there is any excellence
beyond it, in some other of Dryden's works that excellence
must be found. Compared with the ode on Killigrew, it
may be pronounced perhaps superior in the whole, but without any single part equal to the first stanza of the other.

It is said to have cost Dryden a fortnight's labour; but it
30 does not want its negligences; some of the lines are without
correspondent rhymes; a defect which I never detected but
after an acquaintance of many years, and which the enthusiasm of the writer might hinder him from perceiving.

His last stanza has less emotion than the former; but is
not less elegant in the diction. The conclusion is vicious;
the music of Timotheus, which *raised a mortal to the skies,*

had only a metaphorical power ; that of Cecilia, which *drew an angel down*, had a real effect : the crown therefore could not reasonably be divided.

In a general survey of Dryden's labours, he appears to have a mind very comprehensive by nature, and much enriched with acquired knowledge. His compositions are the effects of a vigorous genius operating upon large materials.

The power that predominated in his intellectual operations was rather strong reason than quick sensibility. Upon all occasions that were presented, he studied rather than felt, and produced sentiments not such as nature enforces, but meditation supplies. With the simple and elemental passions, as they spring separate in the mind, he seems not much acquainted ; and seldom describes them but as they are complicated by the various relations of society, and confused in the tumults and agitations of life.

What he says of love may contribute to the explanation of his character :

> Love various minds does variously inspire :
> It stirs in gentle bosoms gentle fire,
> Like that of incense on the altar laid ;
> But raging flames tempestuous souls invade ;
> A fire which every windy passion blows,
> With pride it mounts, or with revenge it glows.

Dryden's was not one of the *gentle bosoms* : Love, as it subsists in itself, with no tendency but to the person loved, and wishing only for correspondent kindness ; such Love as shuts out all other interest, (the Love of the Golden Age, was too soft and subtle to put his faculties in motion.) He hardly conceived it but in its turbulent effervescence with some other desires ; when it was inflamed by rivalry, or obstructed by difficulties ; when it invigorated ambition, or exasperated revenge.

He is therefore, with all his variety of excellence, not often pathetic ; and had so little sensibility of the power of effusions purely natural that he did not esteem them in others. Simplicity gave him no pleasure; and for the first part of his life he looked on Otway with contempt, though at last, indeed very late, he confessed that in his play *there* was *Nature, which is the chief beauty.*

We do not always know our own motives. I am not certain whether it was not rather the difficulty which he found in exhibiting the genuine operations of the heart than a servile submission to an injudicious audience, that filled his
10 plays with false magnificence. It was necessary to fix attention; and the mind can be captivated only by recollection, or by curiosity; by reviving natural sentiments, or impressing new appearances of things : sentences were readier at his call than images; he could more easily fill the ear with some splendid novelty than awaken those ideas that slumber in the heart.

The favourite exercise of his mind was ratiocination ; and, that argument might not be too soon at an end, he delighted to talk of liberty and necessity, destiny and contingence ;
20 these he discusses in the language of the school with so much profundity, that the terms which he uses are not always understood. It is indeed learning, but learning out of place. When once he had engaged himself in disputation, thoughts flowed in on either side : he was now no longer at a loss ; he had always objections and solutions at command ; *verbaque provisam rem*—give him matter for his verse, and he finds without difficulty verse for his matter.

In Comedy, for which he professes himself not naturally qualified, the mirth which he excites will perhaps not be
30 found so much to arise from any original humour, or peculiarity of character nicely distinguished and diligently pursued, as from incidents and circumstances, artifices and surprises ; from jests of action rather than of sentiment. What he had of humorous or passionate, he seems to have had not from nature, but from other poets ; if not always as a plagiary, at least as an imitator.

Next to argument, his delight was in wild and daring
sallies of sentiment, in the irregular and eccentric violence of
wit. He delighted to tread upon the brink of meaning,
where light and darkness begin to mingle ; to approach the
precipice of absurdity, and hover over the abyss of unideal
vacancy. This inclination sometimes produced nonsense,
which he knew ; as

> Move swiftly, Sun, and fly a lover's pace,
> Leave weeks and months behind thee in thy race,
>
> Amariel flies   10
> To guard thee from the demons of the air ;
> My flaming sword above them to display,
> All keen, and ground upon the edge of day.

And sometimes it issued in absurdities, of which perhaps he
was not conscious :

> Then we upon our orb's last verge shall go,
> And see the ocean leaning on the sky ;
> From thence our rolling neighbours we shall know,
> And on the lunar world securely pry.

These lines have no meaning ; but may we not say, in 20
imitation of Cowley on another book,

> 'Tis so like *sense* 'twill serve the turn as well ?

This endeavour after the grand and the new produced
many sentiments either great or bulky, and many images
either just or splendid :

> I am as free as Nature first made man,
> Ere the base laws of servitude began,
> When wild in woods the noble savage ran.

> —'Tis but because the living death ne'er knew,
> They fear to prove it as a thing that's new :   30
> Let me th' experiment before you try,
> I'll show you first how easy 'tis to die.

> —There with a forest of their darts he strove,
> And stood like Capaneus defying Jove ;

With his broad sword the boldest beating down,
While Fate grew pale lest he should win the town,
And turn'd the iron leaves of his dark book
To make new dooms, or mend what it mistook.

—I beg no pity for this mouldering clay ;
For if you give it burial, there it takes   •
Possession of your earth ;
If burnt, and scatter'd in the air, the winds
That strew my dust diffuse my royalty,
10   And spread me o'er your clime ; for where one atom
Of mine shall light, know there Sebastian reigns.

Of these quotations the two first may be allowed to be great,
the two latter only tumid.

Of such selection there is no end. I will add only a few
more passages, of which the first, though it may perhaps not
be quite clear in prose, is not too obscure for poetry, as the
meaning that it has is noble :

No, there is a necessity in Fate,
Why still the brave bold man is fortunate ;   •
20   He keeps his object ever full in sight ;
And that assurance holds him firm and right ;
True, 'tis a narrow way that leads to bliss,
But right before there is no precipice ;
Fear makes men look aside, and so their footing miss.

Of the images which the two following citations afford, the
first is elegant, the second magnificent, whether either be
just, let the reader judge :

What precious drops are these,
Which silently each other's track pursue,
30   Bright as young diamonds in their infant dew ?
—Resign your castle—
—Enter, brave sir ; for, when you speak the word,
The gates shall open of their own accord ; .
The genius of the place its lord shall meet,
And bow its towery forehead at your feet.

These bursts of extravagance Dryden calls the "Dalilahs"

of the theatre ; and owns that many noisy lines of Maxamin
and Almanzor call out for vengeance upon him ; "but I
knew," says he, "that they were bad enough to please, even
when I wrote them." There is surely reason to suspect that
he pleased himself as well as his audience ; and that these,
like the harlots of other men, had his love, though not his
approbation.

He had sometimes faults of a less generous and splendid
kind. He makes, like almost all other poets, very frequent
use of mythology, and sometimes connects religion and fable   10
too closely without distinction.

He descends to display his knowledge with pedantic ostentation ; as when, in translating Virgil, he says, "tack to the
larboard"—and "veer starboard" ; and talks, in another
work, of "virtue spooming before the wind." His vanity
now and then betrays his ignorance :

> They Nature's king through Nature's optics view'd ;
> Reversed, they view'd him lessen'd to their eyes.

He had heard of reversing a telescope, and unluckily reverses
the object.   20

He is sometimes unexpectedly mean. When he describes
the Supreme Being as moved by prayer to stop the Fire of
London, what is his expression ?

> A hollow crystal pyramid he takes,
> In firmamental waters dipp'd above,
> Of this a broad *extinguisher* he makes,
> And *hoods* the flames that to their quarry strove.

When he describes the Last Day, and the decisive tribunal,
he intermingles this image :

> When rattling bones together fly,   30
> From the four quarters of the sky.

It was indeed never in his power to resist the temptation
of a jest. In his Elegy on Cromwell :

No sooner was the Frenchman's cause embraced,
Than the *light Monsieur* the *grave Don* outweigh'd ;
His fortune turn'd the scale——

He had a vanity, unworthy of his abilities, to show, as may
be suspected, the rank of the company with whom he lived,
by the use of French words, which had then crept into conversation ; such as *fraicheur* for *coolness*, *fougue* for *turbulence*, and a few more, none of which the language has incor-
porated or retained.—They continue only where they stood
10 first, perpetual warnings to future innovators.

These are his faults of affectation ; his faults of negligence
are beyond recital. Such is the unevenness of his compositions, that ten lines are seldom found together without
something of which the reader is ashamed. Dryden was no
rigid judge of his own pages ; he seldom struggled after
supreme excellence, but snatched in haste what was within
his reach ; and when he could content others, was himself
contented. He did not keep present to his mind an idea of
pure perfection ; nor compare his works, such as they were,
20 with what they might be made. He knew to whom he
should be opposed. He had more music than Waller, more
vigour than Denham, and more nature than Cowley ; and
from his contemporaries he was in no danger. Standing
therefore in the highest place, he had no care to rise by
contending with himself ; but, while there was no name
above his own, was willing to enjoy fame on the easiest
terms.

He was no lover of labour. What he thought sufficient,
he did not stop to make better ; and allowed himself to leave
30 many parts unfinished, in confidence that the good lines
would overbalance the bad. What he had once written, he
dismissed from his thoughts ; and, I believe, there is no
example to be found of any correction or improvement made
by him after publication. The hastiness of his productions
might be the effect of necessity ; but his subsequent neglect
could hardly have any other cause than impatience of study.

What can be said of his versification will be little more than a dilatation of the praise given it by Pope :

> Waller was smooth ; but Dryden taught to join
> The varying verse, the full-resounding line,
> The long majestic march, and energy divine.

Some improvements had been already made in English numbers ; but the full force of our language was not yet felt ; the verse that was smooth was commonly feeble. If Cowley had sometimes a finished line, he had it by chance. Dryden knew how to choose the flowing and the sonorous 10 words ; to vary the pauses, and adjust the accents ; to diversify the cadence, and yet preserve the smoothness of his metre.

Of Triplets and Alexandrines, though he did not introduce the use, he established it. The triplet has long subsisted among us. Dryden seems not to have traced it higher than to Chapman's Homer ; but it is to be found in Phaer's Virgil, written in the reign of Mary ; and in Hall's Satires, published five years before the death of Elizabeth.

The Alexandrine was, I believe, first used by Spenser, for 20 the sake of closing his stanza with a fuller sound. We had a longer measure of fourteen syllables, into which the Eneid was translated by Phaer, and other works of the ancients by other writers ; of which Chapman's Iliad was, I believe, the last.

The two first lines of Phaer's third Eneid will exemplify this measure :

> When Asia's state was overthrown, and Priam's kingdom stout,
> All guiltless, by the power of gods above was rooted out.

As these lines had their break, or *cæsura*, always at the 30 eighth syllable, it was thought, in time, commodious to divide them : and quatrains of lines, alternately, consisting of eight and six syllables, make the most soft and pleasing of our lyric measures ; as,

G

Relentless Time, destroying power,
Which stone and brass obey,
Who giv'st to ev'ry flying hour
To work some new decay.

In the Alexandrine, when its power was once felt, some
poems, as Drayton's Polyolbion, were wholly written; and
sometimes the measures of twelve and fourteen syllabies
were interchanged with one another. Cowley was the first
that inserted the Alexandrine at pleasure among the heroic
10 lines of ten syllables, and from him Dryden professes to have
adopted it.

The Triplet and Alexandrine are not universally approved.
Swift always censured them, and wrote some lines to ridicule
them. In examining their propriety, it is to be considered
that the essence of verse is regularity, and its ornament is
variety. To write verse, is to dispose syllables and sounds
harmonically by some known and settled rule; a rule however lax enough to substitute similitude for identity, to
admit change without breach of order, and to relieve the
20 ear without disappointing it. Thus a Latin hexameter is
formed from dactyls and spondees differently combined; the
English heroic admits of acute or grave syllables variously
disposed. The Latin never deviates into seven feet, or
exceeds the number of seventeen syllables; but the English
Alexandrine breaks the lawful bounds, and surprises the
reader with two syllables more than he expected.

The effect of the triplet is the same; the ear has been
accustomed to expect a new rhyme in every couplet; but is
on a sudden surprised with three rhymes together, to which
30 the reader could not accommodate his voice, did he not
obtain notice of the change from the braces of the margins.
Surely there is something unskilful in the necessity of such
mechanical direction.

Considering the metrical art simply as a science, and consequently excluding all casualty, we must allow that Triplets
and Alexandrines, inserted by caprice, are interruptions of

that constancy to which science aspires) And though the
variety which they produce may very justly be desired, yet
to make our poetry exact, there ought to be some stated
mode of admitting them.

But till some such regulation can be formed, I wish them
still to be retained in their present state. (They are sometimes grateful to the reader, and sometimes convenient to
the poet.) Fenton was of opinion, that Dryden was too
liberal, and Pope too sparing, in their use.

The rhymes of Dryden are commonly just, and he valued 10
himself for his readiness in finding them, but he is sometimes
open to objection.

It is the common practice of our poets to end the second
line with a weak or grave syllable :

Together o'er the Alps methinks we fly,
Fill'd with ideas of fair Italy.

Dryden sometimes puts the weak rhyme in the first :

Laugh, all the powers that favour *tyranny*
And all the standing Army of the sky.

Sometimes he concludes a period or paragraph with the 20
first line of a couplet, which, though the French seem to do
it without irregularity, always displeases in English poetry.

The Alexandrine, though much his favourite, is not always
very diligently fabricated by him. (It invariably requires a
break at the sixth syllable, a rule which the modern French
poets never violate, but which Dryden sometimes neglected :)

And with paternal thunder vindicates his throne.

Of Dryden's works it was said by Pope, that " he could
select from them better specimens of every mode of poetry
than any other English writer could supply." Perhaps no 30
nation ever produced a writer that enriched his language
with such variety of models.) To him we owe the improvement, perhaps the completion of our metre, the refinement of
our language, and much of the correctness of our sentiments.

By him we were taught *sapere et fari*, to think naturally
and express forcibly. Though Davies has reasoned in rhyme
before him, it may be perhaps maintained that he was the
first who joined argument with poetry. He showed us the
true bounds of a translator's liberty. What was said of
Rome, adorned by Augustus, may be applied by an easy
metaphor to English poetry embellished by Dryden,
lateritiam invenit, marmoream reliquit. He found it brick
and he left it marble.

10   Mr. Dryden, having received from Rymer his Remarks on
the Tragedies of the last Age, wrote observations on the
blank leaves : which, having been in the possession of Mr.
Garrick, are by his favour communicated to the public, that
no particle of Dryden may be lost.

"That we may the less wonder why pity and terror are not
now the only springs on which our tragedies move, and that
Shakspeare may be more excused, Rapin confesses that the
French tragedies now all run on the *tendre*; and gives the
reason, because love is the passion which most predominates
20 in our souls, and that therefore the passions represented
become insipid, unless they are conformable to the thoughts
of the audience.   But it is to be concluded, that this passion
works not now amongst the French so strongly as the other
two did amongst the ancients. Amongst us, who have a
stronger genius for writing, the operations from the writing
are much stronger; for the raising of Shakspeare's passions is
more from the excellency of the words and thoughts, than
the justness of the occasion ; and, if he has been able to pick
single occasions, he has never founded the whole reasonably;
30 yet, by the genius of poetry in writing, he has succeeded.

"Rapin attributes more to the *dictio*, that is, to the words
and discourse of a tragedy, than Aristotle has done, who
places them in the last rank of beauties; perhaps, only last
in order, because they are the last product of the design, of
the disposition or connection of its parts; of the characters,
of the manners of those characters, and of the thoughts pro-

ceeding from those manners. Rapin's words are remarkable:
'Tis not the admirable intrigue, the surprising events, and
extraordinary incidents, that make the beauty of a
tragedy; 'tis the discourses, when they are natural and
passionate: so are Shakspeare's.

"The parts of a poem, tragic or heroic, are,

"1. The fable itself. ,

"2. The order or manner of its contrivance, in relation of
the parts to the whole.

"3. The manners, or decency, of the characters, in 10
speaking or acting what is proper for them, and proper to be
shown by the poet.

"4. The thoughts which express the manners.

"5. The words which express those thoughts.

"In the last of these Homer excels Virgil; Virgil all
other ancient poets; and Shakspeare all modern poets.

"For the second of these, the order: the meaning is, that
a fable ought to have a beginning, middle, and an end, all
just and natural; so that that part, *e.g.* which is the middle,
could not naturally be the beginning or end, and so of the 20
rest: all depend on one another, like the links of a curious
chain. If terror and pity are only to be raised, certainly
this author follows Aristotle's rules, and Sophocles' and
Euripides' example: but joy may be raised too, and that
doubly, either by seeing a wicked man punished, or a good
man at last fortunate; or perhaps indignation, to see wickedness prosperous, and goodness depressed: both these may be
profitable to the end of tragedy, reformation of manners;
but the last improperly, only as it begets pity in the
audience; though Aristotle, I confess, places tragedies of 30
this kind in the second form.

"He who undertakes to answer this excellent critique of
Mr. Rymer, in behalf of our English poets against the Greek,
ought to do it in this manner: either by yielding to him the
greatest part of what he contends for, which consists in this,
that the μῦθος, *i.e.* the design and conduct of it, is more con-

ducing in the Greeks to those ends of tragedy, which
Aristotle and he propose, namely, to cause terror and pity :
yet the granting this does not set the Greeks above the
English poets.

"But the answerer ought to prove two things : first, that
the fable is not the greatest master-piece of a tragedy,
though it be the foundation of it.

"Secondly, That other ends as suitable to the nature of
tragedy may be found in the English, which were not in the
10 Greek.

"Aristotle places the fable first; not *quoad dignitatem, sed
quoad fundamentum*: for a fable never so movingly contrived
to those ends of his, pity and terror, will operate nothing on
our affections, except the characters, manners, thoughts, and
words, are suitable.

"So that it remains for Mr. Rymer to prove, that in all
those, or the greatest part of them, we are inferior to
Sophocles and Euripides : and this he has offered at, in some
measure ; but, I think, a little partially to the ancients.

20   "For the fable itself, 'tis in the English more adorned
with episodes, and larger than in the Greek poets ; consequently more diverting. For, if the action be but one, and
that plain, without any counterturn of design or episode, *i.e.*
underplot, how can it be so pleasing as the English, which
have both underplot and a turned design, which keeps the
audience in expectation of the catastrophe ? whereas in the
Greek poets we see through the whole design at first.

"For the characters, they are neither so many nor so
various in Sophocles and Euripides, as in Shakspeare and
30 Fletcher ; only they are more adapted to those ends of
tragedy which Aristotle commends to us, pity and terror.

"The manners flow from the characters, and consequently
must partake of their advantages and disadvantages.

"The thoughts and words, which are the fourth and fifth
beauties of tragedy, are certainly more noble and more
poetical in the English than in the Greek, which must be

proved by comparing them somewhat more equitably than Mr. Rymer has done.

"After all, we need not yield that the English way is less conducing to move pity and terror, because they often show virtue oppressed and vice punished; where they do not both, or either, they are not to be defended.

"And if we should grant that the Greeks performed this better, perhaps it may admit of dispute, whether pity and terror are either the prime, or at least the only ends of tragedy.

"'Tis not enough that Aristotle has said so; for, Aristotle 10 drew his models of tragedy from Sophocles and Euripides; and, if he had seen ours, might have changed his mind. And chiefly we have to say (what I hinted on pity and terror, in the last paragraph save one), that the punishment of vice and reward of virtue are the most adequate ends of tragedy, because most conducing to good example of life. Now, pity is not so easily raised for a criminal (and the ancient tragedy always represents its chief person such) as it is for an innocent man; and the suffering of innocence and punishment of the offender is of the nature of English tragedy; contrarily, 20 in the Greek, innocence is unhappy often, and the offender escapes. Then we are not touched with the sufferings of any sort of men so much as of lovers; and this was almost unknown to the ancients; so that they neither administered poetical justice, of which Mr. Rymer boasts, so well as we; neither knew they the best common place of pity, which is love.

"He therefore unjustly blames us for not building on what the ancients left us; for it seems, upon consideration of the premises, that we have wholly finished what they began.

"My judgment on this piece is this: that it is extremely 30 learned; but that the author of it is better read in the Greek than in the English poets; that all writers ought to study this critique, as the best account I have ever seen of the ancients; that the model of tragedy, he has here given, is excellent, and extreme correct; but that it is not the only model of all tragedy, because it is too much circum-

scribed in plot, characters, etc.; and, lastly, that we may be
taught here justly to admire and imitate the ancients,
without giving them the preference with this author, in
prejudice to our own country.

"Want of method in this excellent treatise makes the
thoughts of the author sometimes obscure.

"His meaning, that pity and terror are to be moved, is,
that they are to be moved as the means conducing to the
ends of tragedy, which are pleasure and instruction.

10   "And these two ends may be thus distinguished. The
chief end of the poet is to please ; for, his immediate reputation depends on it.

"The great end of the poem is to instruct, which is performed by making pleasure the vehicle of that instruction ;
for, poesy is an art, and all arts are made to profit. *Rapin.*

"The pity, which the poet is to labour for, is for the
criminal, not for those or him whom he has murdered, or
who have been the occasion of the tragedy. The terror is
likewise in the punishment of the same criminal ; who, if he
20 be represented too great an offender, will not be pitied; if
altogether innocent, his punishment will be unjust.

"Another obscurity is, where he says Sophocles perfected
tragedy by introducing the third actor ; that is, he
meant, three kinds of action ; one company singing, or
another playing on the music ; a third dancing.

"To make a true judgment in this competition betwixt
the Greek poets and the English in tragedy :

"Consider, first, how Aristotle has defined a tragedy.
Secondly, what he assigns the end of it to be. Thirdly, what
30 he thinks the beauties of it. Fourthly, the means to attain
the end proposed.

"Compare the Greek and English tragic poets justly, and
without partiality, according to those rules.

"Then, secondly, consider whether Aristotle has made a
just definition of tragedy ; of its parts, of its ends, and of its
beauties ; and whether he, having not seen any others but

those of Sophocles, Euripides, etc., had or truly could determine what all the excellences of tragedy are, and wherein
they consist.

"Next, show in what ancient tragedy was deficient : for
example, in the narrowness of its plots, and fewness of
persons ; and try whether that be not a fault in the Greek
poets ; and whether their excellency was so great, when the
variety was visibly so little ; or whether what they did was
not very easy to do.

"Then make a judgment on what the English have added 10
to their beauties ; as, for example, not only more plot, but
also new passions : as, namely, that of love, scarce touched
on by the ancients, except in this one example of Phædra, cited
by Mr. Rymer ; and in that how short they were of Fletcher !

"Prove also that love, being an heroic passion, is fit for
tragedy, which cannot be denied, because of the example
alleged of Phædra ; and how far Shakspeare has outdone
them in friendship, etc.

"To return to the beginning of this inquiry ; consider if
pity and terror be enough for tragedy to move: and, I 20
believe, upon a true definition of tragedy, it will be found
that its work extends farther, and that it is to reform
manners, by a delightful representation of human life in
great persons, by way of dialogue. If this be true, then
not only pity and terror are to be moved, as the only means
to bring us to virtue, but generally love to virtue, and
hatred to vice; by showing the rewards of one, and punish-
ments of the other; at least, by rendering virtue always
amiable, though it be shown unfortunate ; and vice detestable, though it be shown triumphant.   30

"If, then, the encouragement of virtue and discouragement
of vice be the proper ends of poetry in tragedy, pity and
terror, though good means, are not the only. For all the
passions, in their turns, are to be set in a ferment: as joy,
anger, love, fear, are to be used as the poet's common-places ;
and a general concernment for the principal actors is to be

raised, by making them appear such in their characters, their
words, and actions, as will interest the audience in their
fortunes.

"And if, after all, in a larger sense, pity comprehends
this concernment for the good, and terror includes detestation for the bad, then let us consider whether the English
have not answered this end of tragedy as well as the
ancients, or perhaps better.

"And here Mr. Rymer's objections against these plays are
10 to be impartially weighed, that we may see whether they are
of weight enough to turn the balance against our countrymen.

"'Tis evident those plays, which he arraigns, have moved
both those passions in a high degree upon the stage.

"To give the glory of this away from the poet, and to
place it upon the actors, seems unjust.

"One reason is, because whatever actors they have found, ·
the event has been the same; that is, the same passions
have been always moved; which shows that there is something of force and merit in the plays themselves, conducing
20 to the design of raising these two passions; and suppose
them ever to have been excellently acted, yet action only
adds grace, vigour, and more life, upon the stage; but
cannot give it wholly where it is not first. But, secondly,
I dare appeal to those who have never seen them acted, if
they have not found these two passions moved within them:
and if the general voice will carry it, Mr. Rymer's prejudice will take off his single testimony.

"This, being matter of fact, is reasonably to be established
by this appeal; as, if one man says 'tis night, the rest of
30 the world conclude it to be day, there needs no farther
argument against him, that it is so.

"If he urge, that the general taste is depraved, his arguments to prove this can at best but evince that our poets
took not the best way to raise those passions; but experience
proves against him, that these means, which they have
used, have been successful, and have produced them.

" And one reason of that success is, in my opinion, this, that Shakspeare and Fletcher have written to the genius of the age and nation in which they lived; for though nature, as he objects, is the same in all places, and reason too the same; yet the climate, the age, the disposition of the people, to whom a poet writes, may be so different, that what pleased the Greeks would not satisfy an English audience.

" And if they proceeded upon a foundation of truer reason to please the Athenians, than Shakspeare and Fletcher to please the English, it only shows that the Athenians were 10 a more judicious people; but the poet's business is certainly to please the audience.

" Whether our English audience have been pleased hitherto with acorns, as he calls it, or with bread, is the next question; that is, whether the means which Shakspeare and Fletcher have used, in their plays, to raise those passions before named, be better applied to the ends by the Greek poets than by them. And perhaps we shall not grant him this wholly; let it be granted that a writer is not to run down with the stream, or to please the people by their 20 own usual methods, but rather to reform their judgments, it still remains to prove that our theatre needs this total reformation.

" The faults which he has found in their designs are rather wittily aggravated in many places than reasonably urged; and as much may be returned on the Greeks, by one who were as witty as himself.

" 2. They destroy not, if they are granted, the foundation of the fabric; only take away from the beauty of the sym- metry; for example, the faults in the character of the 30 King and No-King, are not, as he makes them, such as render him detestable, but only imperfections which accom- pany human nature, and are for the most part excused by the violence of his love; so that they destroy not our pity or concernment for him: this answer may be applied to most of his objections of that kind.

"And Rollo committing many murders, when he is
answerable but for one, is too severely arraigned by him;
for, it adds to our horror and detestation of the criminal;
and poetic justice is not neglected neither; for we stab him
in our minds for every offence which he commits; and the
point, which the poet is to gain on the audience, is not so
much in the death of an offender as the raising an horror
of his crimes.

"That the criminal should neither be wholly guilty, nor
10 wholly innocent, but so participating of both as to move
both pity and terror, is certainly a good rule, but not perpetually to be observed; for, that were to make all tragedies
too much alike; which objection he foresaw, but has not
fully answered.

"To conclude, therefore; if the plays of the ancients are
more correctly plotted, ours are more beautifully written.
And, if we can raise passions as high on worse foundations,
it shows our genius in tragedy is greater; for in all other
parts of it the English have manifestly excelled them."

20   The original of the following letter is preserved in the
library at Lambeth, and was kindly imparted to the public
by the reverend Dr. Vyse.   •

. *Copy of an original Letter from John Dryden, Esq., to his
sons in Italy, from a MS. in the Lambeth Library, marked
No. 933, p. 56.*

(*Superscribed*)
    " Al illustrissimo Sigⁿ CARLO DRYDEN Camariere
                    d'Honore A.S.S.
                                        " In Roma.
30 " Franca per Mantoua.
                        " Sept. the 3rd, our style [1697].
    " DEAR SONS,—Being now at Sir William Bowyer's in the
country, I cannot write at large, because I find myself somewhat indisposed with a cold, and am thick of hearing, rather
worse than I was in town.   I am glad to find, by your letter

of July 26th, your style, that you are both in health; but wonder you should think me so negligent as to forget to give you an account of the ship in which your parcel is to come. I have written to you two or three letters concerning it, which I have sent by safe hands, as I told you, and doubt not but you have them before this can arrive to you. Being out of town, I have forgotten the ship's name, which your mother will inquire, and put it into her letter, which is joined with mine. But the master's name I remember: he is called- Mr. Ralph Thorp; the ship is bound to Leghorn, 10 consigned to Mr. Peter and Mr. Tho. Ball, merchants. I am of your opinion, that by Tonson's means almost all our letters have miscarried for this last year. But, however, he has missed of his design in the Dedication, though he had prepared the book for it; for, in every figure of Eneas he has caused him to be drawn like King William, with a hooked nose. After my return to town, I intend to alter a play of Sir Robert Howard's, written long since, and lately put by him into my hands; 'tis called The Conquest of China by the Tartars. It will cost me six weeks study, with the 20 profitable benefit of an hundred pounds. In the meantime I am writing a song for St. Cecilia's Feast, who, you know, is the patroness of music. This is troublesome, and no way beneficial; but I could not deny the Stewards of the Feast, who came in a body to me to desire that kindness, one of them being Mr. Bridgman, whose parents are your mother's friends. I hope to send you thirty guineas between Michaelmas and Christmas, of which I will give you an account when I come to town. I remember the counsel you give me in your letter; but dissembling, though lawful in 30 some cases, is not my talent; yet, for your sake, I will struggle with the plain openness of my nature, and keep in my just resentments against that degenerate order. In the meantime, I flatter not myself with any manner of hopes, but do my duty, and suffer for God's sake; being assured, beforehand, never to be rewarded, though the times should

alter. Towards the latter end of this month, September,
Charles will begin to recover his perfect health, according to
his nativity, which, casting it myself, I am sure is true, and
all things hitherto have happened accordingly to the very
time that I predicted them : I hope at the same time to
recover more health, according to my age. Remember me to
poor Harry, whose prayers I earnestly desire. My Virgil
succeeds in the world beyond its desert or my expectation.
You know the profits might have been more ; but neither
10 my conscience nor my honour would suffer me to take them :
but I never can repent of my constancy, since I am
thoroughly persuaded of the justice of the cause for which I
suffer. It has pleased God to raise up many friends to me
amongst my enemies, though they who ought to have been my
friends are negligent of me. I am called to dinner, and cannot go on with this letter, which I desire you to excuse ;
and am

"Your most affectionate father,

"JOHN DRYDEN."

NOTES.

Page 1, l. 1. **Of the great poet,** etc. This clause is dependent on the word "display" below. Johnson is fond of this inverted opening, as we may call it. Compare "Of the stage, when he had once invaded it, he kept possession for many years," p. 4, l. 3 ; "for of labour, notwithstanding the multiplicity of his productions, there is sufficient reason to suspect that he was not a lover," p. 58, l. 15 ; and " Of Triplets and Alexandrines, though he did not introduce the use, he established it," p. 97, l. 14. It is a mistake to supply, as Ryland does, "of facts" after "display." The phrase, " display of himself," occurs below at p. 61, l. 10.

l. 12. **his last biographer, Derrick.** Derrick's *Life of Dryden* was prefaced to an edition of Dryden's *Miscellaneous Poems*, which appeared in 1760. He consulted Johnson in the undertaking. "I sent Derrick," says Johnson, "to Dryden's relations to gather materials for his life ; and I believe that he got all that I myself should have got " (Boswell's *Life of Johnson*, Globe Edition, p. 156). Derrick is best known now as the hero of one of Johnson's good sayings. "Johnson, for sport perhaps, or from the spirit of contradiction, eagerly maintained that Derrick had merit as a writer. Mr. Morgan argued with him directly in vain. At length he had recourse to this device. ' Pray, sir,' said he, ' whether do you reckon Derrick or Smart the best poet ? ' Johnson at once felt himself roused ; and answered, ' Sir, there is no settling the point of precedency between a louse and a flea ' " (Boswell, p. 599). "Samuel Derrick, an Irishman (1724-1769), was apprenticed to a linen-draper, which useful business he abandoned for the stage, and the stage very soon for literature. He succeeded Beau Nash, as Master of the Ceremonies at Bath, where he was more in his element, but his loose and extravagant life kept him always in want " (Mr. Mowbray Morris' note at Boswell, p. 38).

l. 14. **an anabaptist.** The Anabaptists were a religious sect of the time, who were so called because, believing as they did that the baptism of children was of no efficacy, they insisted on adults who desired to join their communion being baptized again. The

111

modern Baptists are their representatives in English religious
life to-day. The English Anabaptists of Dryden's time are not
to be confounded with the fanatical sect in Germany to whom
the name was first applied. The English Anabaptists were,
Bishop Butler tells us, "generally men of virtue, and of a
universal charity."

Page 2, l. 2. one of the King's scholars. One of those the
cost of whose education was defrayed out of the revenues of the
school. The Westminster scholarships at Cambridge, to one of
which Dryden succeeded, were scholarships endowed in the same
way out of the revenues of Trinity College, Cambridge, to which
only Westminster boys could be appointed. Dr. Richard Busby
(1606-1695), Headmaster of Westminster School, is one of the
most famous of English schoolmasters. Dryden sent his two
sons to be educated by him, and dedicated to him, late in life,
his translation of the *Fifth Satire of Persius.* "There are extant
two letters of Dryden to Busby about his sons when they were
at Westminster, written in 1682, very graceful in their language
of gratitude and deference to his old master" (Christie's Memoir,
prefaced to the Globe Edition of *Dryden's Poetical Works,*
p. xviii).

l. 6. **Lord Hastings.** Son of the Earl of Huntingdon, and a
schoolfellow of Dryden's. He died of small-pox in 1649 at the
age of nineteen. "Ambition" in this sentence is used almost in its
etymological sense of "going about in search of." The phrase
recurs at p. 67, l. 21. For what Johnson means by "conceits"
in it compare his remarks on Cowley and the "Metaphysical
Poets," as he proposed to call them. "They endeavoured to be
singular in their thoughts. ... Their thoughts are often new, but
seldom natural ; they are not obvious, but neither are they just ;
and the reader, far from wondering that he missed them, wonders more frequently by what perseverance of industry they were
ever found. ... The most heterogeneous ideas are yoked by violence
together ; nature and art are ransacked for illustrations, comparisons, and allusions ; their learning instructs, and their
subtilty surprises ; but the reader commonly thinks his improvement dearly bought, and, though he sometimes admires, is
seldom pleased." Dryden's treatment in this poem of the disease
which had carried off his young friend is a good example of the
vicious style referred to. The loathsome pustules of the small-
pox are compared first to rose-buds :

"Blisters with pride swelled, which through his flesh did sprout
    Like rose-buds, stuck in the lily skin about,"

then to gems—

        "Or were these gems sent to adorn his skin,
            The cabinet of a richer soul within ? "

then, in the lines which Johnson quotes, to stars.

l. 7. [**Waller** (1605-1687), **Denham** (1615-1668). The former introduced rhyme into tragedies. He was copied by Dryden, who said "the excellence and dignity of rhyme were never fully known till Mr. Waller taught it; he first made writing easily an art." Dryden said that Denham's *Cooper's Hill* was a poem which for majesty of style is, and ever will be, the exact standard of good writing. C. D. P.]

l. 16. [**public occasions,** important public events. C. D. P.]

l. 21. **he knew how to complain.** A reference to his powers of satire.

In the life of Plutarch, etc. Dryden's *Life of Plutarch* was prefaced to a translation of that Greek author by various hands. In the Preface Dryden says, "I read *Plutarch* in the library of Trinity College in Cambridge, to which foundation I gratefully acknowledge a great part of my education." The prologue at Oxford, from which Johnson goes on to quote, was one of several productions of the kind which Dryden wrote for plays, whether his own or those of other writers, about to be acted before the University.

l. 27. **Thebes,** etc. The rivalry between the two great English Universities is compared to the rivalry between the Greek cities of Athens and Thebes. The lines are not to be taken too seriously. "It was characteristic of Dryden to flatter when he desired to please, and run riot in praise if it suited his purpose of the moment; and a letter of his to John Wilmot, Earl of Rochester, is preserved, in which he avows the insincerity of other similar flattering addresses to an Oxford audience. Sending Rochester copies of a Prologue and Epilogue, written for Oxford in 1673, he says: "I hear they have succeeded, and by the event your lordship will judge how easy 'tis to pass anything upon an University, and what gross flattery the learned will endure" (Christie, p. xxi). "Rude" here is a mistake of Johnson's for "green." Compare the note on p. 99, l. 15.

l. 30. **Heroic Stanzas,** etc. "Heroic" refers to the metre of the poem, a stanza of four decasyllabic iambic lines alternately rhymed. For a criticism of the poem, see below, p. 67. The three poems by Dryden, Sprat, and Waller, on the death of Oliver Cromwell, were published in one volume. "Dryden's poem in praise of Cromwell was published in conjunction with two other poetical eulogies by Waller, an elder poet of established fame, and by 'Mr. Sprat of Oxford,' who was his junior, and who came to be Dean of Westminster and Bishop of Rochester" (Christie, p. xxi).

l. 34. **the other panegyrists of usurpation.** The other writers who had sung Cromwell's praises.

l. 35. **changed his opinion, or his profession.** The words are

H

intended to leave it undecided whether the professed change of opinion was real or not. With the apology which follows compare what Johnson says of the similar case of Waller, where he is much more outspoken. "The poem on the death of the Protector seems to have been dictated by real veneration for his memory. Dryden and Sprat wrote on the same occasion; but they were young men, struggling into notice, and hoping for some favour from the ruling party. Waller had little to expect : he had received nothing but his pardon from Cromwell, and was not likely to ask anything from those who should succeed him. Soon afterwards the Restoration supplied him with another subject ; and he exerted his imagination, his elegance, and his melody, with equal alacrity, for Charles the Second. It is not possible to read without some contempt and indignation poems of the same author ascribing the highest degree of power and piety to Charles the First, then transferring the same power and piety to Oliver Cromwell, now inviting Oliver to take the crown, and then congratulating Charles the Second on his recovered right. Neither Cromwell nor Charles could value his testimony as the effect of conviction, or receive his praises as effusions of reverence; they could consider them but as the labour of invention, the tribute of dependence. Poets, indeed, profess fiction ; but the legitimate end of fiction is the conveyance of truth ; and he that has flattery ready for all whom the vicissitudes of the world happen to exalt, must be scorned as a prostituted mind, that may retain the glitter of wit, but has lost the dignity of virtue." Johnson goes on to tell the story of how Charles the Second twitted Waller with the inferiority of the verses written in his own praise as compared with those the poet had previously written in honour of Cromwell, to which Waller is said to have made the rejoinder that poets succeed better with fiction than with truth.

Sir Walter Scott's remarks on this subject are conspicuously fair to Dryden: "The *Elegy on Cromwell*, although doubtless sufficiently faulty, contained symptoms of a regenerating taste; and, politically considered, although a panegyric on an usurper, the topics of praise are selected with attention to truth, and are, generally speaking, such as Cromwell's worst enemies could not have denied to him. Neither had Dryden made the errors or misfortunes of the royal family and their followers the subject of censure or of contrast. With respect to them, it was hardly possible that a eulogy on such a theme could have less offence in it. This was perhaps a fortunate circumstance for Dryden at the Restoration ; and it must be noticed to his honour, that as he spared the exiled monarch in his panegyric on the usurper, so, after the Restoration, in his numerous writings on the side of royalty, there is no instance of his recalling his former praise of Cromwell."

Page 3, l. 5. It was, however, not totally forgotten, etc. One of the victims of Dryden's satire hit upon the odd piece of vengeance, as Scott calls it, of reprinting the poem with the inscription, "An Elegy on the Usurper, by the author of Absalom and Achitophel, published to show the loyalty and integrity of the poet."

l. 8. The same year. A mistake. *Astræa Redux* was published in 1660, the year of the Restoration, and the poem on the coronation, which is here referred to, in the following year.

l. 12. perhaps with more than was deserved. Critics are not yet at one over this line. The present editor thinks the objection taken to it pure pedantry. No one quarrels with the biblical "darkness that might be felt," or with Milton's "darkness visible." Is it any bolder to speak of the silence that can be "heard" before the burst of the thunder-storm? The stillness takes possession of the ear, and the mind takes the alarm. But Christie, for example, holds that it is not easy to justify the line. Johnson's instances, he says, are not in point. "Death is personified. Stillness may help study or benefit an invalid, as darkness may prevent work, or cold injure plants, but there is decided incongruity in stillness or the absence of all sound *invading* or entering the ear."

l. 14. privation likewise certainly is darkness. Another case of inverted arrangement. Compare the note on p. 11, l. 11.

l. 23. important enough to be formally offered to a patron. In Dryden's time it was still customary for authors to endeavour to ensure a favourable reception for their writings at the hands of the public by choosing a patron, to whom each work was dedicated. The patron enjoyed the distinction of having been singled out for a compliment the worth of which depended on the merits or fame of the author ; and the author in return got, sometimes a money present, but, at all events, such passport to a public hearing as the name of the patron could supply. The custom has long since died out, Dr. Johnson himself having been one of the earliest to repudiate it. He refused to dedicate his *Dictionary* to any one under the following circumstances. When he took the work in hand he put out a plan or prospectus of the undertaking in a letter which he addressed to Lord Chesterfield. In the ordinary course of things the *Dictionary* on its completion would have been dedicated to Lord Chesterfield, and that nobleman fully expected that it would be so dedicated. He was conscious, however, of having in the interval neglected Johnson, if indeed he had not on one occasion treated him with great rudeness. By way of conciliating the author of a work which he saw was likely to prove a great success, Lord Chesterfield wrote a commendatory notice of the *Dictionary* in one of the current journals, and caused it to be intimated to Dr. Johnson

who the writer was.   Upon which Dr. Johnson addressed a
letter to Lord Chesterfield, which was given to the world for the
first time in Boswell's *Life of Johnson*.   In it he spoke of the
neglect with which Lord Chesterfield had treated him after one
interview that would appear to have been of a somewhat cordial
nature.   He went on : "Seven years, my Lord, have passed
since I waited in your outward rooms, or was repulsed from your
door ; during which time I have been pushing on my work
through difficulties, of which it is useless to complàin, and have
brought it at last to the verge of publication, without one act of
assistance, one word of encouragement, or one smile of favour. ...
Such treatment I did not expect, for I never had a patron before.
Is not a patron, my Lord, one who looks with unconcern on a
man struggling for life in the water, and, when he has reached
ground, encumbers him with help?   The notice which you have
been pleased to take of my labours, had it been early, had been
kind ; but it has been delayed till I am indifferent, and cannot
enjoy it ; till I am solitary, and cannot impart it ; till I am
known, and do not want it."

As an illustration of the money relations which often subsisted
between author and patron, with no thought of discredit to either
party, it may be worth adding that Johnson, in taking steps to
secure the ultimate publication of this letter, asked that it might
be noted, with reference to the phrase "without one act of assistance," that he had at one time received from Lord Chesterfield
the sum of £10, "but as that was so inconsiderable a sum, he
thought the mention of it could not properly find a place in a
letter of the kind that this was."

l. 28. **is not certainly known.**   It has been ascertained since
Johnson wrote.   His conjecture that the year was 1663 was
right ; and the play itself contains, in the prologue, an intima-
tion of the day and the hour of its first performance.   "*First
Astrologer reads.* A figure of the heavenly bodies in their
several apartments, Feb. 5th, half an hour after three afternoon,
from which you are to judge the success of a new play, called
The Wild Gallant."   Samuel Pepys, whose famous *Diary* contains many references to Dryden, saw the play acted on the 23rd
February, and has the following note about it : "The play so
poor a thing as I never saw in my life almost, and so little
answering the name that, from the beginning to the end, I could
not, nor can at this time, tell certainly which was the Wild
Gallant.   The King did not seem pleased at all, all the whole
play, nor anybody else."   The play with alterations was reproduced in 1667, and published for the first time in 1669.

l. 33. **collected,** inferred, a meaning which the word has now
almost lost, though the Anglo-Saxon equivalent, 'gathered,' is
still used in that metaphorical sense.

l. 34. **commenced a writer for the stage,** commenced to write plays. This use of the word 'commence' is obsolete. It was a University phrase. The student who took his degree was said to commence a Master of Arts. Compare the word 'commencement' as used at Cambridge for the day on which degrees are conferred.

Page 4, l. 3. **he kept possession for many years.** To keep possession of the stage is to have such a reputation as a playwright that managers will gladly accept your plays, while the public may be counted on as eager to come and give them a trial. He who has possession of the stage is, as Johnson puts it below, at least "secure of a hearing."

l. 20. [**intrinsic,** belonging to the nature of the drama itself. C. D. P.]

[**concomitant,** an external circumstance in some way connected with its publication or performance. C. D. P.]

l. 24. [**Earl of Orrery** had considerable influence. He had worked for the Restoration of Charles II., who made him Lord-Justice of Ireland. C. D. P.]

l. 25. **he made his essay of dramatic rhyme,** used for the first time rhyme in a play.

l. 36. **in the Rehearsal.** See below, p. 27. In the passage referred to, Bayes, who represents Dryden in that burlesque, says, "I'm sure the design's good ; that cannot be denied. And then, for language, egad, I defy 'em all, in nature, to mend it. Besides, sir, I have printed above a hundred sheets of paper to insinuate the plot into the boxes."

Page 5, l. 3. **the description of Night.**

"All things are hushed, as nature's self lay dead ;
The mountains seem to nod their drowsy head ;
The little birds in dreams their songs repeat,
And sleeping flowers beneath the night-dew sweat,
Even lust and envy sleep ; yet love denies
Rest to my soul, and slumber to my eyes."

Wordsworth thought these lines "vague, bombastic, and senseless." But Wordsworth's judgment, whether of his own poems or of those of others, was not always to be depended on. The last couplet here has certainly all the strength and swing of Dryden's manner. Thomas Rymer (1639-1713) was a critic of some note in his day.

l. 10. **who perhaps knew that by his dexterity of versification,** etc. Compare what Dryden himself says about Milton's reason for writing in blank verse. "Neither will I justify Milton for his blank verse, though I may excuse him, by the example of Hanibal Caro, and other Italians, who have used it. For what-

ever causes he alleges for the abolishing of rhyme (which I
have not now the leisure to examine), his own particular reason
is plainly this, that rhyme was not his talent; he had neither
the ease of doing it, nor the graces of it; which is manifest in his
Juvenilia, or verses written in his youth; where his rhyme is
always constrained and forced, and comes hardly from him at an
age when the soul is most pliant ; and the passion of love makes
almost every man a rhymer, though not a poet" (Dedication to
the Translation of Juvenal).

1. 19. The **Annus Mirabilis** was formally dedicated to "the
Metropolis of Great Britain, the most renowned and late flourish-
ing City of London, in its representatives the Lord Mayor and
Court of Aldermen, the Sheriffs and Common Council of it."

1. 25. [**common**, commonplace, and of little value.   c. d. p.]

1. 35. **the Gondibert of Davenant.**   Sir William Davenant was
Ben Jonson's successor and Dryden's predecessor in the poet-
laureateship.   His *Gondibert* was published in 1651.

Page 6, 1. 1. **Of this stanza he mentions the encumbrances.**
"I have chosen to write my poem in quatrains or stanzas of four
in alternate rhyme, because I have ever judged them more noble
and of greater dignity both for the sound and number than any
other verse in use amongst us ; in which I am sure I have your
approbation.... In the necessity of our rhymes I have always
found the couplet verse most easy (though not so proper for this
occasion), for there the work is sooner at an end, every two lines
concluding the labour of the poet; but in quatrains he is to carry
it farther on, and not only so, but to bear along in his head the
troublesome sense of four lines together.   For those who write
correctly in this kind must acknowledge that the last line of the
stanza is to be considered in the composition of the first.
Neither can we give ourselves the liberty of making any part of
a verse for the sake of rhyme, or concluding with a word which
is not current English, or using the variety of female rhymes ;
all which our fathers practised."   Compare the quotation from
Scott given in the note on p. 72, 1. 14.

1. 19. **Here appears a great inconsistency.**   Johnson has forgotten that in the first paragraph of the *Defence of an Essay of
Dramatic Poesy* it is distinctly intimated by Dryden himself that
the *Defence* was written to be prefaced to a second edition of the
Indian Emperor.   There is thus no inconsistency at all; and
Langbaine's statement, to which Johnson refers as helping to
clear the matter up, is taken from the *Defence* itself.

1. 28. **in 1668 he succeeded Sir William Davenant as poet-laureat.**
Davenant died in April, 1668, but Dryden was not appointed to
succeed him until August, 1670.

l. 29. **The salary of the laureat,** etc. A mark was worth 13s. 4d. sterling. A tierce is the third of a pipe of wine, hence the name. Dryden received in 1670 the two appointments of Poet-Laureat and Historiographer Royal, with a consolidated salary for the two posts of £200, and a butt of Canary once a year from the King's cellars.

l. 30. [Jonson, usually known as Ben Jonson, a writer of dramas, had received the pension here mentioned from 1634 till his death in 1637. C. D. P.]

l. 36. [Prior (1664-1721) took an active part in the politics of the reigns of William III. and Anne. C. D. P.]

Page 7, l. 3. **Secret Love, or the Maiden Queen.** This play was brought out in March, 1677, and was a great success. "Nell Gwyn, who had lately begun as an actress, enchanted the audience in the part of Florimel. Pepys went with his wife to see the play on March 2, the first day: the King and the Duke of York were present. 'The play,' says Pepys, 'was mightily commended for the regularity of it, and the strain and wit'; and of Nell Gwyn's acting he says, 'I never can hope to see the like done again by man or woman.' He records a second and a third visit to the play within the month, and each time renews in the same strain his praises both of the play and of Nell Gwyn's acting" (Christie). The student who is still a stranger to Dryden could not do better than begin with this play. It is perhaps the first of his works that does not require reverence for his genius and fame as a poet to hold the attention from beginning to end. Florimel is almost comparable to Shakespeare's Beatrice. The play, besides its merits as a play, is full of passages of great poetical beauty, of which the following is perhaps the most famous :

> "He, who with your possession once is blest,
> On easy terms will part with all the rest.
> All my ambition will in you be crowned ;
> And those white arms shall all my wishes bound.
> Our life shall be but one long nuptial day,
> And, like chafed odours, melt in sweets away ;
> Soft as the night our minutes shall be worn,
> And cheerful as the birds that wake the morn."

l. 12. **Sir Martin Marall.** This play was produced on the 15th of August, 1667. "Thence with much satisfaction, and Sir W. Pen and I to the Duke's house, where a new play. The King and Court there : the house full, and an act begun. ... Up, and at the office all the morning, and so at noon to dinner, and after dinner my wife and I to the Duke's playhouse, where we saw the new play acted yesterday, the *Feign Innocence, or Sir Martin Marr-all* ; a play made by my Lord Duke of Newcastle,

but, as everybody says, corrected by Dryden. It is the most
entire piece of mirth, a complete farce from one end to the other,
that certainly was ever writ. I never laughed so in my life. I
laughed till my head ached all the evening and night with the
laughing; and at very good wit therein, not fooling. The house
full, and in all things of mighty content to me" (Pepys, under
dates the 15th and 16th of August, 1667). "The play was called
the Duke of Newcastle's, and it was published in the following
year without author's name; but, later, Dryden announced it
without dispute as one of his own plays" (Christie). Scott's
version of the matter is that the Duke of Newcastle translated
Molière's *L'Etourdi*, and presented his translation to Dryden,
who adapted it in this play for the stage. The Voiture to whom
Langbaine traced one of the songs introduced into the play by
Dryden was a French poet of some distinction at the time.

l. 16. [**plagiarism**, unacknowledged theft of the literary work
of others. C. D. P.]

l. 19. **The Tempest.** "Up, and at the office hard all the
morning, and at noon resolved with Sir W. Pen to go see *The
Tempest*, an old play of Shakspeare's, acted, I hear, the first
day; and so my wife, and girl, and W. Hewer by themselves,
and Sir W. Pen and I afterwards by ourselves; and forced to sit
in the side balcone over against the musique-room at the Duke's
house, close by my Lady Dorset and a great many great ones.
The house mighty full; the King and Court there: and the most
innocent play that ever I saw; and a curious piece of musique in
an echo of half sentences, the echo repeating the former half,
while the man goes on to the latter; which is mighty pretty.
The play has no great wit, but yet good, above ordinary plays"
(Pepys, under date the 7th of November, 1667). Mr. Saintsbury,
Dryden's latest editor, has some doubt as to whether what Pepys
saw was the original or adapted play, but the reference to the
song shows that it was the adaptation. The song will be found
at Act III., Scene iv. There is nothing to correspond with it in
the original play. Davenant and Dryden's travesty of this great
play is most honourably remembered now on account of the magnificent tribute to Shakespeare's genius in the Prologue.

> "But Shakespeare's magic could not copied be,
>   Within that circle none durst walk but he."

"Much cannot be said for Davenant's ingenuity, in contrasting
the character of a woman, who had never seen a man, with that
of a man, who had never seen a woman, or in inventing a sister
monster for Caliban. The majestic simplicity of Shakespeare's
plan is injured by thus doubling his characters; and his wild
landscape is converted into a formal parterre, 'where each alley
has its brother.'... We are delighted with the feminine sim-

plicity of Miranda; it becomes unmanly childishness in Hippolito: and the premature coquetry of Dorinda is disgusting, when contrasted with the maidenly purity that chastens the simplicity of Shakespeare's heroine. The latter seems to display, as it were by instinct, the innate dignity of her sex; the former to show, even in solitude, the germ of those vices, by which, in a voluptuous age, the female character becomes degraded. The wild and savage character of Caliban is also sunk into low and vulgar buffoonery " (Scott). Johnson is to be taken as anticipating this judgment of Scott's. His reference to "the effect produced by the conjunction of these two powerful minds" is ironical.

l. 24. [the **Latin proverb** as usually expressed in English is "Second thoughts are best." C. D. P.]

l. 26. [**remote**, distant, implying long flights of the imagination. C. D. P.]

l. 34. **About this time**, etc. Johnson here interrupts his account of Dryden's plays, begun with some reluctance (p. 4, l. 15 fg.), to give an inordinately long account of the poet's controversy with Settle. Matthew Arnold takes the excusable liberty of omitting great part of this digression. Compare Christie's remarks. "Dryden involved himself in 1673 in a literary controversy, to an account of which Dr. Johnson has given exaggerated importance and disproportionate space, with Elkanah Settle, an inferior poet and play-writer. Settle's play, *The Emperor of Morocco*, had great success, and, patronized by the capricious Rochester, who had the ear of the King, had been often acted at Court; and Settle published this play in 1673 with many signs of inflated vanity, and with a dedication in which Dryden was disrespectfully spoken of. This led to the publication of a severe and malignant criticism, the joint work of Crowne, Shadwell, and Dryden. Crowne claims to have written three-fourths of this pamphlet, which Johnson treats as if it were almost entirely Dryden's. But Dryden had a part in it, and Settle retorted sharply on him, criticising the *Conquest of Granada*. Settle had by no means the worst of it in the pamphleteering fray, and Dryden gained no increase of reputation by his part in this controversy. Time has decisively settled the question of the relative merits of Dryden and Settle; but the author of *The Emperor of Morocco* then divided not unequally public favour and sympathy with the Laureate. Dennis, who was sixteen years old in 1673, and went up to Cambridge as a freshman in 1676, wrote in 1717 that he remembered Settle at the time of this controversy as a formidable rival to Dryden, and that not only London, but also the University of Cambridge, was much divided in opinion as to which was the superior, and that in both places Settle was the favourite among the younger men."

Page 8, l. 4. sculptures, what we now call engravings. Dryden's *Translation of Juvenal* (1697) is, in the words of the title page, "adorned with sculptures."

l. 6. **[the last blast of inflammation,** the last circumstance which inflamed Dryden's anger. C. D. P.]

l. 13. **deplored,** deplorable.

conversation, knowledge of how to behave himself. "Conversation," in the sense of behaviour, is familiar now chiefly in Biblical language. "Dearly beloved, I beseech you as strangers and pilgrims, abstain from fleshly lusts, which war against the soul, having your conversation honest among the Gentiles" (1 Peter ii. 11). But compare also the form used in admitting candidates to degrees: "By the authority given me as Chancellor of this University I admit you to the degree of Master of Arts; and I charge you that ever in your life and conversation you show yourself worthy of the same."

l. 17. **lewd,** licentious, irregular, not conforming to the rules of poetry. The word is now generally confined to moral lewdness. [The original meaning was "ignorant," and the term was applied to the laity as distinguished from the clergy, who were the only educated classes. C. D. P.]

l. 19. **pudder,** an older form of pother.

l. 28. **have all a certain natural cast of the father,** are all a little like Settle himself.

Page 10, l. 2. Dutch grout, what in Scotland is called porridge.

l. 3. **[to stay,** to satisfy for the moment; literally, to support the stomach while waiting for other food. C. D. P.]

l. 5. **To dish up the poet's broth,** to serve up to the reader the more plentiful mess promised in the last sentence.

l. 31. **[physical,** medicinal. C. D. P.]

l. 33. **[choleric humours.** Choler was one of the four humours (fluids) supposed to exist in the body. The preponderance of choler, or choleric humour, made a man hot-tempered (Lat. *cholera*, bile). C. D. P.]

were it written in characters, etc. A doctor's bill is what we now call a prescription. The quantities of the drugs prescribed and the like were, as they still are, written in characters which are otherwise almost entirely obsolete.

Page 11, l. 14. [Jacks with lanthorns, Jack-o'-lantern, the *ignis fatuus* or false fire sometimes seen over marshy ground, also called will-o'-the-wisp. C. D. P.]

l. 28. **Never was place so full of game,** etc. The three verbs in the next sentence are all taken from the hunter's

art.   To flush a covey of birds is to make them start up in flight;
to start a hare is to make it leave its hiding-place and run off.
For 'unkennel' compare *Merry Wives of Windsor*, III. iii. :

>   "I'll warrant we'll unkennel the fox."

This is the only sentence in the whole of this tedious passage
that looks in the least as if Dryden could have written it.

Page 12, l. 1.   **so imprudent to expose.**   We must now say "so
imprudent as to expose."   'Expose' means 'set out for sale.'
Matthew Arnold prints 'impudent' for 'imprudent,' and Ryland
and Sharp follow this.   It is a misprint in the edition of 1781.
Impudence and arrogance are not easily distinguished.   Settle
was very unwise ("imprudent") to attempt to sell such stuff,
and very impudent ("arrogant") in attempting to defend it
when its worthlessness was pointed out.

l. 5. [**to discover it**, to point it out to others. c. d. p.]

l. 7. **I will not transpose his verse, but by the help of his own
words transnonsense sense.** That is to say, "I will not any
longer turn his verse into prose as I have been doing, but will
now turn sense, by which I mean an emphatic condemnation of
Settle, into nonsense of the kind he writes.   And I will do this by
the help of his own words."   The passage that follows is a close
parody of a passage in *The Empress of Morocco*.   All the editions
of the *Life* seem to read ' transpose' here, and the mistake may
have been Johnson's own.   Dryden wrote 'transprose,' in contemptuous imitation of Settle himself.   Compare, in the Second
Part of *Absalom and Achitophel*, i. 444 :

>   " Instinct he follows and no further knows,
>   For to write verse, with him is to *transprose*."

This refers to a poem of Settle's called *Achitophel Transprosed*.
Compare Sharp's note on this passage.   He quotes the line from
Absalom and Achitophel, and adds : "The terms *transprose* and
transverse occur not unfrequently in the literature of the time,
and are ridiculed in the *Rehearsal*."

l. 17. [**fustian**, boastful words. c. d. p.]

l. 25. [**huffing**.   See note on p. 15, l. 31. c. d. p.]

l. 33. [**cits**, short for *citizens*. c. d. p.]

l. 38. **Gotham**, a village in Northamptonshire which bore a bad
reputation as being inhabited entirely by fools, the so-called
"wise men of Gotham."   "Where the inhabitants in King John's
time made a pretence of being fools to avoid fine and punishment. ..." (Waugh's note).

Page 13, l. 9. [**placed ... claps**, allowed their happiness to
depend upon applause. c. d. p.]

l. 10. **the Mock Astrologer.** This play was produced on the 12th of June, 1668. "It was not very successful. Pepys did not like it, nor did his wife: the Secretary to the Admiralty [Pepys] thought it 'very smutty, and nothing so good as *The Maiden Queen* or *The Indian Emperor* of Dryden's making.' Heringman the publisher told Pepys that Dryden himself called it 'but a fifth-rate play.' The play was dedicated in the usual strain of adulation to the Duke of Newcastle. On the 19th of June, 1668, the same day on which Pepys mentions that his wife went to the theatre and 'saw the new play, *Evening Love*, of Dryden's, which, though the world commends, she likes not,' Evelyn enters the following in his Diary: 'To a new play with several of my relatives, *The Evening Love*, a foolish plot and very profane; it afflicted me to see how the stage was degenerated and polluted by the licentious times.'"

l. 19. **Shakspeare's plots,** etc. "Most of Shakspeare's plays, I mean the stories of them, are to be found in the *Hecatommithi* or *Hundred Novels* of Cinthio. I have myself read in his Italian, that of *Romeo and Juliet*, the *Moor of Venice*, and many others of them" (Preface to the *Mock Astrologer*). Cinthio's book was published in 1565. "Shakespeare seems to have been indebted to Cinthio for hints only in the case of *Othello*, and perhaps *Measure for Measure*" (Ryland).

l. 24. **which is only to say,** etc. Dryden has answered this objection by anticipation. "But now it will be objected, that I patronise vice by the authority of former poets, and extenuate my own faults by recrimination. I answer, that as I defend myself by their example, so that example I defend by reason, and by the end of all dramatic poesy." Dryden is not defending himself against a charge of immoral writing in general, but against the specific objection that in his comedies the wicked go unpunished, or are even rewarded.

l. 26. **Against those that accused him of plagiarism,** etc. "I am taxed with stealing all my plays, and that by some who should be the last men from whom I would steal any part of them. There is one answer which I will not make; but it has been made for me, by him to whose grace and patronage I owe all things,

'Et spes et ratio studiorum in Caesare tantum'—

and without whose command they should no longer be troubled with anything of mine; that he only desired that they, who accused me of theft, would always steal him plays like mine."

l. 31. **Tyrannic Love,** etc. This play was produced in 1669. Johnson does not give the title correctly, one of several proofs that he was not fond of getting up from his desk to check his memory. The right title is *Tyrannic Love, or the Royal Martyr.*

l. 32. **conspicuous for many passages of strength and elegance.**
Scott, who points out that much of the ranting in this play
"conveys at first a dark impression of grandeur and sublimity,
which only vanishes on a critical examination," justly selects the
following passage as one of many instances in which "the impression of sublimity becomes more deep, in proportion to the
attention we bestow upon them :

> "Could we live always, life were worth our cost ;
> But now we keep with care what must be lost.
> Here we stand shivering on the bank, and cry,
> When we should plunge into eternity.
> One moment ends our pain ;
> And yet the shock of death we dare not stand,
> By thought scarce measured, and too swift for sand :
> 'Tis but because the living death ne'er knew,
> They fear to prove it, as a thing that's new.
> Let me the experiment before you try,
> I'll show you first how easy 'tis to die."

For Johnson's opinion of the last four lines of this passage, see
below, p. 93.

l. 33. **many of empty noise and ridiculous turbulence.**   Scott
instances two.   In the first, he says, "our poet appears shorn of
his locks."

> "Look to it, Gods ; for you the aggressors are :
> Keep you your rain and sunshine in your skies,
> And I'll keep back my flame and sacrifice ;
> Your trade of heaven will soon be at a stand,
> And all your goods lie dead upon your hand."

The idea here is more familiar to the Eastern than to the Western
mind.   It is curious to notice that the other passage, which
Scott quotes as one of those which have a fascination for the
reader that blinds him to "the extravagant and bombast" in it,
is the original of two well-known lines in Marmion.   Maximin is
represented as, like Capaneus, deifying Jove :

> "With his broad sword the boldest beating down,
> While fate grew pale, lest he should win the town,
> And turned the iron leaves of its dark book,
> To make new dooms, or mend what it mistook."

Compare :

> "From fate's dark book a leaf been torn,
> And Flodden had been Bannockburn."

l. 35. **if his own confession may be trusted.**   "I remember
some verses of my own Maximin and Almanzor, which cry vengeance upon me for their extravagance. ... All I can say for those

passages, which are, I hope, not many, is that I knew they were
bad enough to please, even when I writ them ; but I repent of
them amongst my sins ; and, if any of their fellows intrude by
chance into my present writings, I draw a stroke over all those
Delilahs of the theatre ; and am resolved I will settle myself no
reputation by the applause of fools " (Dedication to the *Spanish
Friar*).

Page 14, l. 2. **Want of time,** etc.   Dryden has anticipated this
reflection of Johnson's, though not, of course, with the particular
reference.   He says in the preface to his *Fables*: "I will not
trouble my reader with the shortness of time in which I writ it,
or the several intervals of sickness ; they who think too well of
their own performances are apt to boast in their prefaces how
little time their works have cost them, and what other business
of more importance interfered ; but the reader will be as apt to
ask the question, why they allowed not a longer time to make
their works more perfect, and why they had so despicable an
opinion of their judges as to thrust their indigested stuff upon
them, as if they deserved no better."

l. 14. **his malice to the parsons.**   Compare at p. 51, l. 11.
"Dryden indeed discovered, in many of his writings, and
affected an absurd malignity to priests and priesthood."

l. 16. **the Conquest of Granada.**   *Almanzor and Almahide,
or the Conquest of Granada by the Spaniards*, a tragedy in two
parts, was produced in 1670, and published in 1672.

l. 32. [**epilogue**, a speech in verse uttered by one of the principal actors at the end of the performance of a drama.   Similarly,
a **prologue** preceded the performance.   These speeches were
usually in the form of direct addresses by the writer of the play
to his patrons in the theatre.   C. D. P.]

l. 33. **discrediting his predecessors.**   The theme of the epilogue
is that the poet, to be successful, must conform to the age, and
that the comparative success of the poets of Dryden's day, as
compared with older poets, was only the reflex of the improvement on the times.

"They, who have best succeeded on the stage,
Have still conformed their genius to the age.
Thus Jonson did mechanic humour show,
When men were dull, and conversation low ...
Think it not envy that these truths are told ;
Our poet's not malicious though he's bold.
'Tis not to brand them, that their faults are shown,
But, by their errors, to excuse his own.
If love and honour now are higher raised,
'Tis not the poet, but the age is praised."

In the *Defence of the Epilogue*, Dryden, to his lasting discredit as a critic, singled out the *Winter's Tale, Love's Labour Lost,* and *Measure for Measure* as plays of which it could justly be said that they were "either grounded on impossibilities, or at least so meanly written, that the comedy neither caused you mirth, nor the serious part your concernment." Scott charitably supposes that Dryden had not read with any care the plays so summarily condemned by him.

Page 15, l. 13. **But let honest credulity,** etc. Clifford was pleased, and felt himself secure of fame, when Sprat spoke so highly of him. But a following generation forgot both Clifford and Sprat.

l. 16. **were at last obtained.** Dr. Johnson means that he had great difficulty in obtaining sight of a copy. The reader will be apt to wish that Dr. Percy had not lent him one. Dr. Percy, Dean of Carlisle and Bishop of Dromore, is best known as the editor of *Reliques of Ancient Literary Poetry* (1765). He was a great friend of Dr. Johnson's.

l. 21. **a Jack-of-all-trades' shop,** a shop where wares of all sorts are to be had.

l. 26. **that Almanzor is not more copied,** etc. That is to say, that he is no true hero like Achilles, but a swaggering bully like the Pistol whom Shakespeare portrays.

l. 31. **Huffcap,** a braggart. For 'huff,' in the sense of an idle boast, compare p. 19, l. 4.

Page 17, l. 9. **I'll venture to start,** etc. The metaphor is again from the art of hunting. Settle means 'start and run down.' Compare the note on p. 11, l. 28.

l. 13. **The Phoenix-daughter of the vanquisht old.** "The old ship the 'London,' one of the navy of the Commonwealth, had perished by fire, and the city of London now presented the King with a new ship, called the 'Loyal London'" (Christie's note on the passage). The legend about the phoenix bird was that, when its time to die was come, it lay down on a funeral pyre which was lit by itself, and that from its ashes the next phoenix arose.

l. 17. [**sanguine,** scarlet, blood-coloured (Lat. *sanguis,* blood). C. D. P.]

l. 29. **was not in his altitudes, to compare ships to floating palaces,** could not reach the heights of fancy he rose to afterwards, when he compared ships not to wasps but to floating palaces. The passage referred to is that in which the wondering Mexicans, who had never seen a ship before, reported the arrival on the coast of the Spanish ships to their sovereign. The expression 'floating palace,' for a magnificent ship, has almost passed into common speech.

"*Montezuma.* What forms did these new wonders represent?
"*Guyomar.*   More strange than what your wonder can invent.
The object, I could first distinctly view,
Was tall straight trees, which on the waters flew;
Wings on their sides, instead of leaves did grow,
Which gathered all the breath the winds could blow;
And at their roots grew floating palaces,
Whose outblowed bellies cut the yielding seas."

Page 18, l. 4. **if he had designed,** etc., if his object really was to belittle my play, thought by him to be senseless, he should have tried to find instances of pedantry like those three found by me in his own.

l. 13. [**fustian.**   See p. 12, l. 17.   C. D. P.]

[**canting,** hypocritical.   *Cant* was at first mock humility. Here the words are described as fustian or bombastic because they include ideas taken from logic, and yet hypocritical because of an apparent pretence of ignorance and humility.   C. D. P.]

l. 24. **Poor Robin,** the name assumed by the author of *Poor Robin's Almanack,* an annual which was published first about 1661.   "On the title-page we read, 'Written by Poor Robin, Knight of the Burnt Island, a well-wisher to Mathematicks'" (Ryland).   This explains the following 'Philomathematics' (well-wishers to mathematics).

Page 19, l. 4. [**huff,** mere bluster and empty boasting.   C. D. P.]

l. 25. [**foreright,** in a direct line.   The prefix *fore* (for) is intensive.   We now sometimes use "right" in a similar way. C. D. P.]

l. 28. [**lights of,** alights on; if he finds in another writer's works any idea like the one in his mind, he is almost certain to borrow the words which express the idea.   C. D. P.]

l. 32. [**the fate of Simoeis,** to be dried up by fire.   The line is taken from the verses describing the great fire of 1666.   Homer describes the Scamander, into which the Simoeis flowed, as being burnt up by Vulcan during the siege of Troy.   C. D. P.]

Page 20, l. 21. **Enough of Settle.**   "More than enough of Settle," the reader will be apt to rejoin.   The passage is difficult to print correctly on account of the way in which Johnson mixes up Dryden, Settle, and himself in it.   For example, on page 16, lines 16 to 20 are from Settle's pamphlet, the extract beginning with a quotation made by Settle from Dryden.   The seven lines which follow are Johnson's own, and include two quotations, one from Settle and one from Dryden on Settle. Then follows (l. 27) the second extract from Settle's pamphlet, "So sphere must not be sense," etc. Matthew Arnold, Ryland, and Sharp all print the intermediary paragraph as if it were itself an extract. Cunningham has it right. Cunningham, indeed, prints the whole passage with a care and exactitude, both in the matter of indicating where the extracts from Settle begin and finish, and in that of keeping the quotations from Dryden distinct from one another, which render Ryland's remarks about the remissness in both respects of all editors previous to himself singularly unfair as far as Cunningham is concerned.

l. 22. [Marriage Alamode (or Marriage à-la-mode). c. d. p.] This and the following play were both produced in 1672.

l. 25. The Earl of Rochester, etc. "The patron, whom Dryden here addresses, was the famous John Wilmot, Earl of Rochester, the wittiest, perhaps, and most dissolute, among the witty and dissolute courtiers of Charles II. It is somewhat remarkable, and may be considered as a just judgment upon the poet, that he was, a few years afterwards, waylaid and severely beaten by bravoes, whom Lord Rochester employed to revenge the share which Dryden is supposed to have had in the *Essay on Satire*. ... Perhaps, joined to a certain envy of Dryden's talents, the poet's intimacy with Sheffield, Earl of Mulgrave, gave offence to Rochester. It is certain they were never afterwards reconciled; and even after Rochester's death, Dryden only mentions his once valued patron as ' a man of quality whose ashes he will not disturb'" (Scott). The quotation is from the preface to Dryden's *Juvenal*.

l. 30. against the opinion, etc. "It succeeded ill in the representation, against the opinion of many of the best judges of our age, to whom you know I read it, ere it was presented publicly. Whether the fault was in the play itself, or in the lameness of the action, or in the number of its enemies, who came resolved to damn it for the title, I will not now dispute. That would be too like the little satisfaction which an unlucky gamester finds in the relation of every cast by which he came to lose his money. I have had formerly so much success, that the miscarriage of this play was only my giving Fortune her revenge; I owed it her, and she was indulgent that she exacted not the payment long before" (From Dryden's Dedication to Sedley). Sir Charles Sedley was another of the "mob of gentlemen" writing "with ease" who gave Charles' Court all the lustre that has survived.

Page 21, l. 2. though the author thought not fit, etc. Compare the passage at p. 14, l. 2 fg., and the note there.

l. 4. It was a temporary performance, it was a work written

I

to suit a purpose of the time. Dryden wanted to make the Dutch War, on which Charles the Second was entering, somewhat less unpopular than it was, and, with that intention, tried to inflame popular hate against the Dutch by a dramatic representation of a massacre which had taken place in the East fifty years before. Scott calls *Amboyna* the worst production Dryden ever wrote. It was produced in 1673.

l. 7. **as he declares in his epilogue.**

> " A poet once the Spartans led to fight,
> And made them conquer in the muse's right ;
> So would our poet lead you on this day,
> Showing your tortured fathers in this play."

" The style and tone of the Prologue and Epilogue are execrable. It is not to be forgotten that the now fierce abettor of this Dutch war, begun and carried on by the so called Cabal Ministry, was a few years later as fierce a reviler of Shaftesbury for his share in promoting this very war. Both in *Absalom and Achitophel* and in *The Medal* is this war in alliance with France against Holland made a chief indictment against Shaftesbury by Dryden, who now, while the war was in progress, gloated over the French alliance against Holland, and prayed for the degradation and ruin of the Dutch republic. These are the concluding lines of the Epilogue, chiming with Shaftesbury's *Delenda est Carthago* of the same year :

> ' Yet is their empire no true growth but humour,
> And only two kings' touch can cure the tumour.
> As Cato did his Afric fruits display,
> So we before your eyes their Indies lay ;
> All loyal English will like him conclude,
> Let Caesar live, and Carthage be subdued.' "

(Christie.)

Amboyna is one of the Molucca islands. The massacre of the English merchants of the factory there took place in 1622. Shaftesbury used Cato's phrase to the Romans, *Delenda est Carthago*—"'Carthage must be destroyed" in recommending the Dutch War to his countrymen. When later he had to fly to Holland as a political refugee, he asked the citizens of Amsterdam to enrol him among their number, in order that he might be safe from Charles II. The story goes that they sent him his ticket of citizenship with the mocking inscription, *Ab nostra Carthagine nondum deleta salutem accipe*—" Take safety from our Carthage not yet destroyed."

l. 8. [**Tyrtæus** (about B.C. 700-660). His poems exercised an important influence upon the Spartans in the second Messenian war, by assuaging dissensions at home and animating their courage in the field. C. D. P.]

l. 11. **Troilus and Cressida.** "Dryden's adaptation of Shakespeare's *Troilus and Cressida,* a decided deterioration, was brought out at Dorset Gardens in April, 1679" (Christie, p. 439). "Mr. Godwin has justly remarked, that the delicacy of Chaucer's ancient tale has suffered even in the hands of Shakespeare ; but in those of Dryden it has undergone a far deeper deterioration. Whatever is coarse and naked in Shakespeare has been dilated into ribaldry by the poet laureate of Charles the Second ; and the character of Pandarus, in particular, is so grossly heightened, as to disgrace even the obliging class to whom that unfortunate procurer has bequeathed his name. So far as this play is to be considered as an alteration of Shakespeare, I fear it must be allowed that our author has suppressed some of his finest poetry, and exaggerated some of his worst faults" (Scott).

l. 17. **the Spanish Friar.** "Dryden's tragi-comedy *The Spanish Friar,* one of his best plays, was produced at Dorset Gardens in 1681 : it was published in November, 1682. Dryden called this 'a Protestant play.' It is a severe attack on the Roman Catholic priesthood. *The Religio Laici* was published by Dryden in the interval between the first representation and the publication of *The Spanish Friar.* This play was prohibited by James II., and Dryden having then become a Roman Catholic, would not have wished that it should be acted. After the Revolution, it was the first play ordered to be represented by Queen Mary in her presence : her Protestant zeal brought punishment on this occasion, for she was greatly disconcerted by passages in the play, bearing hard on her own position, with reference to her exiled father, the bearing of which struck the audience" (Christie, p. 444). Scott quotes a contemporary account of this incident which tells how the Queen, at these 'unhappy expressions' (*e.g.* 'Very good; she usurps the throne, keeps the old king in prison, and at the same time, is praying for a blessing on her army') "was put in some disorder, and forced to hold up her fan, and call for her palatine and hood, and anything she could next think of ; while those who were in the pit before her, turned their heads over their shoulders, and all in general directed their looks towards her, whenever their fancy led them to make any application of what was said."

Eminent for the happy coincidence and coalition of the two plots. The way in which the tragic and the comic plots fall in with each other (coincidence) and help each other (coalition). Compare Scott's remarks. "*The Spanish Friar ; or, The Double Discovery,* is one of the best and most popular of our poet's dramatic efforts. The plot is, as Johnson remarks, particularly happy, for the coincidence and coalition of the tragic and comic parts. ... The felicity of Dryden's plot, therefore, does not consist in the ingenuity of his original conception, but in the minutely artificial strokes, by which the reader is perpetually reminded of the dependence of the one part of the play ꞯn the other.   These are so frequent, and appear so very natural, that the comic plot, instead of diverting our attention from the tragic business, recalls it to our mind by constant and unaffected allusion."

l. 22. [risible, comical, that which excited laughter (Lat. *risus*, laughter).   c. d. p.]

l. 31. the Duke of Guise.   "This play, a joint composition of Dryden and Lee, was first represented December 4, 1682.   It was the first new play brought out by the united company.   The apparent application of the play to the political circumstances of England at that time, and more especially points of resemblance in the history of the Duke of Guise to that of Monmouth, led the Lord Chamberlain (the Earl of Arlington) to withhold his license for some months.   The King's partiality for Monmouth and fear of what might be the effect on the public of a play which might be understood as predicting for Monmouth an assassination like that of Guise were the causes of the Court's unwillingness to allow the play to be acted.   The Court's scruples, however, gave way.   The play was received with discordant feelings by the Whig and Tory portions of the audience; and at first the disapprobation decidedly predominated" (Christie).

l. 32. Œdipus.   Produced in the latter part of 1678.   See Christie, p. 438.

l. 33. the remnant of the Covenanters.   The Solemn League and Covenant was a document pledging all who signed it to establish and maintain the Presbyterian form of church government.   It was put forward by the General Assembly of the Scotch Church in August, 1643, and was subscribed by the English Parliament and the Westminster Assembly of Divines in September of the same year.   But the Covenant and its principles never made any real headway in England.

Page 22, l. 11. [the Leaguers of France, a Catholic organisation under the Guises, with the King of France at its head (1576).   c. d. p.]

l. 14. Albion and Albanius.   "The opera of *Albion and Albanius* was written before the death of Charles II., and privately represented several times in his presence; but it was not brought before the public till after Charles' death. It was first acted publicly, June 3, 1685.   It is a political piece, and was intended to celebrate the victory of Charles II. over the Whigs.   'Albion' is Charles, and 'Albanius' his brother James.   The opera was brought out after James' accession to the throne with great splendour, and at very great expense.   On the sixth night of the representation, June 13, news came to London of the landing of Monmouth, which stopped the career of the play, and caused great loss to the theatre " (Christie, p. 465).

l. 17. **The State of Innocence and Fall of Man.** This is the story of Milton's *Paradise Lost* told in rhyme. Dryden called the piece au opera, but it was never acted or intended to be acted. It was published in 1674. The most interesting thing about it now is the story of how Milton gave Dryden permission to make the proposed use of his poem. " It is reported by Mr. Audrey that the step was not taken without Dryden's reverence to Milton being testified by a personal application for his per- mission. The aged poet, conscious that the might of his versification could receive no addition even from the flowing numbers of Dryden, is stated to have answered with indiffer- ence, 'Ay, you may *tag* my verses if you will'" (Scott). Johnson's criticism of the Dedication to the Duchess of York is a great deal too harsh. It is a very graceful bit of writing, and could not have been misunderstood as "an attempt to mingle earth and heaven " even by the lady addressed. Compare the note on p. 48, l. 11.

l. 36. **Heroic verse,** heroic or epic poetry.

Page 23, l. 5. overpassed, we now say 'passed over.'

l. 14. **seek an apology in falsehood.** Johnson lets his indig- nation at the preface carry him too far here. Dryden's statement is by no means so incredible as to warrant Johnson in dismissing it in this unhesitating way as pure fiction.

l. 16. **Aureng Zebe.** "*Aureng Zebe* was produced at the Theatre Royal in 1675. It is the last of Dryden's rhyming tragedies ; and in the Prologue he says that he grows weary of rhyme, which he had before so zealously defended. He also, in the Prologue, speaks of retiring from the stage ; and nearly two years elapsed before he produced his next play. *Aureng Zebe* was published in 1676 " (Christie, p. 427).

l. 17. **[a great prince then reigning.** Aurung Zebe (d. 1707) had a long and glorious reign, and was the most successful of a line of Indian Emperors known as Great Moguls. Delhi was his capital. C. D. P.]

l. 29. **The complaint of life is celebrated.** " The passage descriptive of life has been distinguished by all critics, down to Dr. Johnson :

> *Aur.* When I consider life, 'tis all a cheat ;
> Yet, fooled with hope, men favour the deceit ;
> Trust on, and think to-morrow will repay :
> To-morrow's falser than the former day ;
> Lies worse, and when it says we shall be blest
> With some new joys, cuts off what we possest.

Strange cozenage ! none would live past years again,
Yet all hope pleasure in what yet remain ;
And from the dregs of life think to receive
What the first sprightly running could not give.
I'm tired of waiting for this chymic gold,
Which fools us young and beggars us when old.

Nor is the answer of Nourmahal inferior in beauty :

> *Nour.* 'Tis not for nothing that we life pursue ;
> It pays our hopes with something still that's new :
> Each day's a mistress, unenjoyed before ;
> Like travellers, we're pleased with seeing more.
> Did you but know what joys your way attend,
> You would not hurry to your journey's end.

It might be difficult to point out a passage in English poetry in
which so common and melancholy a truth is expressed in such
beautiful verse, varied with such just illustration " (Scott).   The
first passage had a fascination for Johnson.   " He used frequently to observe that there was more to be endured than
enjoyed in the general condition of human life, and frequently
quoted those lines of Dryden, 'Strange cozenage,' etc.   For his
part, he said, he never passed that week in his life which he
would wish to repeat, were an angel to make the proposal to
him " (Boswell, Globe edition, p. 217).

l. 31. **the Earl of Mulgrave.**   "John Sheffield, Earl of Mulgrave.
afterwards created Marquis of Normanby, and at length Duke
of Buckingham, made a great figure during the reigns of Charles
II., of his unfortunate successor, of William III., and of Queen
Anne.   His bravery as a soldier, and abilities as a statesman,
seem to have been unquestioned, but for his poetical reputation
he was probably much indebted to the assistance of those wits
whom he relieved and patronized.   As, however, it has been
allowed a sufficient proof of wisdom in a monarch that he could
choose able ministers, so it is no slight commendation to the
taste of this rhyming peer that in youth he selected Dryden to
supply his own poetical deficiencies, and in age became the
friend and eulogist of Pope.... After the grave of Dryden had
remained twenty years without a memorial, this nobleman had
the honour to raise the present monument at his own expense,
being the latest, and certainly one of the most honourable, acts
of his life.... It may be worthy the attention of the great to
consider the value of that genius which can hand them down to
posterity in an interesting and amiable point of view, in spite of
their own imbecilities, errors, and vices.   While the personal
character of Mulgrave has nothing to recommend it, and his
poetical effusions are sunk into oblivion, we still venerate the
friend of Pope and the protector of Dryden" (Scott).   Sheffield

was Duke of Buckinghamshire, though Pope also shortens the
title to 'Buckingham':

"Muse, 'tis enough ; at length thy labour ends,
And thou shalt live, for Buckingham commends."

l. 34. his intention to write an epic poem. "Some little hopes
I have yet remaining, and those too, considering my abilities,
may be vain, that I may make the world some part of amends,
for many ill plays, by an heroic poem. Your lordship has been
long acquainted with my design ; the subject of which you know
is great, the story English, and neither too far distant from the
present age, nor too near approaching it. Such it is in my
opinion, that I could not have wished a nobler occasion to do
honour to my king, my country, and my friends ; most of our
ancient nobility being concerned in the action" (Scott). The
subject referred to was the conquest of Spain by Edward the
Black Prince. See Christie's *Memoir*, p. xxxviii. Notice again
that Johnson is content to quote from memory. Compare the
note at p. 13, l. 31.

l. 36. purloined, as, he says, happened to him. See p. 50,
l. 5 fg.

Page 24, l. 5. All for Love. "*All for Love, or the World well
Lost*—universally considered the best of Dryden's plays—was
produced at the King's Theatre at the beginning of 1678. The
concluding couplet of the Prologue shows that it came out in
winter. In the Prologue to *Aureng Zebe*, in 1675, Dryden had
confessed his intention of renouncing rhymed tragedies, and in
this he abandons rhyme.

' He fights this day unarmed, without his rhyme ' " (Christie).

Compare the following from Dryden's Preface to this play, and
notice the grace of the reference to Shakespeare : "In my style,
I have professed to imitate the divine Shakespeare ; which that
I might perform more freely, I have disencumbered myself from
rhyme ... I hope I may affirm, and without vanity, that, by
imitating him, I have excelled myself throughout the play ; and
particularly, that I prefer the scene betwixt Antony and
Ventidius in the first act, to anything which I have written in
this kind."

l. 21. Limberham. The play takes its name from Mr. Limberham, the chief character, "a tame, foolish keeper, persuaded by
what is last said to him, and changing next word." By 'keeper'
is meant a man who keeps a mistress. "It is a singular mark of
the dissolute manners of those times, that an audience to whom
matrimonial infidelity was nightly held out, not only as the most
venial of trespasses, but as a matter of triumphant applause,
were unable to brook any ridicule upon the mere transitory union

formed between the keeper and his mistress" (Scott). The play
was produced in 1678, and had to be withdrawn after the third
acting.

l. 28. Œdipus. See reference given at p. 21, l. 32. Johnson
would appear to have forgotten that he had already mentioned
Œdipus.

l. 29. [Sophocles (born B.C. 495), a celebrated Greek tragic
poet, wrote two tragedies on Oedipus. C. D. P.]

[Seneca (died A.D. 65), a celebrated Roman philosopher ; his
language is clear, forcible, and full of thought. C. D. P.]

l. 30. [Corneille (1606-1684), the first French writer of heroic
plays, which are considered the progenitors of those of Dryden.
C. D. P.]

l. 32. Don Sebastian. "Dryden had not produced a play
for four years, when his tragedy of *Don Sebastian* was brought
out in 1690 : and it was his first appearance on the stage after
the Revolution, which had deprived him of Court favour, and of
his offices of Poet Laureate and Historiographer Royal. He refers
in the opening of the Prologue to his altered position, and
endeavours to propitiate the audience by an appeal to their
magnanimity. The play was not very successful in representation, but it is one of the best of Dryden's plays. It was published
also in 1690, with a dedication to the Earl of Leicester, the elder
brother of Algernon Sydney, who himself as Lord Lisle had in
early life acted with Cromwell, and was now, without being
prominent in politics, a supporter of William and Mary's throne"
(Christie, p. 467). Scott justly complains of Johnson's "meagre
commendation" of the play. "Shakespeare laid aside, it will be
perhaps difficult to point out a play containing more animatory
incident, impassioned language, and beautiful description, than
Don Sebastian. Of the former, the scene betwixt Dorax and the
king, had it been the only one ever Dryden wrote, would have
been sufficient to ensure his immortality" (Scott).

Page 25, l. 3. the distresses of princes, and the vicissitudes of
empires. The play deals with the adventures supposed to have
befallen Sebastian, King of Portugal, after the fatal battle of
Alcazar. Sebastian fell in that fight, but, as his body was not
recovered, there were as many legends about, his subsequent
adventures in captivity, and as much hope of his ultimate return
to Portugal, as in the similar case of James the Fourth of Scotland after Flodden.

l. 12. Amphitryon. "Dryden had now set to work again
diligently for the stage ; and *Don Sebastian* was quickly followed
by the comedy of *Amphitryon, or the Two Sosias*, which was very
successful" (Christie, p. 470). *Amphitryon* was produced in the
same year as the last-mentioned play. The plot of the play

makes Jupiter and Mercury visit the house of the Theban
General Amphitryon in the disguise of Amphitryon himself and
his servant Sosia. The play is still "a very diverting entertainment" to the reader.

[**Plautus**, the most celebrated comic poet of Rome, born
about B.C. 254. C. D. P.]

l. 13. [**Molière** (d. 1673) was one of the chiefs of French literature. He wrote numerous comedies. C. D. P.]

l. 16. **Cleomenes.** "The tragedy of *Cleomenes* was first
represented in May, 1692. There had been some delay in
bringing it out; Queen Mary, who was acting as Regent during
William's absence in Ireland, having objected to its being
licensed. Cleomenes, King of Sparta, defeated by the Achæans,
took refuge in Egypt; and the resemblance of his story to the
exile of James II. in France made Queen Mary fear the effect of
the representation of this play. The Queen, however, was persuaded, chiefly by Rochester (to whom, in consequence, Dryden
dedicated the play when it was published), to withdraw her
objection ... " (Christie, p. 476). Johnson does not even care to
damn *Cleomenes* with faint praise, but it is, as Mr. Saintsbury
says, in parts extremely fine and noble. The following song
from it is quoted here as one example of the many exquisite
lyrics of Dryden which unfortunately lie for the most part
hidden now in his plays :

"No, no, poor suffering heart, no change endeavour,
Choose to sustain the smart, rather than leave her;
My ravished eyes behold such charms about her,
I can die with her, but not live without her;
One tender sigh of hers to see me languish,
Will more than pay the price of my past anguish :
Beware, O cruel fair, how you smile on me,
'Twas a kind look of yours that has undone me.

"Love has in store for me one happy minute,
And she will end my pain, who did begin it;
Then no day void of bliss, or pleasure, leaving,
Ages shall slide away without perceiving :
Cupid shall guard the door, the more to please us,
And keep out Time and Death, when they would seize us :
Time and Death shall depart, and say, in flying,
Love has found out a way to live by dying."

l. 17. [**the Guardian**, Steele's paper, which followed the
Spectator (1713). C. D. P.]

l. 20. **left alone with a young beauty.** Cleomenes is tempted
by Cassandra, the mistress of Ptolemy, King of Egypt, and
repels her advances.

l. 24. **King Arthur.** "*King Arthur, or the British Worthy,* called by Dryden 'a dramatic opera,' was produced at the Theatre Royal in 1691. The music was by Purcell, and the opera was a great success. Dryden had meditated an epic poem on King Arthur, but the necessity, as he himself said, of working for subsistence, and probably even more his nature, which made him work impulsively and under excitement, prevented the fulfilment of that design. This opera had been originally composed, like *Albion and Albanius*, at the end of Charles II.'s reign: it was much changed before it was produced in the reign of William and Mary" (Christie, p. 473).

l. 26. **it does not seem to have been ever brought upon the stage.** This is incorrect and inconsistent also with Johnson himself four lines below. Moreover it was not during a performance of this opera that the news of Monmouth's landing reached the capital. That true story applies to an opera previously mentioned, *Albion and Albanius*. See note on p. 22, l. 14. It looks as if two additional remarks on the operas, jotted down by Johnson after the completion of his first draft, had by accident got inserted in the wrong places. It was *The State of Innocence and Fall of Man* that was never acted; and it was a performance of *Albion and Albanius* which was interrupted in the way described. The error was not noticed, and "Arthur" was accordingly written at p. 25, l. 32. Scott notes that *King Arthur* was still occasionally performed in his time, "being the only one of Dryden's numerous plays which has retained possession of the stage."

l. 28. [**Marquis of Halifax,** Chancellor of the Exchequer, and leader of the Whigs. He had opposed the Duke of York in the reign of Charles II. C. D. P.]

l. 31. [**Monmouth had landed.** This was in June, 1685, therefore six years before the publication of this opera. C. D. P.]

l. 33. **Love Triumphant.** "*Love Triumphant,* a tragi-comedy, Dryden's last play, was brought out in the beginning of 1694. It was a great failure. A letter, preserved by Malone, written by one who was evidently a bitter enemy of Dryden's—'huffing Dryden' he calls him—says that the play 'was damned by the universal cry of the town.' Dryden returned on this occasion to rhyme, which he had long discarded for tragedy, in some of the tragic parts. In the Prologue Dryden formally announces his intention of giving up writing for the stage: and the Epilogue opens with the conceit that 'the poet's dead'" (Christie, p. 479).

Page 26, l. 4. he began and ended his dramatic labours with ill success. Scott quotes this, and finely adds, "a fact which may secure the inexperienced author from despondence, and teach him who has gained reputation how little he ought to presume on its stability." Scott joins in the general condemnation of this play, but with a word of praise for it too. "It is impossible to dismiss the performance of Dryden without some tribute of praise. The verse, where it is employed, possesses, as usual, all the dignity which numbers can give to the language; and the 'Song upon Jealousy,' as well as that in the character of a Girl, have superior merit." The "Song for a Girl" runs as follows:

> "Young I am, and yet unskilled
> How to make a lover yield:
> How to keep, or how to gain,
> When to love, and when to feign.

> "Take me, take me, some of you,
> While I yet am young and true;
> Ere I can my soul disguise,
> Heave my breasts, and roll my eyes.

> "Stay not till I learn the way
> How to lie and to betray:
> He that has me first is blest,
> For I may deceive the rest.

> "Could I find a blooming youth,
> Full of love, and full of truth,
> Brisk, and of a jaunty mien,
> I should long to be fifteen."

l. 17. **the poet had, for a long time, but a single night.** The word "night" in this and the next sentence is an anachronism. In Dryden's time plays were performed in the afternoon, and not at night. The meaning here is that the "takings" of one performance were the poet's perquisite. The performance selected was the third, which gave time for the poet to share to the full in the good or ill success of the play. The state of the house on the third day was therefore a matter of some interest to the author. Compare the lines in Pope's *Dunciad*, l. 113:

> "Now (shame to Fortune!) an ill run at play
> Blank'd his bold visage, and a thin third day:
> Swearing and supperless the hero sate,
> Blasphem'd his gods, the dice, and damn'd his fate."

A good attendance on the important day is spoken of in the same poem (l. 57) as "a warm third day."

l. 19. [**Southern** (1660-1746) produced his best tragedies *The Fatal Marriage* and *Oroonoko* in the reign of William III. c. d. p.]

[**Rowe** (1673-1718) wrote several tragedies, but is best known as the first editor of Shakespeare (1709). He was poet-laureate from 1715 till his death. c. d. p.]

l. 20. **arts of improving a poet's profit, which Dryden forbore
to practise.** This is obscure. Ryland quotes Milnes, "Johnson
alludes, perhaps, to Southerne, who used to solicit people to buy
tickets for the performance of the plays, and use every means for
the increase of his profits. Dryden was annoyed to hear him
own that he had made £700 by one play." But Johnson's
language seems to point to something more discreditable than
merely soliciting people to take tickets. Perhaps something like
blackmail is meant.

l. 23. **the accumulated gain of the third night, the dedication,
and the copy.** The "copy" is the manuscript of the play, from
which it was first produced on the stage, and afterwards
published. Compare below, l. 30, where "copies" is used in the
sense of printed copies of the play.

[**the dedication.** This was expected to produce a donation
from the one to whom the play was dedicated. The amount
depended on the degree of flattery employed. See p. 40, ll. 15-20.
C. D. P.]

l. 30. **To increase the value of his copies,** etc. Compare Swift's
lines :

> " Read all the Prefaces of Dryden
> For these our critics much confide in ;
> Though merely writ at first for filling,
> To raise the volume's price a shilling."
> *On Poetry,* a Rhapsody.

l. 35. [By studying the prefaces the public would learn lessons
in the art of criticising and judging poetry, and therefore would
become more difficult to please. C. D. P.]

Page 27, l. 4. **His prologues had such reputation,** etc. Scott
points out that prologues (and epilogues) to plays had, in Dryden's
time, a degree of consequence attached to them which they did
not possess before, and which has not since been given to them.
" They were not only used to propitiate the audience ; to apolo-
gise for the players or poet ; or to satirise the follies of the
day, which is now their chief purpose ; but they became, during
the collision of contending factions, vehicles of political tenets
and political sarcasm, which could at no time be insinuated with
more success than when clothed in nervous verse and delivered
with all the advantages of elocution to an audience, whose
numbers rendered the impression of poetry and eloquence more
contagious."

"It is not surprising," Scott goes on, "that Dryden soon
obtained a complete and absolute superiority in this style of
composition over all who pretended to compete with him. While
the harmony of his verse gave that advantage to the speaker

which was wanting in the harsh, coarse, broken measure of his contemporaries, his powers of reasoning and of satire left them as far behind in sense as in sound. This superiority, and the great influence which he had in the management of the theatre, made it usual to invoke his assistance in the case of new plays, many of which he accordingly furnished either with prologues or epilogues. The players also had recourse to him upon any remarkable occasion; as when a new house was opened; when the theatre was honoured by a visit from the King or Duke; when they played at Oxford during the public Acts; or, in short, in all cases when an occasional prologue was thought necessary to grace the performance."

l. 15. **It is certain,** etc. The statement that Dryden published six plays in the course of the year 1678 is an error which Johnson borrowed from Langbaine. See previous notes for the true dates of the six plays cited. The Spanish dramatist, Lopez de Vega (1562-1635), is said to have written from 1500 to 2000 dramas altogether, and to have been able to write a play from beginning to end in three hours.

l. 28. **characterised him,** almost equivalent to "caricatured him," but with the suggestion that there was a good deal of truth in the representation.

l. 30. [**Butler** (1612-1680). His *Hudibras* was a severe satire against the Puritans. C. D. P.]

l. 32. **then his chaplain,** private chaplain to the Duke of Buckingham.

l. 33. **the length of time,** etc. As Johnson says below, "Bayes, in the *Rehearsal,* was originally meant for Sir William Davenant, who, however, died three years before it was put upon the stage."

l. 35. [**artifice of action,** adaptation of the performance so as to suit it to ridicule of a later poet. For example, in 1717, it was reproduced with the alterations necessary to ridicule Pope. C. D. P.]

Page 28. l. 12. **These contradictions show how rashly satire is applied.** Johnson means that the critics were mistaken who saw in the *Rehearsal* allusions to the plays named. But his dates are again wrong. *Tyrannic Love* and *The Conquest of Granada* appeared before the *Rehearsal, Marriage Alamode* and the *Assignation* about the same time. He forgets also that a play may be well known before it is published. And the *Rehearsal,* as he had it and we have it, is not the play acted in 1671. Alterations and additions were made to it from time to time. See next note.

l. 25. **The design was probably to ridicule the reigning poet, whoever he might be.** "Unquestionably, and this continued a stage custom with the *Rehearsal* long after Dryden's death, and was even made the means of annoying Pope. 'To the character of Bayes,' says Cibber in his letter to Pope, 'there had always been allowed such ludicrous liberties of observation upon anything new or remarkable in the state of the stage as Mr. Bayes might think proper to make.' Cibber, therefore, in acting Bayes (and it was one of his favourite characters), 'had a fling' at the *Three Hours of Marriage*. This fling, as Cibber himself relates, gave him his first place in the deathless satire of Pope, who had at least one finger in the unfortunate *Three Hours of Marriage*" (Cunningham).

l. 28. **Bayes probably imitated the dress**, etc. "The poet Bayes of the farce was Dryden; his dress and manners were imitated, his favourite phases freely used, and a number of passages of his plays parodied; Buckingham is said to have taken great pains with the actor Lacey to teach him how to recite various passages" (Christie, *Memoir*, p. xxxiii).

l. 30. **the cant words**, words used without any particular meaning, interjectional phrases, and the like. One meaning of "cant" in the dictionaries is, "the special phraseology or speech peculiar to any profession, trade, or class." Johnson here speaks of the cant words in the sense of words continually in the mouth of an individual.

l. 32. **is blooded and purged.**

"*Bayes*. Pray, sir, how do you do when you write?
"*Smith*. Faith, sir, for the most part, I am in pretty good health.
"*Bayes*. Ay, but I mean what do you do when you write?
"*Smith*. I take pen, ink, and paper, and sit down.
"*Bayes*. Now, I write standing, that's one thing; and then another thing is, with what do you prepare yourself?
"*Smith*. Prepare myself! what the devil does the fool mean?
"*Bayes*. Why, I'll tell you now what I do. If I am to write familiar things, as sonnets to Armida and the like, I make use of stew'd prunes only; but when I have a grand design in hand, I ever take physic, and let blood; for, when you would have pure swiftness of thought and fiery flights of fancy, you must have a care of the pensive part. In fine, you must purge the stomach.
"*Smith*. By my troth, sir, this is a most admirable receipt for writing.
"*Bayes*. Ay, 'tis my secret; and, in good earnest, I think one of the best I have.

"*Smith*. In good faith, sir, and that may very well be" (*The Rehearsal*, ii. 1).

l. 36. **keeps Prince Volscius in a single boot.** He has sat down to put on his boots, with a view of starting to join his army, when the sight of his mistress distracts him as he sits with one boot on and the other off.

> " How has my passion made me Cupid's scoff !
> This hasty boot is on, the other off.
> And sullen lies, with amorous design,
> To quit loud fame and make that beauty mine. . . .
> Shall I to honour or to love give way ?
> Go on, cries honour ; tender love says, nay ;
> Honour aloud commands, plucks both boots on ;
> But softer love doth whisper, put on none." . . .

In the end he "goes out hopping, with one boot on, and t'other off."

Page 29, l. 2. [**lost Dublin,** in 1647. Ormond was in command of the Royalists, and, having to choose between surrendering Dublin to the Irish or the Parliament, chose the latter course. C. D. P.]

l. 4. **The Earl of Rochester,** etc. Johnson repeats here a good deal that has been already said at p. 7, l. 34 fg.

l. 23. [**by opposing a shield of adamantine confidence,** by shielding himself with a confidence in himself which no attack could shake. " To oppose a shield " is here " to place the shield between himself and his opponents." C. D. P.]

l. 27. **injuriously,** unjustly.

l. 28. [**he would,** etc., if he denied a part, and not the whole, of the accusation it would be assumed that he was unable to deny the rest, and the partial denial would be equivalent to a confession. C. D. P.]

l. 31. [**perplexity which generality produces,** the confusion raised in the mind of a reader by an indefinite accusation. C. D. P.]

l. 33. [**unless provoked by vindication,** unless his attempt to justify himself should cause readers to look closer into the facts. C. D. P.]

Page 30, l. 9. **they procured Dryden to be waylaid and beaten.** This cowardly night attack on Dryden took place on the 16th of December, 1679. " As the poet was returning to his residence in Long Acre that evening through Rose Street, Covent Garden, he was attacked and cudgelled by a party of ruffians, who escaped after perpetrating the assault. A reward of £50 was offered for the discovery of the offender, and later, the same reward and a pardon were offered to the offender himself if he would make known the instigator. Neither offender nor instigator was discovered. It seems to have been always believed that Rochester was the instigator of the assault, and the *Essay on Satire* the cause of anger" (Christie's *Memoir*, p. xlii).

l. 12. **the true writer**, that is, of the above-mentioned *Essay on Satire*.

l. 21. [**versions**, translations into English. c. d. p.]

l. 24. **such a charge**, that he professed to be translating from the Latin original when in reality he was only making an English version of a French translation.

l. 26. [**wanted the literature**, lacked the education. c. d. p.]

l. 28. **Hidden in a crowd**. The *Tacitus* was, like the *Lucian* and the *Plutarch*, the work of "different hands." Dryden was only one of several authors.

l. 32. **among which one was the work of Dryden**. Dryden translated two of the Epistles himself, and a third in conjunction with Mulgrave.

l. 35. **who on such occasions was regularly summoned**. Compare what has been already said of the way in which Dryden was employed to write prologues to plays, p. 27, l. 4 fg.

Page 31, l. 1. **the liberty that it now enjoys.** "There is undoubtedly a mean to be observed. Dryden saw very early that closeness best preserved an author's sense, and that freedom best exhibited his spirit; he therefore will deserve the highest praise who can give a representation at once faithful and pleasing, who can convey the same thoughts with the same graces, and who, when he translates, changes nothing but the language" (Johnson in the *Idler*, No. 69, quoted here by Cunningham). Compare, too, what Dryden says, in the preface to the translation of Juvenal of which he was a part author, of the work of Holiday, a previous translator. "And if we are not altogether so faithful to our Author, as our predecessors Holiday and Stapylton, yet we may challenge to ourselves this praise, that we shall be far more pleasing to our readers. We have followed our authors at greater distance, though not step by step, as they have done. For oftentimes they have gone so close, that they have trod on the heels of Juvenal and Persius, and hurt them by their too near approach. A noble author would not be pursued too close by a translator. We lose his spirit, when we think to take his body. The grosser part remains with us, but the soul is flown away, in some noble expression, or some delicate turn of words, or thought. Thus Holiday, who made this way his choice, seized the meaning of Juvenal; but the poetry has always escaped him."

l. 3. [**shackles of verbal interpretation**, the cramped style produced by translating word by word instead of rendering phrases and clauses by their equivalent English idioms. C. D. P.]

l. 5. **The authority of Jonson**, etc. Ben Jonson translated parts of Horace: George Sandys translated Ovid's *Metamorphoses*; and Barten Holiday, to whom reference has just been made, translated Juvenal and Persius. Of the quartette of free translators who are here opposed to these, Sir Richard Fanshaw translated Camoens; Sir John Denman, part of the *Aeneid*; Edmund Waller, parts of Virgil; and Abraham Cowley, parts of Horace, Martial, and other Latin poets.

l. 12. **Absalom and Achitophel.** In this "memorable satire," perhaps the greatest of all his works, Dryden took the biblical story of Absalom's revolt against his father David, and applied it to the party who at the time were endeavouring to secure the succession to the crown for Monmouth, the illegitimate son of Charles, to the exclusion of James, brother to the King, and his rightful successor. Absalom's evil counsellor Achitophel supplied the prototype of Shaftesbury, who was at the head of that faction, and who, at the moment of the publication of the poem, was lying a prisoner in the Tower awaiting trial as a traitor. He escaped that danger through the action of the grand jury, who "ignored," or threw out the bill against him. See p. 32, l. 12 fg. Dryden's character of Achitophel in this satire has for nervous strength never been surpassed, either by himself or by any one else.

"Of these the false Achitophel was first,
    A name to all succeeding ages curst:
For close designs and crooked counsels fit,
Sagacious, bold, and turbulent of wit,
Restless, unfixed in principles and place,
In power unpleased, impatient of disgrace;
A fiery soul, which working out its way,
Fretted the pigmy body to decay,
And o'er-informed the tenement of clay.
A daring pilot in extremity,
Pleas'd with the danger, when the waves went high,
He sought the storms, but, for a calm unfit,
Would steer too nigh the sands to boast his wit.
Great wits are sure to madness near allied
And thin partitions do their bounds divide;
Else why should he," etc.

The poem is full of writing of the same high order, and it is not difficult to understand the sensation which a satire of this sort, dealing with a quarrel in which all Englishmen of the time took one side or the other, created. The first edition appeared in

November, 1681. A second edition was called for before the end of the year, and there were no less than seven editions of the poem issued in Dryden's lifetime.

l. 20. **Sacheverell's trial**   Dr. Sacheverell was in 1709 impeached before the House of Lords for a sermon preached at St. Paul's, in which he had maintained that the King could do no wrong, and that resistance to him was a crime against God. This doctrine was in effect a condemnation of the Revolution of 1688, and the Whig ministry unwisely resolved to put Sacheverell on his trial for it. "An outburst of popular enthusiasm in Sacheverell's favour showed what a storm of hatred had gathered against the Whigs and the war. The most eminent of the Tory Churchmen stood by his side at the bar, crowds escorted him to the court and back again, while the streets rang with cries of 'The Church and Dr. Sacheverell.' A small majority of the peers found the preacher guilty, but the light sentence they inflicted was in effect an acquittal, and bonfires and illuminations over the whole country welcomed it as a Tory triumph" (Green).

l. 21. **Addison has attempted to derive.** "In No. 512 of the *Spectator*" (Ryland).

l. 31. **his person**, attacks similar to that which Dryden himself made, for example, on the person of Lord Shaftesbury in the line quoted above:

"Fretted the pigmy body to decay."

l. 33. **drew blood**, made Dryden very angry.

l. 35. **Ascribed ... to Somers.** "The author has never been discovered" (Malone, p. 165). That Somers was not the author may be fairly assumed from the fact of his contributing a translation of one of Ovid's *Epistles* (Dido to Aeneas) to the translation of 1680 known as Dryden's *Ovid*" (Cunningham).

[**Somers**, a Whig leader, became Lord Chancellor in 1696. C. D. P.]

Page 32, l. 8. [**to him**, *i.e.* Elkanah Settle. C. D. P.]

l. 10. **This is a difficulty which I cannot remove.** It is known now that the first of these two attempts at replying to Dryden was by one Samuel Pordage, and the second by Settle.

l. 13. **Lord Shaftesbury's escape from a prosecution**, etc. See note on p. 31, l. 12. "The rejection by the London grand jury, on November 24, 1681, of the bill of high treason presented against Lord Shaftesbury, was celebrated by a medal, having on one side a portrait of Shaftesbury, and on the other a sketch of London from the other bank of the river, showing the Bridge and the Tower, with the sun rising and shining through a cloud, and the inscription, 'Laetamur' (we rejoice). The event had been a great victory for the Whig party, and a great discomfiture for the Court. When the foreman of the grand jury announced their decision with the word Ignoramus (we throw out the bill), the hall rang with cheers, which were caught up and prolonged for an hour by the multitude assembled without, and in the evening bonfires were lighted through the city" (Christie). There is a story to the effect that it was Charles himself who suggested this poem to Dryden.

l. 20. **he left the palm doubtful, and divided the suffrages of the nation.** Compare the note at p. 7, l. 34.

l. 21. **Such are the revolutions of fame,** etc. Johnson here sums up Settle's subsequent history. Compare Christie's note on the lines in the Second Part of *Absalom and Achitophel*, in which Settle is attacked under the name of Doeg :

> " Doeg, though without knowing how or why,
> Made still a blundering kind of melody ;
> Spurred boldly on, and dashed through thick and thin,
> Through sense and nonsense, never out nor in ;
> Free from all meaning, whether good or bad,
> And, in one word, heroically mad," etc.

"Settle was the city poet. He had been a Tory ; he went over to the Whigs, and wrote *The Character of a Popish Successor* on their side of the question, and in 1683 he again joined the Tory party. He had made himself notorious by directing pope-burnings in the city, to which Dryden alludes in what he says of fireworks and a puppet-show. But some years after, Settle, being very poor, became assistant to the keeper of a puppet-show of Bartholomew Fair, and even performed as a dragon. These lines in Young's *Epistle to Pope* refer to him :

> ' Poor Elkanah, all other changes past,
> For bread in Smithfield dragons hissed at last,
> Spit streams of fire to make the butchers gape,
> And found his manners suited to his shape.'

Settle died, a pensioner of the Charter-house, in 1724." There is a touch of exaggeration in Johnson's professed inability to decide whether the final judgment of the world on Settle's claim to compete as a poet with Dryden was capricious or not. Scott is more decided. He quotes some lines of Settle's and adds, "Such were the strains once preferred to the magnificent verses of Dryden, whose very worst bombast is sublimity compared to them."

l. 26. [**epithalamium**, a marriage song. C. D. P.]

Page 33, l. 3. Judge Jefferies, "A man to all succeeding ages curst" for the cruelties practised by him upon the adherents of Monmouth in the West of England, after the failure of Monmouth's insurrection.

l. 4. [**zealot for prerogative,** advocate of the divine right of kings, as claimed by James II. and his predecessors. Jefferies carried out his Assizes after Monmouth's rebellion by order of the king and contrary to all principles of law and justice. C. D. P.]

l. 14. **Dryden declared himself a convert to popery.** The question of Dryden's sincerity in the change is a vexed one. Johnson, by the clause immediately preceding this one, makes it pretty clear what his opinion was, though he expressly declines to pass a categorical condemnation on Dryden. Macaulay does not shrink from doing that, and there is more passion than argument in what Christie calls the "disrespectful comment," which later biographers of Dryden have made on the passage in which Macaulay sums up the case, and gives judgment against the poet. It is not easy to understand how Ryland, for example, can say that "there is no adequate reason to doubt Dryden's sincerity." "Dryden," says Macaulay, "was poor and impatient of poverty. He knew little and cared little about religion. If any sentiment was deeply fixed in him, that sentiment was an aversion to priests of all persuasions, Levites, augurs, muftis, Roman Catholic divines, Presbyterian divines, divines of the Church of England. He was not naturally a man of high spirit, and his pursuits had been by no means such as are likely to give elevation or delicacy to his mind. He had during many years earned his daily bread by pandering to the vicious taste of the pit, and by grossly flattering rich and noble patrons. Self-respect and a fine sense of the becoming were not to be expected from one who had led a life of mendicancy and adulation. Finding that if he continued to call himself a Protestant his services would be overlooked, he declared himself a Papist."

l. 19. **to retire for quiet to an infallible church,** to seek peace for mind and soul by submission to a church accepted by him as an infallible guide in faith and morals. Sir Kenelm Digby was a well-known literary man of the generation previous to Dryden. The two Rainolds are the heroes of the odd story to which Johnson refers. They belonged to the differing faiths, and engaged in hot controversy with such success that each converted the other. Chillingworth is the well-known divine.

l. 33. [**Information may come,** etc., the knowledge necessary to produce a change of opinion may be obtained at the time which may be most advantageous. C. D. P.]

l. 34. [**fatal,** unchangeable, fixed by fate. C. D. P.]

Page 34, l. 12. [came unprovided, approached the controversy without any established convictions of his own.   C. D. P.]

l. 19. **the controversial papers found in the strong box of Charles the Second.**   "James II. had published copies of papers found in Charles II.'s strong box in favour of the Roman Catholic faith, and with them a copy of a paper by his first wife, Anne Hyde, giving the reasons of her conversion to the same faith.   This publication had been answered by Stillingfleet, then Dean of St. Paul's.   The king caused a Defence of the Papers to be published, and Dryden here states that he was the author of that part of the Defence which defended the late Duchess of York's paper" (Christie, note on the preface to *The Hind and the Panther*).

l. 23. **With hopes of promoting popery,** etc.   The translation referred to was done to the order of Charles II., and was published two years before Dryden's conversion.

l. 25. **Life of Francis Xavier.**   "Another task executed by Dryden in the cause of his new religion was a translation of the *Life of St. Francis Xavier*, a Jesuit missionary and worker of miracles of the sixteenth century, whom the Roman Catholic Church had made a saint.   In dedicating this work to the Queen, Dryden seriously announced that this saint had been chosen by her Majesty for one of her patrons, that her prayers to him had not been unprofitable, and that the nation might expect a son and heir for James through these prayers.   When the Queen gave birth to a son, on June 10, 1688, all the adversaries of James and his religion believed the child to be an imposture, and Dryden's prediction came to be counted as evidence of deceit" (Christie's *Memoir*, p. lxi).

l. 28. [**pious fraud,** deception employed in producing some good result.   C. D. P.]

l. 35. **He was supposed,** etc.   The translation referred to was advertised as having been taken in hand by Dryden, but it was never published.   The Revolution probably put an end to the project.   The original was a comprehensive account of all the heresies from the Roman Catholic Church, and the early English Reformers were, of course, not very tenderly dealt with in it. The Burnet of this passage is the famous Bishop of Salisbury, who was one of the confidants of William III., and who accompanied him in his expedition to England.   His *History of his own Time* is one of the best accounts we have of the events which led up and followed the Revolution of 1688.

Page 35, l. 1. **to have written an Answer.**   "Johnson is in error in supposing that Dryden replied to Burnet's *Reflections* on Varillas.   The *Answer* to Burnet was by Varillas himself. Dryden had nothing to do *publicly* with Varillas or his *History*" (Cunningham).

l. 4. and several other things.   Burnet probably means Dryden's licentious style of writing and his change of religion.

l. 8. his Answer.   "If Johnson had printed a preceding paragraph in Burnet, he and his readers would have seen that *his Answer* meant Varillas, not Dryden, as here given" (Cunningham).

l. 10. the conversation that he had set on between the Hinds and Panthers.   See below, p. 36, l. 10 fg.

l. 17. grace.   In the theological sense of the goodness that is a free gift (*gratia*) from God, and finds favour with God.   It is the same as "morals" in l. 21 below.

l. 22. wreaked his malice on me.   In *The Hind and the Panther.*

l. 34. his last employment.   His poem of *The Hind and the Panther.*

Page 36, l. 6. the Hind and Panther.   "Dryden's greatest effort in the cause of his new religion was in poetry.   *The Hind and the Panther*, the most brilliant perhaps of all Dryden's poems, and showing the greatest variety of power, in which the milk-white Hind, representing the Church of Rome, argues the cause of that Church with the spotted Panther, representing the Church of England, occupied Dryden during the greater part of the year 1686, and was published in April, 1687.   It is easy to ridicule the plan of this poem : the congruity of a theological dialogue between two quadrupeds will not bear serious discussion.   But all the more admirable is the triumph of Dryden's art.   Power of argument and beauty of language and verse are equally conspicuous in this fascinating poem" (Christie, *Memoir*, p. lx). For a criticism by Johnson of the poem, see below, p. 83, l. 10 fg.

l. 11. it was accordingly ridiculed, etc.   "The appearance of *The Hind and the Panther* was a signal for a new volley of attack on Dryden, and his recent conversion naturally increased the ire of his opponents, and gave them much assistance for assault.   Of many replies which came forth one only has acquired fame.   Two young men, destined to become afterwards distinguished in literature and politics, Charles Montagu, the future Earl of Halifax, and Matthew Prior, combined to make a burlesque on Dryden's poem, under the title of *The Hind and the Panther transversed to the Story of the Country Mouse and the City Mouse. The Hind and the Panther* lent itself easily to parody.   Bayes, Smith, and Johnson, of the *Rehearsal*, reappeared in this truly witty performance of Dryden's two young friends, for the two young men were frequenters of Will's, where Dryden, sitting in his great chair, now almost a throne, had been kind to them : and it is said that Dryden felt much hurt by their ridicule, and spoke, with tears in his eyes, of their ingratitude" (Christie, *Memoir*, p. lxi).   The story referred to is one of several about

Dryden that have come down to us in Spence's *Anecdotes*.
Spence got it from Dr. Lockier, Dean of Peterborough : "Dryden
was most touched with *The Hind and the Panther Transversed*.
I have heard him say, 'for two young fellows that I have always
been very civil to, to use an old man in misfortunes in so cruel a
manner!' And he wept as he said it." The title of the parody
is borrowed from a story told by Horace in which a city mouse
enjoys a visit from a country mouse, and both are disturbed by
human assailants just as the former is praising the superior advantages of his lot.

l. 17. **the facetious Thomas Brown.** This writer is only known
for the attacks on Dryden cited here.

l. 24. **Bayes.** The name by which Dryden was ridiculed in the
Rehearsal. See p. 28.

l. 28. [**deficient in literature,** lacking in learning. See p. 30,
l. 26. C. D. P.]

Page 37, l. 3. **as many cow-hides,** etc. In Homer Ajax
carries a shield made of sevenfold hides.

l. 7. **worse than,** etc. Worse than a bailiff does a defaulting
debtor. The wit of the passage that follows lies in the insinua-
tion that all the copies of *The Hind and Panther* have already
been put to the ordinary uses of waste-paper.

l. 16. [**can quote,** etc., can give his 'prentice a long lecture on
thrift. C. D. P.]

l. 22. **with a very indifferent religion.** An allusion to the belief that Dryden was an Anabaptist to begin with. See p. 1, l. 14.

l. 24. **which appeared first in a Tyrant's quarrel.** *The Heroic
Stanzas on the Death of Oliver Cromwell.* See p. 2, l. 30.

l. 27. **the birth of the Prince.** See the note on p. 34, l. 25.

l. 31. [**a poem,** *Britannia Rediviva, i.e.* Britain brought to life
again. C. D. P.]

Page 38, l. 5. **celebrated the intruder's inauguration,** etc.
Johnson is out in his dates here. Dryden attacked Shadwell in
Mac Flecknoe before he attacked him, as Og, in the second part
of *Absalom and Achitophel.* The former poem was published in
October, and the latter in November, 1682. Both attacks then
were long prior to the time when Dryden had to yield the
laureateship to one whom he already so cordially despised. In
Mac Flecknoe Dryden describes Flecknoe, an otherwise obscure
poet of that name, as choosing a successor who is to be as dull as
himself. His choice falls on Shadwell, who is accordingly styled
Mac Flecknoe, or son of Flecknoe :

"Shadwell alone my perfect image bears,
Mature in dulness from his tender years ;
Shadwell alone of all my sons is he
Who stands confirmed in full stupidity.

The rest to some faint meaning make pretence,
But Shadwell never deviates into sense.
Some beams of wit on other souls may fall,
Strike through and make a lucid interval ;
But Shadwell's genuine night admits no ray,
His rising fogs prevail upon the day."

l. 10. **It is related by Prior**, etc.   Christie points out that
"there is obviously error and exaggeration in this statement :
'Dryden himself acknowledges the bountiful present' which
Dorset made him at this time, but in terms which make it impossible to believe that Dorset made up to him for the whole loss
he suffered in losing his appointment" (*Memoir*, p. lxiii).

l. 16. **a public infliction**, the loss of an income given and
withdrawn on public grounds.

l. 18. **His patron might**, etc.   Dryden's silence on the point is
no proof that Dorset did not do as Prior said he did, as Dorset
may have enjoined it on him to say nothing about it.

l. 31. **Don Sebastian.**   See note on p. 24, l. 32.

l. 32. **four dramas more**, *Amphitryon* (note on p. 25, l. 12) ;
King Arthur (note on p. 25, l. 24) ; *Cleomenes* (note on p. 25,
l. 16) ; and *Love Triumphant* (note on p. 25, l. 33).

Page 39, l. 4. [the design.   See p. 23, l. 24.   c. d. p.]

l. 18. **as Boileau observes.**   Boileau was a contemporary
French poet and critic.   Dryden quotes his remark that the
plot of Tasso's poem, for example, "is a very unequal match
for the poor devils, who are sure to come by the worst of it
in the combat ; for nothing is more easy than for an Almighty
Power to bring his old rebels to reason when he pleases."

l. 22. [**Rinaldo**, a hero in Tasso's *Jerusalem Delivered*.   c. d. p.]

l. 32. [**our numbers**, English poetry.   It would probably have
added some new and useful feature to English verse.   c. d. p.]

l. 35. [**manners**, morals (Lat. *mores*).   c. d. p.]

Page 40. l. 4. **he charged Blackmore with stealing.**   In the
preface to his *Fables.*   "But I will deal more civilly with his
two poems, because nothing ill is to be spoken of the dead, and
therefore peace to the manes of his Arthurs.   I will only say,
that it was not for this noble knight that I drew the plan of an
epic poem on King Arthur in my preface to the translation of
Juvenal.   The guardian angels of kingdoms were machines too
ponderous for him to manage, and therefore he rejected them, as
Darys did the whirlbats of Eryx when they were thrown before
him by Entellus.   Yet from that preface he plainly took his
hint, for he began immediately upon the story, though he had the

baseness not to acknowledge his benefactor but, instead of it, to traduce me in a libel."

l. 8. **he borrowed two months**. This is Dryden's own phrase on the subject. "The translation of Virgil, as a whole, was commenced in the end of 1693, and was finished about the end of 1696. It was published in July 1697.... During three years Dryden worked with great assiduity at his great translation; one diversion only of importance occurred while he was translating Virgil. In 1695 he (to use his own expression), 'borrowed two months' for a translation in prose of Du Fresnoy's *Art of Painting*, the work, he said, of twelve mornings" (Christie, *Memoir*).

l. 16. **that no opportunity of profit might be lost**. See note on p. 26, l. 23.

l. 19. **economy**, judicious distribution.

l. 26. **a contract now in the hands of Mr. Tonson**. It is given below, p. 53.

l. 30. **the well-known ode on St. Cecilia's day**. St. Cecilia's day is the 22nd of November. She is the patron saint of musicians, and it was for many years usual to celebrate her day by a concert at which an ode written for the occasion was sung. Dryden wrote two such odes. It is the later and more celebrated of the two that is here referred to. It was written for the festival of 1697. Dryden called it *Alexander's Feast, or the Power of Music*. For a notice of Dryden's first ode for St. Cecilia's day see p. 80.

Page 41. l. 3. **into what hands Homer was to fall**. The reference is to Pope's translation of Homer.

l. 6. **On the first of May, 1701**, etc. The real date is just a year earlier. "During the greater part of the months of March and April Dryden was confined to his house by gout; the immediate cause of death was neglected inflammation of a toe which brought on mortification. Hobbs, the famous surgeon of the day, advised at once amputation of the toe, to which Dryden would not consent, and when the evil had spread over the leg Hobbs again advised amputation of the limb, which the old man refused also. Death was then inevitable. The illness was short. A London newspaper announced on the 30th of April, 'John Dryden, Esq., the famous poet, lies a-dying.' At three in the following morning, May 1, he expired" (Christie, *Memoir*).

l. 9. **There is extant a wild story**, etc. It has long been recognized that there is not a word of truth in the romance which follows. Compare Christie's account of the funeral. "The poet who died thus poor had a splendid funeral. There appears

to have been in the first instance an intention of a quiet private
interment; the state of the body rendered quick measures
necessary; and it is said that Charles Montagu promptly offered
to pay the expenses of the burial. But it appeared to others,
among whom Lord Jefferies, the son of the chancellor of bad fame,
was prominent, and of whom Dryden's life-long friend, Dorset,
was also one, that the poet merited burial in Westminster Abbey
and a public funeral; and by their desire the body was embalmed,
and application was made through Garth, a poet and physician,
to the President and Censors of the College of Physicians for
permission to deposit the body in the College until the funeral.
So the body lay in state for several days in the College of
Physicians. The funeral took place on May 13; it was preceded
by a ceremony at the College, in the course of which Garth
delivered a funeral oration in Latin, and the Ode of Horace
beginning 'Exegi monumentum aere perennius' was sung to
music. Then there was a long procession from the College to
Westminster Abbey, Dryden's friends who attended filling nearly
fifty carriages, and the whole number of carriages that followed
being about a hundred; music preceded the hearse, drawn by six
horses. Dryden was buried in Poet's Corner, by the graves of
Chaucer and Cowley." Scott notices the story which Johnson
has given unfortunate prominence to, traces it to a somewhat
spiteful account of the real ceremony from the pen of the
dramatist Farquhar, and adds: "It must be a well-conducted
and uncommon public ceremony, where the philosopher can find
nothing to condemn, nor the satirist to ridicule; yet, to our
imagination, what can be more striking than the procession of
talent and rank which escorted the remains of Dryden to the
tomb of Chaucer."

l. 16. [**Lady Elizabeth Howard**, sister of Sir R. Howard mentioned on p. 28. c. d. p.]

Page 43. l. 28. in a letter of Farquhar. "Farquhar, the dramatic
author, who attended the funeral, wrote an ill-natured account
of it, which is in print: 'I come now from Mr. Dryden's funeral,
where we had an Ode of Horace sung instead of David's Psalms;
whence you may find that we don't think a poet worth Christian
burial. The pomp of the ceremony was a kind of rhapsody, and
fitter, I think, for Hudibras than him; because the cavalcade
was mostly burlesque; but he was an extraordinary man, and
buried after an extraordinary fashion, for I do believe there was
never such another burial seen. The oration, indeed, was great
and ingenious, worth the subject, and like the author, whose pre-
scriptions can restore the living, and his pen embalm the dead.
And so much for Mr. Dryden: whose burial was the same as his
life, variety and not of a piece; the quality and mob, farce and
heroics; the sublime and ridiculous mixed in a piece; great

Cleopatra in a hackney-coach.' This is evidently a letter written for effect, and an ill-natured criticism. It is difficult to eliminate the vulgar and the ludicrous from the solemnity of any funeral: and the more splendour is attempted, the more difficult is perfect congruity " (Note in Christie's *Memoir*). Christie does not admit the legend into the text of his *Life*, and it is to be wished that Johnson had excluded it from his, as indeed he once intended to do (see l. 26). Johnson inserted the story partly for the sake of the pleasure writing the paragraph that follows gave him.

l. 29. [tumultuary, disturbed by tumults. c. d. p.]

l. 35. [event, result, consequence. c. d. p.]

l. 36. [justled, a variation of *jostled*. c. d. p.]

Page 44, l. 6. He was buried among the poets in Westminster Abbey. A part of the Abbey has been for ages set aside as a burying-place for great poets. In our day Browning and Tennyson have each found a grave in "Poets' Corner," as the place is called.

l. 14. with circumstances, etc. "The marriage probably took place under circumstances not happy and auspicious. There are many broad insinuations in the printed productions of Dryden's many assailants against the purity of his wife's character before her marriage; and one distinctly taunts him with having been hectored into marriage by the lady's brothers in order to save her character. A letter, which time has revealed, written by Dryden's wife before her marriage to a licentious young nobleman, the second Earl of Chesterfield, places it beyond reasonable doubt that she had an intrigue with him before her marriage. It is hardly likely that, if her character had been unsullied, she would have married Dryden, who, though of good family, was poor, and living by his pen. There is no doubt that they were an ill-assorted pair, and that the marriage was unhappy" (Christie). For "the satire imputed to Lord Somers," see p. 31, l. 34.

l. 20. He is said to have died at Rome. "John, the second son, died at Rome, very soon after his father's death, in January, 1701" (Christie, *Memoir*, p. lxxxii).

l. 21. Henry entered into some religious order. "Erasmus Henry, the youngest, called 'Harry' in his father's letters, succeeded in May, 1710, to the baronetcy on the death of his cousin, Sir John Dryden, and died on December 4 of the same year" (Christie).

l. 25. the translators of Juvenal. See p. 39, l. 1.

l. 29. the portrait (of his mind) which has been left by Congreve. Congreve edited for the publisher Tonson an edition of Dryden's dramatic works in six volumes in 1735. The quotation which follows is from the preface, which took the form of a Dedication to the Duke of Newcastle. Johnson has altered some

parts of the passage and omitted others. There was great friendship between the old poet and the young one. Congreve, as he
himself says in this Dedication, was very conversant, and as
intimately acquainted, with Mr. Dryden as the great disproportion in their years could allow them to be. When Congreve's
Double-Dealer appeared, Dryden hailed it publicly with generous
warmth as better than anything he himself had written :

> "Well then the promised hour is come at last,
> The present age of wit obscures the past "—

and in the closing lines of the *Epistle to my dear friend, Mr.
Congreve, on his comedy called the Double-Dealer*, of which these
are the opening lines, commended to his young friend the care of
his own reputation, in verses which cannot be read yet without
emotion—

> "Already I am worn with cares and age,
> And just abandoning the ungrateful stage :
> Unprofitably kept at Heaven's expence,
> I live a rent-charge on His providence :
> But you, whom every Muse and Grace adorn,
> Whom I foresee to better fortune born,
> Be kind to my remains ; and oh, defend,
> Against your judgment, your departed friend !
> Let not the insulting foe my fame pursue,
> But shade those laurels which descend to you :
> And take for tribute what these lines express ;
> You merit more, nor could my love do less."

l. 36. [**He was ... access**, it was very easy for others to approach
him, and his reception of them was pleasing. c. d. p.]

Page 45, l. 11. [**pedantic**, introduced for the mere purpose of
showing his learning. c. d. p.]

l. 20. [**the fondness of friendship**, the kindly forbearance produced by Congreve's friendship for Dryden. c. d. p.]

Page 46, l. 13. [**insidiousness**, underhanded meanness. c. d. p.]

l. 14. [**Creech** (1659-1701) had obtained a fellowship at Oxford
for his translation of *Lucretius*, but his translation of Horace's
Odes did not sustain his credit. c. d. p.]

l. 28. [**saturnine**, silent and grave. Astrologers attribute this
character to the influence of the planet Saturn at birth. c. d. p.]

Page 47, l. 15. **It is related**, etc. Carte wrote a *Life of the
Duke of Ormond*. The Duke was a great soldier and statesman
kept in high employments under Charles I., Charles II., and
James II. He died before the Revolution.

l. 21. **Horace will support him in the opinion**, etc.

> "Principibus placuisse viris non ultima laus est."
> Horace's *Epistles*, i. 17.

Page 48, l. 1. **Of the mind that can trade in corruption,** etc.
With Johnson's dignified rebuke of the moral filth in which
Dryden's pen was unhappily from time to time dipped compare
Scott's lines in the Introduction to the first canto of *Marmion* :

" Dryden in immortal strain
Had raised the Table Round again,
But that a ribald King and Court
Bade him toil on, to make them sport ;
Demanded for their niggard pay,
Fit for their souls, a looser lay ;
The world defrauded of the high design,
Profaned the God-given strength, and marr'd
    the lofty line. "

l. 2. [**ideal wickedness,** the imaginary acts of wickedness described in Dryden's dramas.   c. d. p.]

l. 6. **What consolation can be had,** etc.   In 1698, two years
before Dryden's death, appeared the famous work of Jeremy
Collier, a non-juring clergyman, on the immorality and profaneness of the English stage.   Dryden was singled out for special
condemnation.   Two passages in which Dryden says all that he
felt could be said for himself are in Johnson's mind here.   In
a poetical epistle to his friend, Mr. Motteux, on that writer's
tragedy called *Beauty in Distress*, Dryden in two lines admits
that Collier's attack was not undeserved :

" What I have loosely or profanely writ
Let them to fires, their due desert, commit. "

See p. 49, ll. 30-36.

l. 9. **he did not want examples,** etc.   Johnson is referring
here to the passage in Dryden's answer to Collier, which follows
that cited in the note above.   Dryden suggests that Collier took
too great a pleasure in searching out impurities in plays ancient
and modern, and goes on, " A divine might have employed his
pains to better purpose than in the nastiness of Plautus and
Aristophanes ; whose examples, as they excuse not me, so it
might be possibly supposed that he read them not without some
pleasure.   They who have written commentaries on these poets,
or on Horace, Juvenal, or Martial, have explained some vices,
which, without their interpretation, had been unknown to
modern times.   Neither has he judged impartially betwixt the
former age and us.   There is more bawdry in one play of
Fletcher's, called *The Custom of the Country*, than in all ours
together.   Yet this has been often acted on the stage in my
remembrance. "

l. 11. **the meanness and servility of hyperbolical adulation,**
etc.   In the remarks which follow Johnson allows his own

feelings of sturdy independence of all patrons (compare the note on p. 3, l. 23), to make him unfair to Dryden. In his dedications the poet merely wrote after the manner of his age. He no more meant his flattery to be taken in earnest than the favoured recipients of it supposed he did. Scott has well compared this eulogistic style of writing to the practice which makes the modern writer of official letters declare at the foot of each that he is the "humble, obedient servant" of the person he is addressing. Scott quotes Johnson here, and, after observing that perhaps no writer has equalled Dryden in the profusion and elegance of his adulation, goes on, "It may be noticed in palliation of Johnson's heavy charge, that the form of address to superiors must be judged of by the manners of the times; and that the adulation contained in dedications was then as much a matter of course as the words of submissive style, which still precede the subscription of an ordinary letter. It is probable that Dryden considered his panegyric as merely conforming with the fashion of the day, and rendering unto Cæsar the things which were Cæsar's, attended with no more degradation than the payment of any other tribute to the forms of politeness and usage of the world." Dryden enjoyed writing these dedications, and they are still readable, which is proof enough that there is more in them than the vulgar desire to please a nobleman, which was all that Johnson could see in them. The Afra Behn, to whom Johnson assigns a bad pre-eminence in flattery, was a woman writer of the time, who is remembered now chiefly for the gross immorality of the greater part of her writings.

l. 27. [encomiastic, full of praise and commendation. c. d. p.]

Page 49, l. 7. [formed for duration, destined to endure after the writer's death. c. d. p.]

l. 11. [this principle, the principle just laid down by Johnson. Dryden did not often name his enemy, but complained in a general manner. c. d. p.]

l. 14. [adverse name, the name of an adversary. c. d. p.]

l. 17. his libel remains injurious only to himself, his attack on Settle only shows how seriously Settle had contrived to annoy him.

l. 20. [to obviate, to turn aside. c. d. p.]

l. 26. [the claps of a playhouse. See p. 13, l. 9. c. d. p.]

l. 29. [glosses, comments on Dryden's writings. c. d. p.]

l. 30. [he confesses, "I shall say the less of Mr. Collier because in many things he has taxed me justly." This preface appeared in 1700, two years after Collier's criticism. See note on p. 48, l. 6. c. d. p.]

Page 50, l. 1. **a reflection on Collier of great asperity.**   In the beginning of the tale of *Cymon and Iphigenia.*

"Old as I am, for lady's love unfit,
The power of beauty I remember yet,
Which once inflamed my soul, and now inspires my wit.
If love be folly, the severe divine
Has feet that follow, though he censures mine;
Pollutes the pleasures of a chaste embrace,
Acts what I write, and propagates in grace,
With riotous excess, a priestly race."

To Dryden, as a Roman Catholic, a married priest was an abomination.

l. 3. **Blackmore he represents,** etc.   "As for the City Bard or Knight Physician, I hear his quarrel to me is that I was the author of *Absalom and Achitophel,* which he thinks is a little hard on his fanatic patrons in London.   But I will deal the more civilly with his two poems, because nothing is to be spoken of the dead, and therefore peace be to the manes of his Arthurs."   The "Arthurs" are Blackmore's two epic poems, *Prince Arthur* and *King Arthur,* which were already dead in Dryden's times, and have never been revived since.   The rest of the attack on Blackmore has been given already in the note to p. 40, l. 4.

l. 13. [**masters of assay,** those who test the weight of coins before they are issued.   All the terms of this sentence apply first to coinage and then by metaphor to wit.   C. D. P.]

l. 20. [**allay,** an old spelling of *alloy.*   C. D. P.]

Page 51, l. 11. [**discovered,** displayed.   C. D. P.]

l. 12. **malignity to priests and priesthood.**   Compare above, p. 14, l. 14, "Thus foolishly could Dryden write, rather than not show his malice to the parsons."

l. 17. **Trapp.**   See p. 68, l. 28.

[**the author,** *i.e.* Virgil, the author who suffered by this error in Dryden's translation.   C. D. P.]

l. 18. **as if any reproach,** etc.   See note on p. 68, l. 28.   [As if any reflection upon the actions of pagan priests could be considered as also a reflection on Christian priests.   Trapp was claiming reverence for the office of priest irrespective of the priest's creed.   See p. 88, l. 30.   C. D. P.]

l. 29. **with all the allowance,** etc.   Dryden, or his admirers, would fain defend the passages referred to on the ground that the language is not to be taken as expressing the poet's own sentiments, but is made to suit the character and the occasion.

Page 52, l. 9. **the indignation of merit,** etc.   A letter is extant which Dryden wrote in 1683 to the then first commissioner of the Treasury, Hyde, Earl of Rochester, begging for the more punctual payment of his salary. "I know not whether my Lord Sunderland has interceded with your lordship for half of my salary, but I have two other advocates, my extreme wants even to arresting, and my ill health, which cannot be repaired without immediately retiring into the country. A quarter's allowance is but the Jesuit's powder [quinine] to my disease; the fit will return a fortnight hence. If I durst, I would plead a little merit, and some hazards of my life from the common enemies; my refusing advantages offered by them, and neglecting my beneficial studies for the King's service; but I only think I merit not to starve. ... 'Tis enough for one age to have neglected Mr. Cowley and starved Mr. Butler."

l. 19. **to which King James added the office of Historiographer.** This is a mistake. Dryden received the two appointments of Poet-laureate and Historiographer-Royal at the same time, in August, 1670. See note on p. 6, l. 29.

l. 21. [**casual**, dependent upon events, uncertain. c. d. p.]

Page 53, l. 8. [169⅜. According to the Old Style the year began on March 25th, and according to the New Style on January 1st. The New Style did not become universal till 1752, and dates from January 1st to March 24 were accompanied by both numbers to avoid ambiguity. Here the date is 1698 (Old Style), 1699 (New Style). c. d. p.]

Page 54, l. 29. [**the economy of government**, the management of the money required to carry on the government. c. d. p.]

l. 30. **the payments of the exchequer,** etc. Compare the last note but one.

Page 55, l. 1. **Of the only two men,** etc. "Talking of the great difficulty of obtaining authentic information for biography, Johnson told us, ' When I was a young fellow I wanted to write the " Life of Dryden," and in order to get materials I applied to the only two persons then alive who had seen him ; these were old Swinney and old Cibber. Swinney's information was no more than this, ' That at Will's coffee-house Dryden had a particular chair for himself, which was set by the fire in winter, and was then called his winter-chair; and that it was carried out for him to the balcony in summer, and was then called his summer-chair. Cibber could tell no more but 'That he remembered him a decent old man, arbiter of critical disputes at Will's'" (Boswell's *Life of Johnson*, Globe ed., p. 380).

l. 3. [**Will's coffee-house,** on the north side of Russell Street, at the end of Bow Street, was, in Dryden's day, called the " Wits' Coffee-house," and was much resorted to by literary men. Johnson tells us that Pope, when a child, persuaded some friends to take him there in order to see Dryden. c. d. p.]

l. 12. **He put great confidence in the prognostications of judicial astrology.** Compare below, p. 110, l. 1. "Towards the latter end of this month, September, Charles will begin to recover his perfect health, according to his nativity, which, casting it myself, I am sure is true." Astrologists divided their art into "Natural Astrology," which predicted changes in the weather, and "Judicial Astrology," which foretold the destinies of men or of nations.

l. 14. **the Life of Congreve.** The book referred to already at p. 46, l. 29.

l. 20. **The utmost malice, etc.** The quotation is from the *Annus Mirabilis.* "The stars," in the first line, should be "their stars." The poet is not speaking of the malice of the stars in general, but of the baneful influence of the stars ruling over the destinies of the city of London. For the rest, compare Christie's note, "A trine, or conjunction of planets in the form of a triangle, was considered fortunate by astrologers; and to 'frequent trines' Dryden adds another happy omen, the planet Jupiter in ascension. Dryden was learned in astrology, and a firm believer. The verb *succeed* here has an active meaning, *make to succeed.* "Those weights took off" is an absolute construction, *took* being used for *taken.*

l. 25. [**the planetary powers**, the influence which astrologers say is exercised by the planets over earthly affairs. c. d. p.]

l. 27. [**obliquely**, indirectly. c. d. p.]

by attributing the same to some of the Ancients. "Both Ovid and Chaucer were knowing in astronomy, of which Ovid's book of the *Roman Feasts,* and Chaucer's treatise of the *Astrolabe,* are sufficient witnesses. But Chaucer was likewise an astrologer, as were Virgil, Horace, Persius, and Manilius" (Globe edition of Dryden, p. 497).

l. 35. [**first taught us.** See p. 26, l. 30 fg. c. d. p.]

Page 56, l. 2. **the greatest dramatist,** Shakespeare. Compare with Johnson's judgment here the well-known lines of Milton in *L'Allegro:*

    "Or sweetest Shakespeare, Fancy's child,
    Warble his native wood-notes wild."

Compare also Johnson here, below, p. 63, l. 13.

l. 3. [**conducted** applies to dramatist (l. 2). c. d. p.]

l. 9. **Essay on dramatic poetry,** published in 1668. See page 6, above. The real title of the work is *Essay of Dramatic Poesy.*

Page 57, l. 1. [**laboured** (here used transitively), elaborated, worked upon so as to make perfect. c. d. p.]

l. 12. **The praise lavished by Longinus,** etc. Longinus (died 273 A.D.) was a Greek writer, author of a treatise on the *Sublime,*

L

which has come down to us (unless, indeed, the work we have
be a forgery, as is possible). Johnson is referring to the praise
Longinus lavishes on a particular passage in one of Demosthenes'
orations, in which the orator excited the Athenians to the highest
pitch of military enthusiasm by an invocation addressed to the
dead heroes of Marathon.

l. 14. [**so curious in its limitations**, so carefully limited and
qualified. *Curious* is here used in its original sense of *full of
care*. C. D. P.]

l. 18. [**their emulation of reverence**, their attempts to exceed
Dryden's expressions of veneration for Shakespeare. C. D. P.]

l. 25. [**censor**, critic. The critic might not have been able to
produce a passage so good as the one in which he found a fault.
But, as Johnson says just below, Dryden proved his right to
judge Shakespeare by showing his own power of writing. C. D. P.]

l. 31. **Rymer**. Already mentioned, p. 5, l. 3.

l. 33. **malim**, etc. "I would rather err with Scaliger than
judge rightly with Clavius." The saying is, at least, as old as
Cicero, who makes a character in one of his dialogues say that he
would rather be in the wrong with Plato than in the right with
any one else.

Page 58, l. 17. **con amore**, with love, with a real enjoyment
of the labour for its own sake.

l. 29. [**Palamon and Arcite** ; or, *The Knight's Tale*, one of the
Canterbury Tales of Chaucer. C D. P.]

Novimus, etc. "We know what Dryden said of a certain poem of Chaucer's, a beautiful poem without doubt, and one
worthy of much praise, but which Dryden, forsooth, declared to
be not only written in true epic style, but the equal, if not the
superior, of the *Iliad* or the *Aeneid*. But we know at the same
time that the criticisms of that great man were not always of the
most accurate sort, or in accordance with the severest rules of
the art : in his opinion, that is apt to be best which is at the
moment before him, and on which he is then engaged." Trapp
has been mentioned before, p. 51, l. 17.

Page 59, l. 1. **constant to himself**, consistent with himself.

His defence and desertion of dramatic rhyme. For the defence, see p. 6, l. 10 fg. *Aureng Zebe* was the last of Dryden's
rhyming tragedies. In the Prologue he begins by condemning
himself his play, because it is written in rhyme :

" Our author by experience finds it true,
    'Tis much more hard to please himself than you ;
    And, out of no feigned modesty, this day
    Damns his laborious trifle of a play ;

> Not that it's worse than what before he writ,
> But he has now another taste of wit ;
> And, to confess a truth, though out of time,
> Grows weary of his long-loved mistress, Rhyme."

l. 3. **Spence**, etc. Joseph Spence, Professor of History at Ox- ford, wrote, among other works of a critical kind, an essay on *Pope's Translation of the Odyssey*, to a passage in which Johnson is here referring.

l. 9. **When he has any objection**, etc. The first half of this sentence expands the statement above (p. 58, l. 26) that Dryden's occasional and particular positions were sometimes interested : the second, that they were sometimes negligent.

l. 14. **when he cannot disown**, etc. Mr. Sharp points out that Johnson is probably thinking here of a passage in the preface to Dryden's *An Evening Love* : "It is charged upon me that I make debauched persons (such as, they say, my Astrologer and Gamester are) my protagonists, or the chief persons of the drama ; and that I make them happy in the conclusion of my play, against the law of comedy, which is to reward virtue and punish vice. I answer, first, that I know no such law to have been constantly observed in comedy, either by the ancient or modern poets." If this is the passage referred to it will be seen that Johnson has not accurately reproduced the point. Dryden is not talking of the grossness of his plays, and his statement as to the practice of writers of comedy, so far from being the des- perate sophistry of a dialectician run to earth is, as Dryden has no difficulty in showing, literally true.

l. 19. **Sewell**. ' Preface to Ovid's *Metamorphoses*" (Johnson's note).

l. 21. [**Statius** was a Latin poet of the first century. His chief work was the *Thebais*. C. D. P.]

l. 24. **Quæ**, etc. The first line of the *Sylvæ* of Statius.

l. 27. **condemned him to straw**, said that he was undoubtedly mad. The phrase refers to the layers of straw that were in those days thought beds good enough for lunatics.

l. 29. [**imprest**, forced, pressed. C. D. P.]

l. 30. **He cited Gorbuduc, which he had never seen**. In the Dedication of *The Rival Ladies*, Dryden refers to *The Tragedy of Queen Gorbuduc* as an early example of a rhymed play, though the play he means is written in blank verse, and Gorbuduc is the king in it, not the queen.

l. 31. **gives a false account**, etc. In the Preface to his *Annus Mirabilis* Dryden cites Chapman's translation of Homer as one of several works in English written in verses of six feet, whereas Chapman's metre is one of seven feet.

l. 32. **discovers, in the preface,** etc. "You never cool while you read Homer, even not in the second book (a graceful compliment to his countrymen); but he hastens from the ships, and concludes not that book till he has made you an amends by the violent playing of a new machine." "Machine" here is used in the technical sense of a supernatural intervention in the plot of a poem. Dryden was certainly nodding in this passage, as the catalogue of the ships, which is the chief theme of the second book of the *Iliad*, is continued to the very end of that book, and the third book does not even begin with a "machine" of the kind he had in his mind. But Johnson should have said "without remembering" rather than "without knowing." It would be quite easy to put together a similar list of Johnson's own careless quotations or references.

Page 60, l. 1. [**literature,** learning. See p. 30, l. 26. c. d. p.]

l. 27. **shows what he wanted,** shows what he had not got to give. Compare "to want book-learning" in the sense of "to be without book-learning," next page, l. 19.

l. 29. **unprovided of matter.** We must now say, "unprovided with matter."

l. 32. [**faculty,** scientific profession or study. The term is now more commonly applied to the members of a scientific profession. c. d. p.]

l. 33. [**images,** figures of speech. c. d. p.]

Page 61, l. 3. [**accidental intelligence,** information obtained by accident. c. d. p.]

[**various,** varied, conversation on many subjects and with many persons. c. d. p.]

[**a quick apprehension,** the power of quickly grasping an idea. c. d. p.]

l. 5. [**powerful digestion,** great power of adapting ideas to his needs. c. d. p.]

l. 16. [**desultory,** irregular, inconstant. c. d. p.]

l. 17. [**fortuitous,** dependent upon chance. c. d. p.]

l. 22. [**parts,** abilities. The quotation is from *Threnodia Augustalis*, ll. 337-345, a funeral poem in memory of King Charles II. c. d. p.]

Page 62, ll. 9-11. [Johnson utters the same sentiments on p. 46, ll. 5-10. c. d. p.]

l. 19. **another and the same.** The same, yet not the same. Johnson is translating the Latin phrase "alter et idem."

l. 20. **nor appears to have any art other,** etc. Johnson is referring to the dictum of Horace, that the poet's highest art lies in concealing the fact that he is employing any art.

l. 25. [**discriminative characters**, peculiar features which serve to distinguish his style from that of others. C. D. P.]

l. 27. [**overcharged**, exaggerated. C. D. P.]

l. 33. **forced thoughts.** See the note on p. 2, l. 6.

l. 35. [**Waller and Denham.** See note on p. 2, l. 7. C. D. P.]

Page 63, l. 10. [**scholastic,** polished and accurate. C. D. P.]

[**popular,** colloquial, such as would be used in ordinary conversation and therefore not always accurate. C. D. P.]

l. 11. [**gross,** coarse and vulgar. C. D. P.]

l. 14. **to whom their own original rectitude,** etc. Compare p. 56, l. 2.

l. 21. **terms appropriated to particular arts,** technical terms.

l. 23. **defeat the purpose of a poet.** Johnson returns to this subject below at p. 74, l. 24.

. **Page 64,** l. 5. [**affluence,** wealth of words. C. D. P.]

[**comprehension,** comprehensiveness, that is, the vast number of ideas which can be expressed by the language. C. D. P.]

l. 8. **Ben Jonson thought it necessary,** etc. With the passage which follows compare that at pp. 30, 31, where the same theme is treated.

l. 9. [**to copy Horace word by word,** to translate each word separately instead of taking phrases and sentences as wholes. C. D. P.]

l. 10. [**Feltham** "was the author of a book very popular in its day—*Resolves: Divine, Political, and Moral*" (M. Arnold). C. D. P.]

l. 12. [**Sandys** (1577-1643) is known chiefly by the translation here referred to. C. D. P.]

l. 13. [**versifier,** translator. C. D. P.]

l. 15. [**verses,** lines of verse. C. D. P.]

[**Holyday** (1593-1661), chaplain to Charles I., a learned man, left a translation of *Juvenal and Persius* into poor verse with many learned illustrative notes. See p. 86, l. 32 fg. C. D. P.]

l. 22. [**left his authors,** ceased to give a literal translation, and introduced ideas of his own. C. D. P.]

l. 24. [**poetical liberty,** the extent to which a poetical translation might deviate from a literal rendering of the original. C. D. P.]

l. 30. [**divaricate** (a word now obsolete), diverge; literally, step in different directions (Lat. *varicare*, to spread the legs apart). C. D. P.]

l. 31. [**correspondence,** similarity of idiom. C. D. P.]

l. 33. [**paraphrase** is a rendering which preserves the meaning without respect to the words or idioms employed ; *metaphrase* is a rendering which preserves the order and nature of the words and idioms.   c. D. P.]

Page 65, l. 7. [**A translator is to be like his author,** the language used by the translator is to resemble that used by the author whose work is translated.   c. D. P.]

l. 11. **Sir Edward Sherburne,** author of *A Translation of the Dramas of Seneca,* to which he prefixed a *Brief Discourse concerning Translation.* The passage in Horace referred to is in that writer's *Ars Poetica*:

> "Nec verbo verbum curabis reddere fidus
> Interpres "

("Nor will you be anxious only to give word for word as a faithful interpreter").

l. 18. [**reason wants,** etc., if the arguments put forward by Sir E. Sherburne are reasonable, there is no need to support them by quoting Horace.   c. D. P.]

l. 22. [**exigencies,** conditions of poverty. See pp. 52-54. c. D. P.]

l. 36. [That which might have been is not known, that which exists can be seen.   c. D. P.]

Page 66, l. 4. [**occasional,** produced by the requirements of some special occasion.   c. D. P.]

l. 8. **arbitrary.** Chosen freely by himself.

l. 14. [**ardent,** hasty, produced in the *heat* of the moment. c. D. P.]

l. 18. [**The occasional poet,** the poet who writes only as required by occasion. See l. 4, above.   c. D. P.]

l. 34. **attended.** Waited for.

Page 67, l. 15. [**Davenant** (1605-1668) succeeded Ben Jonson as court poet, and shared exile with the Stuarts. After the Commonwealth he was poet-laureate. His *Gondibert,* a heroic poem, was written about 1649.   c. D. P.]

l. 18. [**versification,** style in which his lines were written. c. D. P.]

l. 19. [**Donne** (1573-1631), a poet who delighted men of fashion, but his style was unreal, and sacrificed sense to ingenuity. c. D. P.]

l. 20. **the ambition of forced conceits.** See the note on p. 2, l. 6.

l. 21. [**forced conceits,** unnatural ideas. A conceit is a *conception* of the mind.   c. D. P.]

l. 23. **He, toss'd by Fate.** This is the beginning, not the end of a line, in the original.

" He, toss'd by Fate, and hurried up and down,
Heir to his father's sorrows with his crown,
Could taste," etc.

The conceit here is not perhaps very forced. Religion teaches that man's life is a pilgrimage, a hard and toilsome journey from the first day to the last. The truth is hidden, as a rule, from the young man, who finds all around him pleasant ("youth's desired age ") ; but his early trials revealed it to Charles.

l. 28. **Well might the ancient poets,** etc. The conceit this time is so forced that no one has been able to say with certainty what Dryden meant. " Euphrone, a Greek name for night, is probably meant. It may be translated ' well-minded ' or ' well-judging ' " (Christie). " Christie supposes the reference to be to the word euphrone, which, however, means rather ' kind ' than counsellor.' That ' night brings counsel ' is a well-nigh universal sentiment " (Saintsbury). The saying is, of course, common enough, but it has nothing to do with the teaching of adversity. It refers to the opportunity for quiet deliberation which night affords. Saintsbury's interpretation is, therefore, to be rejected, but it is not certain that Christie's is right.

l. 35. **'Twas Monk,** etc. The whole passage is a glorification of the skill with which Monk prepared and waited for the right moment in which to attempt the restoration of Charles II. It was his task (p. 68, l. 11 fg.) to be to the body politic what the brain, nerves, and muscles are for the body natural. The muscles and the nerves convey through their "viewless conduits " the spirits, which, rising in the brain, set the body in motion. Monk had to be both brain and conduit in the task of rousing the English nation to call back its king.

Page 68, l. 1. **The blessed saints,** etc., a biblical idea. The author of the Epistle to the Hebrews, after a long enumeration of saints of old time who had " died in faith," goes on, " Wherefore seeing we also are compassed about with so great a cloud of witnesses ... let us run with patience the race that is set before us " (*Hebrews* xii. 1).

l. 3. **To see small clues,** etc. Clues are threads, and pencils are paint brushes. In themselves they are small things, but, rightly applied, they can produce great effects.

l. 7. **With ease,** etc. Others had dreamt of a restoration of the king, but their dreams could no more be made to take the shape of action than can the false gold, which alchemists make, survive the trial of the mint.

l. 11. **How hard,** etc. See note above on the first line of this passage. Christie has the merit of having removed a mark of

punctuation after " see " which made nonsense of the passage.
"At once" means 'at one and the same time' (brain and
conduit).

l. 19. **Strook.** Gave the line a jerk with the view of fixing the
hook fast in the fish.

l. 21. [**labours,** works upon. See p. 57, l. 1. c. d. p.]

l. 23. [**leeches,** doctors. c. d. p.]

l. 24. [While increasing pains show that the disease is not
fully developed. c. d. p.]

l. 25. [**they wait upon the ill,** they watch the progress of the
disease. c. d. p.]

l. 28. **the improper use of mythology.** Johnson had a strong
objection to any collocation of Christian and non-Christian ideas
that might seem to suggest that the two stood in any way on
the same plane. Compare the passage at p. 51, l. 18. "Trapp's
anger arises from his zeal, not for the author, but the priest ; as
if any reproach of the follies of paganism could be extended to
the preachers of truth." Notice, also, how in the present
passage, l. 34, the word "religion" is used, in the exclusive sense,
of "the Christian religion," and is opposed to "mythology."
His complaint against Dryden is, therefore, that the poet in this
passage passes from mythology to religion without any hint of
the gulf that separates the two. The meaning is obscured by
the way in which Johnson printed the passage. From "After
having rewarded " down to "Sacred history" is one sentence,
and should be printed as such.

l. 30. **With Alga,** etc. Scott has the note, " The ceremonies of
classical antiquity, observed by those who escaped from ship-
wreck, are here detailed. The *alga*, or seaweed, sprinkled on
the altar, alluded to the cause of their sacrifice. Portunus,
otherwise called Portumnus, was a sea god of some reputation.
The Greeks called him Palæmon, which was formerly his earthly
name. He is mentioned by Virgil :

> ' Et Pater ipse, manu magna, Portunus euntem
> Impulit.' "

l. 34. **in the language of religion.** In the quotation which
follows, "Heaven itself is took by violence," is taken from a
text of Scripture, "The kingdom of heaven suffereth violence,
and the violent take it by storm " (*Matthew* xii. 12). Compare
the passage quoted at p. 84 below from Dryden's *Lament for
King Charles* (*Threnodia Augustalis*), where there is the same
jumbling of Christian and Pagan ideas which Johnson is condemning here.

l. 37. **one of the most awful passages of Sacred History.**
Johnson's objection is to any intermingling in one and the same

poem of sacred and pagan ideas. The fact, therefore, that he leaps here from line 144 of the poem to line 262 ought not to have proved the stumbling-block it has. There is not anything in the interval which could possibly have been described by Johnson as mention made of one of the most awful passages of Sacred History. At line 262 the clemency shown by Charles is compared by the poet to the mercy shown by God to the Israelites.

> " Thus, when the Almighty would to Moses give
> A sight of all he could behold and live ;
> A voice before his entry did proclaim
> Long-suffering, goodness, mercy in His name."

The original of this is one of the most sublime passages in the Bible. See *Exodus* xxxiii. 18, and following verses.

Ryland thinks Johnson is referring to the words "heaven's prefixed hour not come," two lines below, but that is a mere isolated phrase, though it is used, as Sharp points out, in a very solemn context having reference to the death of Christ. The reference to *John* ii. 4, which Ryland (perhaps by a slip) gives, is certainly wrong.

Page 69, l. 4. **And, glass-like, clearness mix'd with frailty bore.** The commas before and after "glass-like," which are found in some editions, were inserted by Scott. They do not appear to be wanted. The construction is, "and bore glass-like clearness with glass-like frailty," that is, "facility for re-producing what appeared before us, combined with liability to weakness." Christie compares

> " *Angelo.* 　　　　　　　　　 Nay, women are frail too.
> *Isabel.* Ay, as the glasses where they view themselves,
> Which are as easy broke as they make forms."

l. 17. **Malherbe,** a French poet and critic (1555-1628).

l. 27. [**synod,** council which consulted on religious affairs. C.D.P.]

l. 30. **there is not another.** " Dr. Johnson hastily expressed his belief that this is the only instance in Dryden's poems of such a rhyme, which was common with his predecessors and early contemporaries. Another example occurs in his earliest poem, the *Elegy on Lord Hastings* :

> ' No comet need foretell his change drew on,
> Whose corps might seem a constellation.'

The following instance is from the second part of the *Conquest of Granada*, Act IV., Sc. iii. :

> ' This with the dawn of morning shall be done :
> You haste to make her execution.' "
> 　　　　　　　　　　 Christie's note on this passage.

l. 32. [**fruition** is to be uttered as a word of four syllables, fru-i-ti-on, the last syllable rhyming with *lone* in *alone*.   C. D. P.]

Page 70, l. 6. [**bounds our eye,** interrupts the view.   C. D. P.]

l. 10. [**Our sight is limited,** our view terminates.   C. D. P.]

l. 13. [**orbs,** globes, or spheres, symbolical of the extent of their power.   One globe is supposed to be placed within the other, and to exactly fill the internal space.   C. D. P.]

Page 71, l. 17. [**unsociable matter,** ideas which ought not to be, or which cannot readily be, associated with one another.   The word is now usually applied to persons, and *dissociable*, or *discordant*, would be used.   C. D. P.]

l. 30. [**quatrain,** a stanza of four lines rhyming alternately. C.D.P.]

l. 32. **he complains of its difficulty.**   See in passage at p. 6, l. 1, and the note there.

Page 72, l. 7. **transferred the invention of fire-arms,** etc. *Paradise Lost,* Bk. vi., l. 568 fg.

l. 12. [**incidental disquisition,** turning aside from the subject in hand to enlarge upon some topic or event only incidentally mentioned.   For example, stanzas 155 to 164 form a digression on shipping and navigation, which is followed by an apostrophe to the Royal Society.   C. D. P.]

l. 14. **The general fault is,** etc.   Scott has pointed out that the metre of the poem proved a continual snare to Dryden as regards the point to which Johnson is referring.   "This structure of verse has often laid him under an odd and rather unpleasing necessity, of filling up his stanza, by coupling a simile, or a moral, expressed in the last two lines, along with the fact which had been announced in the two first.   When these comments, or illustrations, however good in themselves, appear to be intruded upon the narrative or description, and not naturally to flow out of either, they must be considered as defects in composition ; and a kind of versification, which compels frequent recurrence to such expedients for filling up the measure, has a disadvantage for which mere harmony can hardly compensate."

l. 21. "**Orbem jam totum,**" a poem attributed to the Latin poet Petronius Arbiter.   [One of the chosen companions of the Emperor Nero, and director-in-chief of the imperial pleasures, hence his title *Elegantiae Arbiter*.   Matthew Arnold, however, suggests that the poem is the *Pharsalia* of Lucan, a Latin poet of the first century A.D.   C. D. P.]

l. 26. **Proteus,** a sea god to whom Neptune confided the care of his scaly flock, the fishes.   He is mentioned in Wordsworth's sonnet, *The World is too much with us,*

" Have sight of Proteus rising from the sea,
     Or hear old Triton blow his wreathed horn."

l. 28. **It would not be hard,** etc. It is not easy to follow Johnson here. Modern taste certainly sees no such difference, either between the two couplets of this verse or between this verse as a whole and the verse which follows it, as appears self-obvious to him. Of the two verses, indeed, most modern critics would prefer the first. It ought to be noted, as Dryden himself points out, that in the two lines about Proteus the poet is quoting Virgil, *Georg.* iv. 387-8.

l. 36. **For tapers made two glaring comets rise.** "A comet was seen on the 14th of December, 1664, which lasted almost three months; and another, the 6th of April, 1665, which was visible fourteen days. Appendix to Sherburn's *Translation of Manilius,* p. 241" (Scott).

Page 73, l. 1. the attempt at Bergen. Bergen is a seaport of Norway. Two Dutch fleets coming, the one from the Levant, the other from the East Indies, afraid to risk the passage through the English Channel, had attempted to reach Holland unmolested ·by the route round the north of Scotland. Finding that also barred, they put in for safety at Bergen. The attempt of the English, under the Earl of Sandwich, to cut them out was a disastrous failure, the real character of which is very faintly concealed in Dryden's reference to the affair.

l. 5. **And precious sand from southern climates brought.** Dryden himself notes that by "southern climates" he means Guinea, and Scott adds that "the war began by mutual aggression on the coast of Guinea." The precious sand is sand with gold in it.

l. 7. **conscious of their store.** The castor, or beaver, was believed to be aware of the reason why he was hunted, and to be capable on occasion of mutilating himself, that the hunter might take what he wanted and leave off pursuit. The ships here, of course, are compared to castors not yet reduced to that last extremity but still seeking to find safety in flight.

l. 18. **Besiege the Indies, and all Denmark dare.** The Indies were there in the shape of the ships with their costly Indian cargoes. Bergen belonged to the King of Denmark, and the attempt to violate the neutrality of the port was an invasion of his rights. The story at the time was that the King of Denmark had consented to the enterprise, but had, whether by accident or by design, failed to notify his purpose to the governor of the place.

l. 19. [**These,** the latter, *i.e.* the enemy. C. D. P.]

[**those,** the former, *i.e.* the English. C. D. P.]

l. 22. [**hazard to destroy,** run the risk of destroying.]

l. 25. [**shatter'd porcelain:** part of the cargo from the East; por-

celain was imported from China before the process of manufacture
was discovered in England.   c. d. p.]

l. 27. [by tempests, etc., the battle was stopped by a storm
which prevented the English from capturing the enemy's fleet.
c. d. p.]

Page 74, l. 5. The account of the different sensations, etc.
The passage which follows is part of the account of the three
days' fight in the Downs between the English under the Duke of
Albemarle (the "great leader" referred to in the second verse)
and Prince Rupert, and the Dutch under De Ruyter.   The
English fleet had separated, Prince Rupert having received
instructions to go off in search of the French fleet, and Albemarle (Monk) and his detachment had to bear the brunt of the
first day's fighting.

l. 11. [doubtful moonlight, the indistinctness of objects when
seen by moonlight.   c. d. p.]

l. 24. appropriated terms of art.   What are commonly called
"technical terms."

l. 27. not liberal, mechanical, such as, in the present case,
shipbuilding.

Page 75, l. 2. in the dock, when describing the process of
refitting the injured ships.

l. 10. And shake them from the rising beak in drops.   The ship
plunges headlong into the sea.   If the seams had not been
properly stopped, as described, the waves would find entrance.
As it is, when the beak rises out of the water the waves are seen
to be falling back from the seams in drops.   Saintsbury prints
"shakes," and says that Christie prints "shake" without
authority.   He adds that "the singular is barely possible
(taking the previous line as parenthetical), and would express
the result of the stopping."   I find this more unintelligible than
Dryden.

l. 11. Some the gall'd ropes, etc.   "Marline, a piece of
untwisted rope, dipped in pitch, and wrapped round a cable to
guard it" (Scott).   "Searcloth" in the next line is a verb.   Sir
Thomas Browne has "cereclothed" (searclothed) in the sense of
wrapped in cerecloths.   Tarpauling is pitched canvas.

l. 19. [Royal Society, founded in 1663 as the "Royal Society of
London for promoting Natural Knowledge."   c. d. p.]

l. 20. seasonable excursion and artful return, that is, from and
to his subject proper.

[seasonable excursion, appropriate and well-timed departure
from the subject in hand.   c. d.-p.]

l. 22. One line, however, leaves me discontented, etc.   It is
perhaps fair to remark that Johnson is a little inconsistent here.

If Dryden had done what Johnson wishes he had done, and "laboured science into poetry by explaining longitude," he would again have committed the fault for which Johnson has just blamed him. For "measure of longitudes" Dryden wrote in the first edition "knowledge of longitudes." Improved methods of finding the longitude from time to time during the ship's voyage are what is meant. Notice that "commerce" has the accent here on the second syllable.

l. 32. **a mind better formed to reason than to feel.** Johnson returns to this thought below, p. 91, l. 9 fg.

Page 76, l. 13. **is taken from Seneca.** This is not quite accurate. In the passage which Johnson has in his mind the elder Seneca records a tradition to the effect that Ovid was in the habit of saying that the line of Varro (not Virgil)—

" Omnia noctis erant placida composta quiete "—

would have been much improved if the last three words had been omitted. Dryden, doubtless, took the hint for his phrase from the passage in Seneca.

l. 19. **The ghosts of traitors,** etc. "This most beautiful stanza requires but little illustration. London Bridge, as early as Shakespeare's time, was a place allotted for affixing the heads of persons executed for treason. Thus Catesby to Hastings :

' The princes both make high account of you,
For they account his head upon the bridge.'

The skulls of the regicides of the Fifth Monarchy insurgents, of Philips, Gibb, Tongue, and other fanatics executed for a conspiracy in 1662, were placed on the Bridge, Tower Hill, Temple Barr, and other conspicuous places of elevation ; that of the famous Hugh Peters, in particular, was placed upon the Bridge. The 'Sabbath notes,' imputed to this assembly of fanatic spectres, are the infernal hymns chanted at the witches' Sabbath—a meeting concerning which antiquity told and believed many strange things " (Scott).

l. 24. [**event,** fulfilment (L. *eventus*, result). C. D. P.]

l. 26. **The poem concludes with a simile that might have better been omitted.** The verse is as follows :

" Thus to the eastern wealth through storms we go,
But now, the Cape once doubled, fear no more ;
A constant trade wind will securely blow,
And gently lay us on the spicy shore."

This prediction was as unfortunate in the event as the other was the reverse. In the very next year the Dutch, by the surprise of Chatham, inflicted the greatest humiliation of the war on

England. Johnson's language is ambiguous, but the context would seem to indicate that he is objecting to the verse, not as a simile, but as a prophecy.

Page 77, l. 2. **Harte.** "Walter Harte (1707-74), of St. Mary's Hall, Oxford, had been tutor to Lord Chesterfield's natural son, Philip Stanhope, to whom the famous letters were written" (Croker's note on Boswell, p. 215). Harte, who was one of Johnson's friends, was Canon of Windsor, and author of a *History of Gustavus Adolphus*.

l. 11. **independent on**, not dependent on. We must now say 'independent of.'

l. 13. **the description of Night.** See note on p. 5, l. 3.

l. 14. **the rise and fall of empire.** The reference is to the opening lines of the second part of the *Conquest of Granada*:

" At length the time is come, when Spain shall be
From the long yoke of Moorish tyrants free.
All causes seem to second our design,
And heaven and earth in their destruction join. '
When empire in its childhood first appears,
A watchful fate o'ersees its tender years ;
Till, grown more strong, it thrusts and stretches out,
And elbows all the kingdoms round about :
The place thus made for its first breathing free,
It moves again for ease and luxury ;
Till, swelling by degree, it has possessed
The greater space, and now crowds up the rest ;
When, from behind, there starts some petty state,
And pushes on its now unwieldy fate ;
Then down the precipice of time it goes,
And sinks in minutes, which in ages rose."

l. 22. [**promulgated the laws.** See p. 30, l. 31 fg. c. d. p.]

l. 26. **Absalom and Achitophel.** See p. 31, and the notes there.

l. 27. [**particular**, detailed, criticism of the parts of the poem. c. d. p.]

Page 78, l. 12. [**action ... power**, it was not within the poet's power to invent the scenes depicted, nor to select his own climax, because history had already decided both. c. d. p.]

l. 19. **the king makes a speech**, etc. Johnson omits to notice that Dryden, who was probably quite conscious himself of the disproportion between the king's speech and the effects attributed to it, has recourse to supernatural agency. The whole passage runs :

" He said : the Almighty, nodding, gave consent,
And peals of thunder shook the firmament.

Henceforth a series of new times began,
The mighty years in long procession ran ;
Once more the god-like David was restored,
And willing nations knew their lawful lord."

l. 26. **there is a long insertion**, that is, a long passage contributed by Dryden to Tate's work.

l. 33. [**discovers**, shows. C. D. P.]

Page 79, l. 5. a man. Sir Anthony Ashley Cooper, afterwards Lord Shaftesbury, had been a member of the Council of State after the dissolution of Barebone's Parliament in 1653. In the beginning of the Civil War he had supported Charles I. c. D. P.]

[**propensions**, propensities, natural inclinations. C. D. P.]

l. 17. [**his fanatic years**, the time during which he supported Cromwell. C. D. P.]

l. 18. [**gears**, dress. He was so accustomed to deceive that he was uneasy when playing the part of an honest man. C. D. P.]

l. 21, [**first bias**, early inclination to evil. C. D. P.]

Page 80, l. 2. nor was he serious enough to keep heathen fables out of his religion. See note on p. 68, l. 28.

l. 10. [**the giant's war.** The Titans, sons of Uranus (Heaven) and Ge (Earth), having been expelled from heaven, fought against their father and deposed him, establishing Cronus (Saturn) in his place. C. D. P.]

l. 12. [**like Hezekiah's.** See 2 *Kings* xx. 6. C. D. P.]

l. 18. [**Mrs.** (or, as we should now say, Miss) **Killigrew** was maid of honour to the Duchess of York, and died of small-pox in 1685, in the twenty-fifth year of her age. C. D. P.]

l. 21. **Fervet immensusque ruit.** Horace's description of Pindar's style.

l. 28. **the word diapason is too technical.** See the passage at p. 74, l. 24 fg.

Page 81, l. 7. [According to the Pythagorean system, the world is a piece of harmony, and man is the full chord, the whole octave. The word *diapason* means "through all," and man is supposed to touch Deity, pass through all the planets, and touch earth. C. D. P.]

l. 9. [**it can owe little to poetry**, poetry can do little to add to its awfulness. C. D. P.]

l. 22. [**Eleonora**, Countess of Abingdon, died May 31, 1691, in her thirty-third year. C. D. P.]

ll. 27-30. [These lines are descriptive of a Roman general's triumph. C. D. P.]

l. 30. [**his pomp to crowd**, to crowd all the magnificence of the procession into one day. C. D. P.]

Page 83, l. 13. The scheme of the work is injudicious, etc.
See this objection already stated at p. 36, l. 10 fg. In what
follows Johnson is referring to a passage at the beginning of the
Second Part of the poem. The Panther has asked where "that
wondrous wight, Infallibility," is lodged :

> " First seat him somewhere, and derive his race,
>   Or else conclude that nothing has no place ";

to which the Hind rejoins :

> " Suppose though I disown it, said the Hind,
>   The certain mansion were not yet assigned ;
>   The doubtful residence no proof can bring
>   Against the plain existence of the thing.
>   Because philosophers may disagree,
>   If sight by emission, or reception be,
>   Shall it be thence inferred, I do not see ?
>   But you require an answer positive,
>   Which yet, when I demand, you dare not give,
>   For fallacies in universals live.
>   I then affirm that this unfailing guide.
>   In Pope and General Councils must reside ;
>   Both lawful, both combined," etc.

l. 22. is afraid to drink at the common brook.

> " Among the rest the Hind, with fearful face,
>   Beheld from far the common watering-place,
>   Nor durst approach, till with an awful roar
>   The sovereign Lion bade her fear no more."

The "Lion" being the King.

l. 26. the City Mouse and Country Mouse. See p. 36, l. 11 fg.

l. 33. bribed by the subject, since Pope was a Catholic.
[*Bribed* is here used in the sense of *biassed* or *prejudiced.* C. D. P.]

Page 84, l. 16. [the pause, the stop in the middle of each line,
except the fifth. C. D. P.]

l. 24. More haughty than the rest, etc. "The personal
appearance of the Presbyterian clergy was suited by an
affectation of extreme plainness and rigour of appearance. A
Geneva cloak and band, with the hair close cropped, and covered
with a sort of black skull-cap, was the discriminating attire of
their teachers. This last article of dress occasioned an unseemly
projection of their ears, and procured those who affected it the
nickname of prick-eared fanatics, and the still better known
appellation of Roundheads " ... (Scott). "Predestinating ears "
are ears that showed, by the peculiarity Scott has described,
that the wearer was one of those who accepted Calvin's doctrine
of predestination.

l. 25. [This line refers to the Puritan objection to feasting and merriment. C. D. P.]

l. 34. **stand like Adam naming every beast.** "And out of the ground the Lord God formed every beast of the field, and every fowl of the air; and brought them unto Adam to see what he would call them: and whatsoever Adam called every living creature, that was the name thereof. And Adam gave names to all cattle, and to the fowl of the air, and to every beast of the field " (*Genesis* ii. 19).

Page 85, l. 1. **Who, far from steeples,** etc. "The dregs of the fanaticism of the last age fermented during that of Charles II. into various sects of sullen enthusiasts, who distinguished themselves by the different names of Brownists, Families of Love, etc., etc. In many cases they rejected all the usual aids of devotion, and, holding their meetings in the open air and in solitary spots, nursed their fanaticism by separating themselves from the more rational part of mankind. Dryden has elsewhere described them with equal severity :

' A numerous host of dreaming saints succeed,
Of the true old enthusiastic breed ;
'Gainst form and order they their powers employ,
Nothing to build, and all things to destroy.'

In Scotland, large conventicles were held in the mountains and morasses by the fiercest of the Covenanters, whom persecution had driven frantic. These men, known now by the name of Cameronians, considered popery and prelacy as synonymous terms, and even stigmatised as Erastians and self-seekers the more moderate Presbyterians whe were contented to exercise their religion as tolerated by the Government " (Scott).

l. 7. **Souls that can scarce ferment their mass of clay.** Compare Dryden's description of the Dutch sailors as

"Vast bulks, which little souls but ill supply "

(p. 74, l. 19).

l. 8. **so divisible are they,** divisible, and therefore material. Spirit is indivisible.

l. 9. [allay, alloy. C. D. P.]

l. 10. **Such souls as shards produce.** "Shard here means excrement or dung, and it probably has the same meaning where Shakespeare speaks of 'the shard-born beetle' (*Macbeth*, Act III. Sc. ii.) ..." (Christie). So "slimy-born and sun-begotten tribe" (p. 84, l. 36).

l. 22. **to wait her,** to wait on her, attend her, accompany her. Compare the term 'waiter' for a servant who attends on you at meals.

l. 25. [motion, proposal. C. D. P.]

M

Page 86, l. 6. [constitutional absurdity, absurdity in the con-
stitution (construction) of the poem.   c. d. p.]

l. 18. [impropriety, inappropriateness, unsuitability.   c. d. p.]

l. 22. [ratiocination, process of reasoning from cause to effect.
c. d. p.]

l. 24. poem on the Birth of the Prince of Wales.   See p. 37,
l. 27 fg.

Page 87, l. 25. his version, etc.   *The Pollio* is a name given
to one of Virgil's *Eclogues*; the episodes mentioned are in the
same poet's *Aeneid.*

Page 88, l. 11. [arguments, summaries of the subject-matter.
c. d. p.]

l. 18. Milbourne, a clergyman, attacked it.   See p. 40,
l. 21 fg.

l. 24. and sometimes licentious.   Licentious here means free,
not sticking closely enough to the original.   See also p. 77,
l. 35, "some lines are inelegant or improper, and too many are
irreligiously licentious."   The word is used in what is now its
most common meaning of lewd, impure, at p. 47, l. 33.

l. 30. [Trapp (1679-1747), an eminent divine.   He translated
the *Aeneid* into blank verse (blank version, l. 32).   See pp. 51, 58.
c. d. p.]

l. 36. the clandestine refuge of school-boys.   A 'crib,' as the
school-boys call it, a translation which they use in secret.

Page 89, l. 6. [by opposing, etc., by setting lines of one
version side by side with those of another for the purpose of
comparison.   c. d. p.]

l. 14. [The improvement in the parts may injure the whole.
c. d. p.]

l. 24. [this predomination, this power of enchaining the attention of the reader.   Dryden should be judged by the extent
("his proportion ") to which he can command the reader's attention.   c. d. p.]

l. 26. [Ariosto (1474-1533), an Italian poet, is chiefly known by
his *Orlando Furioso*, a life work, published in sections at various
periods during his life and after his death.   The poem was
written with the greatest care, in an easy and graceful style.
c. d. p.]

Page 90, l. 13. [still, always.   c. d. p.]

l. 21. [The Ode for St. Cecilia's Day, published in 1697, and
usually known as *Alexander's Feast.*   Dryden wrote a previous
Ode for St. Cecilia's Day in 1687.   See p. 80.   c. d. p.]

l. 30. [does not want, etc., is not lacking in lines which betray
negligence.   c. d. p.]

1. 35. **The conclusion is vicious**, etc.   The lines are :

   " Let old Timotheus yield the prize,
     Or both divide the crown ;
   He raised a mortal to the skies,
     She drew an angel down."

Page 91, 1. 2. [**the crown**, etc.   Johnson thinks the merit of the real effect produced by the Christian saint is greater than the fanciful effect produced by the heathen musician, hence it is not reasonable for Dryden to suggest that they should share the crown between them.   C. D. P.]

Page 92, 1. 3. [Otway (1651-1685) wrote tragedies and comedies. He appealed to the higher feelings of his audience, and *The Orphan* was very popular as a touching picture of innocence and beauty in distress.   The truth of nature in this play drew natural tears from many who found only artificial excitement in the heroic plays of the time.   C. D. P.]

1. 14. [**images**, illustrations which arouse the imagination. C. D. P.]

1. 17. [**ratiocination**.   See p. 86, 1. 22.   C. D. P.]

1. 19. [**contingence**, accidental circumstances.   C. D. P.]

1. 25. **verbaque provisam rem**, the half of a quotation from Horace.   The words which follow are a free translation.

1. 35. [**a plagiary**, one who steals the literary work of another. C. D. P.]

Page 93, 11. 8, 9. [See criticism by Settle, p. 18.   C. D. P.]

1. 20. **These lines have no meaning**, etc.   Scott says that Dryden in this verse is unintelligible, because he had conceived an idea approaching to nonsense, while the words themselves are both poetical and expressive.   Christie quotes Johnson on the verse, and says that it is difficult to perceive the resemblance to sense in it.

1. 34. [**Capaneus**, one of the seven heroes who marched against Thebes.   Jupiter struck him with lightning because he dared to scale the walls of Thebes in defiance of the god's command.   See note on p. 13, 1. 33.   C. D. P.]

Page 94, 1. 15. **though it may not perhaps be quiet clear in prose.**   "I cannot see why Johnson has thought there was any want of clearness in this passage even in prose.   Addison has given us almost the very same thought in very good prose : ' If we look forward to Him (the Deity) for help, we shall never be in danger of falling down those precipices which our imagination is apt to create.   Like those who walk upon a line, if we keep our eye fixed upon one point we may step forward securely ; whereas an imprudent or cowardly glance on either side will infallibly destroy us' " (Note by "J. B." in Murphy's edition of *Johnson's Works*).

l. 27. [just. In the first, the reference to "young diamonds" is contrary to nature; in the second, the genius (guardian spirit) of the castle is confused with the castle itself, and said to "bow its towery forehead. c. d. p.]

Page 95, l. 10. connects religion and fable too closely. This charge is brought here against Dryden for the third time in the *Life*. See the note on p. 68, l. 28.

l. 15. "When virtue spooms before a prosperous gale,
    My heaving wishes help to fill the sail."
                        Hind and Panther, Part III., 96.

l. 19. **He had heard of reversing**, etc. Johnson has mistaken the construction. "Revers'd" is an absolute construction, and means 'when Nature's optics had been revers'd.' All this criticism is petty.

l. 24. **A hollow crystal pyramid**, etc. "The love of conceit and point, that inveterate though decaying disease of the literature of the time, has not failed to infect the *Annus Mirabilis*. That monstrous verse, in which the extinction of the fire is described, cannot be too often quoted, both to expose the meanness of the image, and the confusion of the metaphor ; for it will be noticed, that the extinguisher, so unhappily conceived, is not even employed in its own mean office. The flames of London are first a tallow candle; and secondly hawks, which, while pouncing on their quarry, are hooded with an extinguisher" (Scott).

Page 97, l. 14. Of Triplets and Alexandrines, etc. A Triplet is a combination of three lines with the same rhyme in place of the couplet that is the rule in the heroic stanza. An Alexandrine is a line of twelve, instead of the usual ten syllables. There is an example of both in the passage quoted above, p. 94, l. 22.

" True, 'tis a narrow way that leads to bliss,
    But right before there is no precipice ;
    Fear makes men look aside, and so their footing miss."

l. 24. [**was the last.** This *Iliad* was published in 1598. c. d. p.]

Page 98, l. 8. Cowley was the first that inserted the Alexandrine at pleasure, etc. "This is an error. The Alexandrine inserted among heroic lines of the syllables is found in many of the writers of Queen Elizabeth's reign" (Murphy).

l. 13. [**wrote some lines**, the last three lines of *A Description of a City Shower* written in 1710, and first published in the *Tatler*. c. d. p.]

l. 31. **the braces of the margins**. The brackets, as we now call them, put at the side to show that three lines have a common rhyme. The use of these brackets has been almost entirely given up in modern printing.

l. 35. [casualty, accidental changes of metre. A science is governed by fixed laws, and therefore does not admit of casualty or chance. C. D. P.]

Page 99, l. 7. [grateful, pleasing. C. D. P.]

l. 8. **Fenton.** Elijah ·Fenton, a poet clean forgotten now, but in his own day of some reputation. He translated four books of the *Odyssey* for Pope.

l. 14. **a weak or grave syllable.** An unaccented syllable.

l. 15. **Together o'er the Alps,** etc. A couplet of Pope's. Johnson, as was common with him, quotes without taking the trouble to see if his memory has served him well. Pope wrote " fir'd " not " fill'd." So in the quotation immediately following Johnson puts " that " where Dryden wrote " who."

Page 100, l. 2. **Davies.** Sir John Davies (1569-1626) was the author of a philosophical poem, *Nosce Teipsum* (Know Thyself).

l. 5. **What was said of Rome,** etc. It was the Emperor Augustus himself, according to Suetonius, who described in this way the improvements he had wrought in Rome.

l. 13. **that no particle of Dryden may be lost.** This is hardly an adequate reason for inserting these observations in a life of Dryden. They are as much out of place there as the long quotation from Milbourne's version of Virgil. Johnson was weary of his task, and was glad to insert anything.

l. 18. [**the tendre,** the affections, the *tender* passion. C. D. P.]

Page 102, l. 11. [**not quoad,** etc., not on account of its superior merit, but as being the primary basis on which to construct the play. C. D. P.]

Page 106, l. 17. [**event,** result. C. D. P.]

Page 108, l. 20. **the Library at Lambeth.** Lambeth Palace, in London, is the official residence of the Archbishop of Canterbury. Dr. Vyse was the librarian there in Dr. Johnson's time.

l. 28. **A.S.S.** That is, *ad Sacram Sedem*, at the Holy See, the Court of the Pope.

l. 31. **our style.** Compare "your style," p. 109, l. 1. When Dryden wrote, England had not yet adopted the Gregorian reformation of the calendar. In all intercommunication, therefore, it was necessary to say whether the date given was according to the English style ("our style") or the style of the greater part of Catholic Europe.

Page 109, l. 14. **he has missed of his design in the Dedication,** etc. Tonson, the publisher, was extremely anxious that Dryden should dedicate his translation of Virgil to King William III.,

which, however, Dryden sturdily refused to do.   In the hope
that Dryden would relent at the last, Tonson had given Aeneas
throughout the pictures in the book the " hooked nose " of King
William.   The story became public, and Cunningham quotes
from the Harleian MSS. an epigram with the heading, "'To be
published in the next edition of Dryden's Virgil."

> " Old Jacob, by deep judgment sway'd,
>   To please the wise beholders,
> Has placed old Nassau's hook-nosed head
>   On poor Aeneas' shoulders.
> To make the parallel hold tack,
>   Methinks there's little lacking ;
> One took his father pick-a-pack,
>   And t'other sent his packing."

l. 22. [St. Cecilia's Feast fell on Nov. 22, 1697.   This song
was *Alexander's Feast*.   See note on p. 90, l. 21.   c. d. p.]

l. 29. **I remember the counsel, etc.**   His sons would appear to
have asked him to write with more charity of the priesthood.
See note on p. 51, l. 12.

Page 110, l. 2. **Charles will begin to recover his perfect health,**
etc.   See the note on p. 55, l. 12.

l. 9. **the profits might have been more.**   If he had dedicated it
to the King may be what is meant.

INDEX.

GLASGOW : PRINTED AT THE UNIVERSITY PRESS BY ROBERT MACLEHOSE AND CO.

MACMILLAN'S
ENGLISH CLASSICS:

A SERIES OF SELECTIONS FROM THE
WORKS OF THE GREAT ENGLISH WRITERS
WITH INTRODUCTION AND NOTES.

The following Volumes, Globe 8vo, are ready or in preparation.

ADDISON—SELECTIONS FROM THE SPECTATOR. By K. DEIGHTON. 2s. 6d.

ADDISON AND STEELE—COVERLEY PAPERS FROM THE SPECTATOR. Edited by K. DEIGHTON. 1s. 9d.

ARNOLD—SELECTIONS. By G. C. MACAULAY. 2s. 6d.

BACON—ESSAYS. By F. G. SELBY, M.A. 3s. ; sewed, 2s. 6d.

—THE ADVANCEMENT OF LEARNING. By F. G. SELBY, M.A. Book I., 2s. ; Book II., 4s. 6d.

—THE NEW ATLANTIS. Edited by A. T. FLUX. Sewed, 1s.

BUNYAN—THE PILGRIM'S PROGRESS. Edited by JOHN MORRISON, M.A. 1s. 9d. ; sewed, 1s. 6d.

BURKE—REFLECTIONS ON THE FRENCH REVOLUTION. By F. G. SELBY, M.A. 5s.

—SPEECHES ON AMERICAN TAXATION ; ON CONCILIATION WITH AMERICA ; LETTER TO THE SHERIFFS OF BRISTOL. By F. G. SELBY, M.A. 3s. 6d.

BYRON—CHILDE HAROLD'S PILGRIMAGE. By EDWARD E. MORRIS, M.A. Cantos I. and II. 1s. 9d. Cantos III. and IV. 1s. 9d.

CAMPBELL—SELECTIONS. By W. T. WEBB, M.A. *[In the Press.*

CHAUCER—SELECTIONS FROM CANTERBURY TALES. By H. CORSON. 4s. 6d.

—THE SQUIERE'S TALE. With Introduction and Notes. By A. W. POLLARD, M.A. *[In the Press.*

—THE PROLOGUE. With Introduction and Notes. By A. W. POLLARD, M.A. *[In the Press.*

—THE KNIGHT'S TALE. With Introduction and Notes. By A. W. POLLARD, M.A. *[In the Press.*

CHOSEN ENGLISH—Selections from Wordsworth, Byron, Shelley, Lamb, and Scott. With short biographies and notes by A. ELLIS, B.A. 2s. 6d.

COWPER—THE TASK, Books IV. and V. By W. T. WEBB, M.A. Sewed, 1s. each.

—THE TASK, Book V. Sewed, 6d.

—LETTERS, SELECTIONS FROM. By W. T. WEBB, M.A. 2s. 6d.

—SHORTER POEMS. Edited by W. T. WEBB, M.A. 2s. 6d.

DRYDEN—SELECT SATIRES—ABSALOM AND ACHITOPHEL ; THE MEDAL; MACFLECKNOE. By J.CHURTON COLLINS,M.A. 1s.9d.

—THE HIND AND THE PANTHER. Edited by Prof. A. WILLIAMS, University of Tasmania. *[In the Press.*

GOLDSMITH—THE TRAVELLER aud THE DESERTED VILLAGE. By ARTHUR BARRETT,B.A. 1s.9d. THE TRAVELLER(separately), sewed, 1s. THE DESERTED VILLAGE (separately), sewed, 1s.

—THE TRAVELLER and THE DESERTED VILLAGE. By Prof. J. W. HALES. 6d.

—VICAR OF WAKEFIELD. By MICHAEL MACMILLAN, B.A. 2s. 6d.

MACMILLAN AND CO., LIMITED, LONDON.

2

GRAY—POEMS. By JOHN BRADSHAW, LL.D. 1s. 9d.

Dublin Evening Mail—"The Introduction and Notes are all that can be desired. We believe that this will rightly become the standard school edition of Gray."

Schoolmaster—"One of the best school editions of Gray's poems we have seen.

—ODE ON SPRING and THE BARD. Sewed, 6d.

—ELEGY IN A COUNTRY CHURCHYARD. Sewed. 6d.

HELPS—ESSAYS WRITTEN IN THE INTERVALS OF BUSINESS. By F. J. ROWE, M.A., and W. T. WEBB, M.A. 1s. 9d.

The Guardian—"A welcome addition to our school classics. The introduction, though brief, is full of point."

JOHNSON—LIFE OF MILTON. By K. DEIGHTON. 1s. 9d.

—LIFE OF DRYDEN. By P. PETERSON. [*In the Press.*

—LIFE OF POPE. By P. PETERSON. [*In the Press.*

LAMB—THE ESSAYS OF ELIA. First Series. Edited by N. L. HALLWARD, M.A., and S. C. HILL, B.A. 3s.; sewed, 2s. 6d.

LONGFELLOW—COURTSHIP OF MILES STANDISH. By W. ELLIOT, M.A. 1s.

MACAULAY—LAYS OF ANCIENT ROME. Edited by W. T. WEBB, M.A. 1s. 9d.

—ESSAY ON ADDISON. Edited by R. F. WINCH, M.A. 2s. 6d.

—ESSAY ON WARREN HASTINGS. Ed. by K. DEIGHTON. 2s. 6d.

—LORD CLIVE. Edited by K. DEIGHTON. 2s.

—ESSAY ON BOSWELL'S LIFE OF JOHNSON. Edited by R. F. WINCH, M.A. 2s. 6d.

—ESSAYS ON WILLIAM PITT, EARL OF CHATHAM. By R. F. WINCH, M.A. 2s. 6d.

—ESSAY ON MILTON. By H. B. COTTERILL, M.A. 2s. 6d.

—ESSAY ON FREDERIC THE GREAT. By A. T. FLUX.
[*In the Press.*

MALORY—MORTE D'ARTHUR. Edited by A. T. MARTIN, M.A. 2s. 6d.

MILTON—PARADISE LOST, Books I. and II. By MICHAEL MACMILLAN, B.A. 1s. 9d. Books I.-IV. separately, 1s. 3d. each; sewed, 1s. each.

The Schoolmaster—"The volume is admirably adapted for use in upper classes of English Schools."

The Educational News—"For higher classes there can be no better book for reading, analysis, and grammar, and the issue of these books of Paradise Lost must be regarded as a great inducement to teachers to introduce higher literature into their classes."

—L'ALLEGRO, IL PENSEROSO, LYCIDAS, ARCADES, SONNETS, &c. By WILLIAM BELL, M.A. 1s. 9d.

The Glasgow Herald—"A careful study of this book will be as educative as that of any of our best critics on Aeschylus or Sophocles."

—COMUS. By the same. 1s. 3d.; sewed, 1s.

The Practical Teacher—"The notes include everything a student could reasonably desire in the way of the elucidations of the text, and at the same time are presented in so clear and distinct a fashion, that they are likely to attract the reader instead of repelling him."

—SAMSON AGONISTES. By H. M. PERCIVAL, M.A. 2s.

The Guardian—"His notes are always of real literary value. . . . His introduction is equally masterly, and touches all that can be said about the poem."

—LYCIDAS. By W. BELL. Sewed, 6d.

—LYCIDAS AND COMUS. By W. BELL. 1s. 6d.

MACMILLAN AND CO., LIMITED, LONDON.

3

MILTON—THE SHORTER POEMS. With Introduction and Notes. By A. J. GEORGE, M.A. 3s. 6d.

—TRACTATE OF EDUCATION. By E. E. MORRIS, M.A. 1s. 9d.

PALGRAVE—GOLDEN TREASURY OF SONGS AND LYRICS. Book Second. By W. BELL, M.A. 3s. 6d.

POEMS OF ENGLAND. A Selection of English Patriotic Poetry, with notes by HEREFORD B. GEORGE, M.A., and ARTHUR SIDGWICK, M.A. 2s. 6d.

POPE—ESSAY ON MAN. Epistles I.-IV. Edited by EDWARD E. MORRIS, M.A. 1s. 3d.; sewed, 1s.

—ESSAY ON MAN. Epistle I. Sewed, 6d.

—ESSAY ON CRITICISM. Edited by J. C. COLLINS, M.A. 1s. 9d.

SCOTT—THE LADY OF THE LAKE. By G. H. STUART, M.A. 2s. 6d.; sewed, 2s. Canto I., sewed, 9d.

—THE LAY OF THE LAST MINSTREL. By G. H. STUART, M.A., and E. H. ELLIOT, B.A. 2s. Canto I., sewed, 9d. Cantos I.-III., and IV.-VI., 1s. 3d. each; sewed, 1s. each.

The *Journal of Education*—"The text is well printed, and the notes, wherever we have tested them, have proved at once scholarly and simple."

—MARMION. By MICHAEL MACMILLAN, B.A. 3s.; sewed, 2s. 6d.

The *Spectator*—" . . . His introduction is admirable, alike for point and brevity."

The *Indian Daily News*—"The present volume contains the poem in 200 pages, with more than 100 pages of notes, which seem to meet every possible difficulty."

—ROKEBY. By the same. 3s.; sewed, 2s. 6d.

The *Guardian*—"The introduction is excellent, and the notes show much care and research."

SHAKESPEARE—THE TEMPEST. By K. DEIGHTON. 1s. 9d.

The *Guardian*—"Speaking generally of Macmillan's Series we may say that they approach more nearly than any other edition we know to the ideal school Shakespeare. The introductory remarks are not too much burdened with controversial matter; the notes are abundant and to the point, scarcely any difficulty being passed over without some explanation, either by a paraphrase or by etymological and grammatical notes."

—MUCH ADO ABOUT NOTHING. By the same. 2s.

The *Schoolmaster*—"The notes on words and phrases are full and clear."

—A MIDSUMMER-NIGHT'S DREAM. By the same. 1s. 9d.

—THE MERCHANT OF VENICE. By the same. 1s. 9d.

—AS YOU LIKE IT. By the same. 1s. 9d.

—TWELFTH NIGHT. By the same. 1s. 9d.

The *Educational News*—"This is an excellent edition of a good play."

—THE WINTER'S TALE. By the same. 2s.

—KING JOHN. By the same. 1s. 9d.

—RICHARD II. By the same. 1s. 9d.

—HENRY IV., Part I. By the same. 2s. 6d.; sewed, 2s.

—HENRY IV., Part II. By the same. 2s. 6d.; sewed, 2s.

—HENRY V. By the same. 1s. 9d.

—RICHARD III. By C. H. TAWNEY, M.A. 2s. 6d.; sewed, 2s.

The *School Guardian*—"Of Mr. Tawney's work as an annotator we can speak in terms of commendation. His notes are full and always to the point."

—HENRY VIII. By K. DEIGHTON. 1s. 9d.

MACMILLAN AND CO., LIMITED, LONDON.

SHAKESPEARE — CORIOLANUS. By K. DEIGHTON. 2s. 6d.; sewed, 2s.

—ROMEO AND JULIET. By the same. 2s. 6d.; sewed, 2s.

—JULIUS CAESAR. By the same. 1s. 9d.

—MACBETH. By the same. 1s. 9d.

The *Educational Review*—"This is an excellent edition for the student. The notes are suggestive, . . . and the vivid character sketches of Macbeth and Lady Macbeth are excellent."

—HAMLET. By the same. 2s. 6d.; sewed, 2s.

—KING LEAR. By the same. 1s. 9d.

—OTHELLO. By the same. 2s.

—ANTONY AND CLEOPATRA. By the same. 2s. 6d.; sewed, 2s.

—CYMBELINE. By the same. 2s. 6d.; sewed, 2s.

The *Scotsman*—"Mr. Deighton has adapted his commentary, both in *Othello* and in *Cymbeline*, with great skill to the requirements and capacities of the readers to whom the series is addressed." .

SOUTHEY—LIFE OF NELSON. By MICHAEL MACMILLAN, B.A. 3s.; sewed, 2s. 6d.

SPENSER—THE FAERIE QUEENE. Book I. By H. M. PERCIVAL, M.A. 3s.; sewed, 2s. 6d.

—THE SHEPHEARD'S CALENDER. By C. H. HERFORD, Litt.D. 2s. 6d.

STEELE—SELECTIONS. By L. E. STEELE, M.A. 2s.

TENNYSON—SELECTIONS. By F. J. ROWE, M.A., and W. T. WEBB, M.A. 3s. 6d. Also in two Parts, 2s. 6d. each. Part I. Recollections of the Arabian Nights, The Lady of Shalott, The Lotos-Eaters, Dora, Ulysses, Tithonus, The Lord of Burleigh, The Brook, Ode on the Death of the Duke of Wellington, The Revenge.—Part II. Oenone, The Palace of Art, A Dream of Fair Women, Morte d'Arthur, Sir Galahad, The Voyage, and Demeter and Persephone.

The *Journal of Education*—"It should find a wide circulation in English schools. . . . The notes give just the requisite amount of help for understanding Tennyson, explanations of the allusions with which his poems teem, and illustrations by means of parallel passages. A short critical introduction gives the salient features of his style with apt examples."

The *Literary World*—"The book is very complete, and will be a good introduction to the study of Tennyson's works generally."

—MORTE D'ARTHUR. By the same. Sewed, 1s.

—THE COMING OF ARTHUR; THE PASSING OF ARTHUR. By F. J. ROWE, M.A. 2s. 6d.

—ENOCH ARDEN. By W. T. WEBB, M.A. 2s. 6d.

—AYLMER'S FIELD. By W. T. WEBB, M.A. 2s. 6d.

—THE PRINCESS. By P. M. WALLACE, M.A. 3s. 6d.

—GARETH AND LYNETTE. By G. C. MACAULAY, M.A. 2s. 6d.

—THE MARRIAGE OF GERAINT; GERAINT AND ENID. By G. C. MACAULAY, M.A. 2s. 6d.

—THE HOLY GRAIL. By G. C. MACAULAY, M.A. 2s. 6d.

—LANCELOT AND ELAINE. By F. J. ROWE, M.A. 2s. 6d.

—GUINEVERE. By G. C. MACAULAY, M.A. 2s. 6d.

WORDSWORTH—SELECTIONS. By W. T. WEBB, M.A. 2s. 6d.; also in two parts, 1s. 9d. each.

MACMILLAN AND CO., LIMITED, LONDON.